As Elizabeth stepped back,

a hand was clamped over her mouth.

"If you call out now, I'm dead for sure,"
Sean Jameson said in her ear.

Elizabeth began to squirm frantically, but he held
her tight.

"Settle down. If you promise you won't yell for the
servants, I'll set you free."

Elizabeth stopped struggling.

Sean's arms fell away, and she whirled to face him.
"How dare you sneak into my house and scare me
like that?" she demanded in a whisper.

"Are you saying I should have come to the door and
called like a gentleman? I've tried that before, and
I'm thinking you'll remember the reception I got for
my trouble."

"So you hid in my room because you wanted to see
me?" she asked, her anger fading. "For a few stolen
minutes, you would take such a chance? How did you
know I wouldn't call for help when I found it was
you?" she continued, lifting her hand to touch
his cheek.

"I didn't know," he said huskily. "I hoped...." He
stared down at her for a long moment, and then he
gathered her fiercely into his arms.

Dear Reader,

The July books from Harlequin Historicals range in setting from the coal mines of Pennsylvania to the French countryside as we, once again, bring you four historical romances.

Readers of our contemporary romances will easily recognize the author of *Torchlight*, Doreen Owens Malek. With this story of a miner and a mine owner's daughter, Ms. Malek tells of a love strong enough to survive social injustice and prejudice.

Lovers of Westerns won't want to miss Elaine Rome's *Stark Lightning*. Valentine Stark is caught unawares when her father's new ranch manager starts probing beneath her rough exterior.

In *The Daring, New York Times* bestselling author Patricia Hagan brings to life a North Carolina farming community in the throes of the Civil War. *Autumn Rose*, by Louisa Rawlings, takes place in France during the seventeenth century.

We hope you will enjoy the greater variety of settings and time periods as well as the many new authors that our expansion to four titles a month has enabled us to offer you.

Yours,

Tracy Farrell
Senior Editor

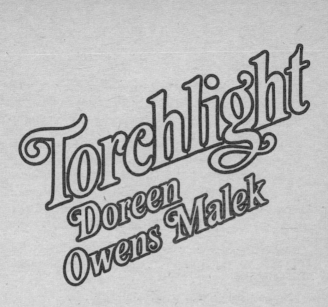

Torchlight

Doreen Owens Malek

Harlequin Books

TORONTO • NEW YORK • LONDON
AMSTERDAM • PARIS • SYDNEY • HAMBURG
STOCKHOLM • ATHENS • TOKYO • MILAN

Harlequin Historicals first edition July 1991

ISBN 0-373-28683-X

TORCHLIGHT

DOREEN OWENS MALEK

is a former attorney who decided on her current career when she sold her fledgling novel to the first editor who read it. Since then, she has gained recognition for her writing, winning honors from *Romantic Times* magazine and the coveted Romance Writers of America Golden Medallion Award. She has travelled extensively throughout Europe, but it was in her home state of New Jersey that she met and married her college sweetheart. They now make their home in Pennsylvania.

Chapter One

Autumn, 1870

Elizabeth Langdon clutched her hat as the coach wheels hit a rut and she was jostled in her seat. For the most part the journey to Langdon from her Aunt Dorothea's house in Wynnewood had been smooth and uneventful. But as soon as they had begun to traverse the coal patch surrounding her father's mine, the carriage had started to rock and plunge like the wooden hobbyhorse she'd had as a child. The road was gouged and pitted like the surface of an orange peel. Elizabeth frowned as she shot out of her seat once more, gasping. She hadn't remembered that the road was this bad.

But then she hadn't been back to Langdon in a long time.

She didn't really think of the town as "home," since she had not been raised there. She had been sent to live with her aunt when she was only two, just after her mother had died. Then, her father had not wanted to be burdened with her and sought only to keep her well maintained and out of his hair. Consequently she felt almost a newcomer to the valley where she was born.

She peered out of the isinglass window to her left at the sagging shanties, the hanging laundry begrimed with coal dust, the ragged children running past with sooty faces and scabby knees. Occasionally a woman attired in a long drab skirt and a fringed shawl looked up from washing clothes in a tub or hoeing a struggling garden to glance curiously at the carriage from the main house, wondering who was inside.

There were no men around; they were either down in the mine or sleeping until the next shift.

Elizabeth drew back from the window, vaguely ashamed to be seen. She'd been at school for six years, taking her vacations at her aunt's house and seeing her father only infrequently. She hadn't been here since she was fourteen, and then only briefly. Had things worsened so much since then, or had she simply been too immersed in her own world to notice the poverty?

Suddenly the ride evened out. She knew before she looked that they were starting the ascent to her father's house at the top of the hill. The drive was level and smooth all the way to the front door and around to the carriage house behind it, just as she recalled. The house was virtually unchanged, also, looming in gingerbread splendor over the town spread out below it. She knew that from the window seat in her bedroom she could see the breastworks of the mine shafts, the straggling alleys where the miners lived and the two wooden buildings they used for worship—Catholic for the Irish and Protestant for the Welsh.

When she was visiting at the house, she and her father had attended the Church of England services in Pottstown, six miles away.

Elizabeth straightened her hat and checked the pins in the bun at the back of her neck. Then she settled her traveling cape on her shoulders and took the lap robe off her knees and put it aside on the seat.

She would soon have her first interview with her father, and she was nervous about it. She had completed the course at Miss Taylor's finishing school in Philadelphia the previous May, and then had spent the summer with her aunt. Ten days ago, at the beginning of September, her father had summoned her home, explaining in a businesslike letter that since she was grown and educated now he expected her to take her place as mistress of his house. It was clear that he also expected her to find a husband from among the young men he considered suitable. His letter had conveyed, with little subtlety, the message that he considered her old enough to be married and thought that serving as his hostess would introduce her to the propertied families in the area.

Elizabeth had many private objections to this plan, but she knew better than to confront her father directly. She saw him as a stern, distant authority figure whose sole function was to step into her life at various times and issue orders: this church for his daughter, that school, such and such a milliner and ladies' shop and bootery on Revere Lane in Philadelphia for her clothes. He paid for everything and made the major decisions about her life, but the man himself she knew hardly at all. She knew enough, however, to realize that the progressive ideas she had picked up at Miss Taylor's and from her Aunt Dorrie would not be tolerated in his home. But he was in control of her destiny and so the appearance of obedience must be preserved.

Todd, the coachman, pulled to a stop in the circle that fronted the house. His family had been in service to hers for generations; his grandfather had come over from England with her grandfather almost fifty years earlier, in 1825. The Todds had always lived in the rooms above the carriage house. Todd still preserved the west country accent of his forebears, disdaining the Americanization of his speech.

"Home all safe and tidy, miss," he said in a satisfied tone.

"Yes, indeed," Elizabeth replied. "Thank you."

When she was little he used to lift her onto his shoulders and carry her into the house, but now he held out his hand for her to take as she stepped down to the ground. She did so graciously, practicing rather self-consciously for her role as the mistress of the manor.

"I'll take this little one in now, miss, and tote the rest up later, by your leave," he said deferentially, lifting her carryall once she had gained her footing.

"That will be fine, Todd," she responded, looking through the glass panels on either side of the cameo door. A brass chandelier, suspended by an extension chain from a plaster medallion in the vaulted ceiling, glowed softly, the flutes of its oil lamps sparkling. The black-and-white tiled floor, reminiscent of the Dutch paintings her father so admired, was spotless. A large blush porcelain vase on the cherry bachelor's chest in the entrance hall was filled with an assortment of late-blooming flowers, and to the left the sliding wooden doors to her father's study were closed. Elizabeth wondered if he were in there, working.

An auburn-haired maid she didn't recognize was dusting the furniture. As she watched, the young woman folded her polishing cloth and ascended the curved oak staircase, disappearing on the second floor.

Todd opened the door and Elizabeth preceded him into the house. They were met in the hall by the house-keeper, Mrs. Tamm. She beamed at Elizabeth, clasping her hands together with delight.

"My, dear, it's so wonderful to have you with us at last," she said. "Your father and I have been looking forward to this for weeks."

"Is he home?" Elizabeth asked.

"No, he's out at a meeting, but he'll be back for dinner."

Mrs. Tamm had been working for the family since Elizabeth was nine, and she occupied a quasi-relative status that elevated her above the rest of the servants—especially in her own mind. She was just releasing Elizabeth from a smothering hug when someone pounded on the door behind them.

"Who's that?" Elizabeth said to Todd, who was blocking her view through the flanking windows.

"Nothing to bother yourself about, miss," Todd said grimly. "I'll take care of it." He turned and yanked open the door as Elizabeth followed curiously. The door was closed firmly in her face, but she went to the window and peered through the sheer lawn curtains despite Mrs. Tamm's restraining arm.

"Him!" the older woman said at her side. Her tone was contemptuous. "That one's trouble."

"Who is it?" Elizabeth said.

"One of those organizers, the big mouth, worst of the lot," the housekeeper said. Her attitude indicated that she considered such people on a level with the vermin she was constantly battling in the root cellar of the house.

A tall, lithe young man was angrily confronting Todd, who instantly assumed an equally belligerent stance.

"Get off with you," Todd sputtered at the new arrival. "I've told you before not to make a nuisance of yourself. You can't come up here to the main house, bold as brass! I'll have the law on you, so help me I will."

"I want to see Langdon," the man demanded.

"In a pig's eye," Todd responded flatly.

Their raised voices carried easily through the wall to where the women were standing. Elizabeth's view was excellent, and she observed the scene closely, noting that both men were so absorbed in their conflict they didn't even notice their audience.

Todd's antagonist appeared to be in his late twenties, with thick chestnut-brown hair. He was dressed in rough clothes with bulky work boots.

"He can't hide forever," the younger man said. "He has to come out and face the real world sometime."

"I'll get the coal police if you start anything. You hark at me, boy," Todd said.

"You tell Langdon I'm here," the other insisted, his eyes blazing. That he was a miner was obvious from his dress, and his speech was the lilting brogue of the immigrant collier.

"I'll tell him nothing at all, you cheeky thug," Todd replied, raising his hand threateningly.

The miner eyed him wearily and shook his head.

"Get wise to yourself, man," he said to Todd. "Langdon's using you as well as me."

"Don't start that kind of talk here," Todd said. "Nobody's listening. I'd take you on if I was twenty years younger."

"But you're not," the other said softly. "And I won't go away. I'll be back, again and again, until even Langdon has to pay attention."

"Do you want to hold your place in the pit?" Todd said craftily. "Still keeping that family of yours, widowed mother and how many bairns? It would go awfully hard with them if you lost your situation. Maura's pittance won't do much."

The young man's mouth went tight. "Don't make threats you can't enforce, old man. If Langdon gave the gate to every miner griping about the working conditions, he'd have an empty pit."

"They're not all flailing away at his front door," Todd pointed out, his hands on his hips.

The younger man studied the older one and then shrugged, as if suddenly seeing the futility of continuing the conversation. He said only, "I'll be back," then turned and set off briskly down the hill, long legs striding purposefully.

"Not if you've got a brain in that thick skull," Todd called after him loudly.

Elizabeth exchanged glances with the housekeeper, who had watched the byplay with her. Mrs. Tamm pursed her lips and shook her head.

"No good will come of this," she said ominously. "I don't understand that boy—his sister's such a lovely girl."

"His sister?" Elizabeth said.

"Maura, the parlor maid. I hired her myself and she's worked out just fine. Quiet and industrious, such a docile nature."

"Is that the red-haired girl I saw as I arrived?"

"The same. She's quite the opposite of that ill-mannered lout who just left."

Elizabeth thought this over as she watched Todd go to the coach and take out one of the larger bags, still muttering to himself. Elizabeth waited for him.

"What was that all about?" she asked when the driver came inside.

He lifted her carryall from the floor with his free hand.

"Don't you pay him any mind, miss, he's just one of those rabble-rousing miners. Nothing for you to worry about. Your father will take care of them right enough."

"What are the miners doing?" Elizabeth asked quietly.

"Getting too big for their britches, if you ask me," Todd replied huffily.

Todd, like Mrs. Tamm, was one of the house servants. He'd always shared that lady's fine disdain for those who went down into the mines, referring to them as "that lot" for as long as she could remember. Now he mumbled, "Trashy goings-on, hammering on doors like a tinker hawking wares." He brushed past Elizabeth and lumbered up the stairs with both bags banging against his legs.

"Let me help you with your cape," Mrs. Tamm said briskly, as if to dismiss the unpleasant scene they had just witnessed. "I must be getting old and forgetful, leaving you standing here in the hall in your traveling clothes."

Elizabeth handed the housekeeper her bonnet and cape as Mrs. Tamm said, "I was thinking of assigning Maura to you, if you have no objection. She's really wasted on cleaning tasks—I can hire a drudge for that.

Of course, she'd not trained to be a lady's maid, but she's quick. All you have to do is instruct her—"

"That will be fine," Elizabeth said quickly. She was curious about the girl's family, which had produced a young man bold enough to confront her father. Few people had the nerve.

"You'd have to share her with me at serving time, but otherwise—"

"It's all right, Mrs. Tamm. It seems foolish to hire someone just for me. I wouldn't have enough for her to do."

Mrs. Tamm nodded and went to the foot of the stairs, calling, "Maura? Maura, come down here."

After a brief pause the girl appeared at the top of the stairs and then descended them gracefully, her long skirt whispering about her ankles. She was dressed as rudely as her brother in a gray linsey-woolsey jumper and a thin cotton blouse that had seen too many washings. But her beauty transcended the common attire; her sibling's roan-colored hair had turned to flame in her case, and she had braided it into an abundant coil, topped by a frilled maid's cap, which betokened her station. She stopped in front of the two women and looked at Mrs. Tamm inquiringly.

"Maura, this is Miss Langdon," Mrs. Tamm began kindly. "She's been away at school, but she's home for good. It will be your main job from now on to look after her."

The girl brightened, then dropped a quick curtsy. "Pleased to meet you, miss," she said shyly, looking up at Elizabeth through coppery lashes a shade darker than her hair. Her skin was milky with a few toasty freckles scattered across her nose.

"Hello, Maura," Elizabeth said.

"Why don't you go with Miss Langdon to her room." Mrs. Tamm said. "You can help her unpack."

"Yes, ma'am," Maura said.

The maid followed Elizabeth up the stairs and down the long upper hall, papered with maroon-and-white stripes and carpeted with a figured Turkish runner. Elizabeth's room was at the end of the corridor, overlooking the valley. It had been aired and dusted for her return and the carpet had been beaten, but it still smelled musty. The cabbage roses on the curtains were repeated in the hangings on the bed, and the china bowl and pitcher Elizabeth remembered still stood on the mahogany dresser. The scrubbed chamber pot, topped with an embroidered cover, peeked from under the flowered bed skirt.

Todd had left the bags on the floor just inside the door. Elizabeth bypassed them and went to the cheval mirror in the corner, examining her wrinkled and travel-stained clothes.

"Oh, dear, I'd better bathe and change for dinner," she said, noting her collapsing chignon and crushed linen shirtwaist. She unpinned her hair and its sable waves cascaded over her shoulders. She stared at the flushed cheeks and large dark eyes reflected in the mirror, wondering what to expect of her readjustment to life in Langdon.

"I'll lay something out for you, miss," Maura said, "and then fetch the water for your bath." She hoisted the larger bag onto the bed and selected a lavender wool dress, spreading out the folds of the fine material on the coverlet.

"You can put the underthings in the dresser drawers and hang up the rest," Elizabeth said to her.

"Yes, miss."

Elizabeth winced and turned to face the other girl. "Do you think you could call me by my first name? After all, we're almost the same age. What are you, eighteen?"

"Nineteen."

"All right, then. I'm twenty."

Maura folded a pair of silk bloomers and shook her head. "Mrs. Tamm would never stand for that, miss. She doesn't hold with the help getting too familiar."

"I'll take care of Mrs. Tamm," Elizabeth said briskly.

"Oh, don't do that, miss. She'll give me the devil." Then Maura smiled, relenting. "Maybe just when it's the two of us alone."

"Good enough," Elizabeth said. She turned from the mirror and began to unbutton her blouse. "I saw your brother today," she said casually.

She was unprepared for the anxious expression that suffused the other girl's face.

"Sean?" Maura said nervously.

"How many brothers do you have?"

"Two, but the younger one is only five. He's kept at home."

"I see."

"What did Sean do?" Maura asked.

"What makes you think he did anything?" Elizabeth countered.

The girl, still flustered, remained silent.

"Maura, it's all right," Elizabeth said gently. "You can talk to me."

Maura went on folding clothes without replying.

Trust, Elizabeth decided, would have to be earned. "What time is dinner?" she went on conversationally, deliberately changing the subject.

"Mrs. Tamm serves at six unless otherwise instructed," Maura answered neutrally.

"I suppose that gives me time for a short rest, then," Elizabeth observed.

"I'll be out of your way in a moment, miss," Maura said, shaking out a fitted jacket and then placing it in the wardrobe.

"I didn't say that to drive you out of the room, Maura," Elizabeth said gently. The girl, for all her deferential attitude, was obviously as sensitive underneath as her firebrand brother.

"Just about done," Maura murmured, hanging the last of Elizabeth's garments in the armoire. "I'll be off for the bath water now." She closed the closet door, dropped a quick curtsy and left the room.

Elizabeth sighed and stretched out across the bed in her chemise, her hair hanging over the edge of the feather-ticking mattress like a midnight curtain.

She felt that she was beginning a new life and that it would be quite different from the one she had left behind.

Sean Jameson kicked his way home through an accumulation of dirt and coal dust, his frustration mounting to fury as he thought about his dismissal at the Langdon house. He should have run down that old fool of a servant and smashed in the door; Langdon was probably hiding in his study like the coward he was, issuing orders to his west country lackey. The coachman should have been on Sean's side, but he was duped, duped like all of them who worked at the house, thinking they were better off because they rubbed shoulders with the quality. He'd have to make sure Maura didn't acquire the same airs. He hated her working at the house, scrubbing Langdon's sheets, but they needed the money.

Sean glanced up at the lowering sky and marked the time. He had only a few hours to get some sleep before his shift began. And tonight he would hold the first secret miners' meeting in the abandoned number nine shaft. If they were ever going to accomplish anything, they had to get organized.

He climbed the wooden steps to the shanty he lived in, not even glancing at the weathered clapboard long since faded to gray, the single streaked window covered with a tattered lace curtain yellowed with age. He pushed the door and saw his young brother, Matthew, at the table in the tiny front room, laboring over a copybook. His mother stood at the fireplace, which heated the room and served as her stove. To his left was the staircase leading to a loft divided into sleeping spaces by makeshift curtains strung on clothesline. And that was the house.

Sean stood on the threshold and promised himself that soon he would get them all out of this place. And he wasn't going to do it by standing hip-deep in murky water chipping coal out of a rock face half a mile underground.

He slammed the door behind him.

Elizabeth smoothed the skirt of her lavender dress and then fingered the straggling ebony wisps at her ears. Her Pre-Raphaelite locks, wayward on the best of days, were proving especially difficult to confine, and she wanted to look neat for this first interview with her father. She took her hair down and repinned it, declining to call Maura, who was doubtless occupied in the kitchen. The ship's clock on the mantel was chiming six, and Elizabeth's father was always punctual.

He was waiting for her in the wainscoted dining room, seated at the head of a carved table set with her mother's best Limoges and the heavy silver she remembered from her childhood. Elizabeth might have thought this was in her honor, but she knew that her father dined in state this way every evening, although he was most often alone.

"My dear," he said, standing. He was wearing a cutaway coat with a ribbed stomacher; he looked heavier and older than Elizabeth remembered.

"Father."

"It's so wonderful to have you home," he added, coming toward her and kissing her on the cheek. His lips were warm and dry.

Mrs. Tamm bustled into the room with a soup tureen as he pulled out Elizabeth's chair.

"It's nice to be here," Elizabeth replied as she sat, feeling as if she were talking to a stranger.

Mrs. Tamm served her father first, and Elizabeth watched as he tasted the bisque and then nodded brusquely. Mrs. Tamm bowed her head and served Elizabeth, then exited quietly, her starched apron crackling.

Arthur Langdon gestured for Elizabeth to pick up her spoon. She did, accepting her role in the choreography. Were they really going to go through this ritual every night?

"Tell me about your school," Langdon said without preliminary. "I'd like to know what I was paying for all that time."

Elizabeth provided him with a capsule summary of her courses and teachers, wondering if he had bothered to read any of her letters, which contained the same information.

"And your summer?" he asked when she was finished.

Elizabeth went on about her activities with Aunt Dorrie, wishing that the interplay felt more like a conversation than an interrogation. Mrs. Tamm cleared the soup bowls and served the roast while Elizabeth finished her description.

"Todd told me that there was an unpleasant incident with one of the miners when you arrived," Langdon said, heaping his plate with slices of meat as her voice trailed into silence.

"Well, it wasn't exactly unpleasant," Elizabeth qualified.

"What happened?" Langdon asked.

Elizabeth knew that he had already gotten Todd's version, so she kept her account as brief and undramatic as possible.

"So Jameson didn't accost you?" Langdon inquired, his gaze bent on his food.

"Jameson?"

"The miner."

"Oh, no, I was already inside the house when he arrived. He and Todd had some words and then he left."

"Very wise of him," Langdon said crisply. "I've a good mind to have him arrested."

"Father, he didn't actually do anything. He just asked to see you and . . ."

"And what?"

"Todd wouldn't let him so he got angry."

"He's always angry," Langdon stated flatly. "The man obviously doesn't know when he's well-off. He could be back in his own country, starving." He chewed industriously. "I've got his sister working here—I should throw her out. Why any of that Jameson spawn is under my roof I'll never know."

"Oh, no," Elizabeth protested, dropping her fork. "Maura shouldn't have to suffer because of her brother."

Her father really looked at her for the first time. "You are so like your mother," he said, sighing. "Very well. Mrs. Tamm hired her before her brother started making trouble, and she gives the girl a good report. But I am sorry you had to be exposed to this on your first day."

"Exposed to what?"

He gestured vaguely. "All this turmoil with the miners."

"What are they complaining about, Father?"

Langdon shrugged. "Conditions, pay, medical care—you name it. As if they had their pick of jobs. They're a bunch of bog trotters not qualified to do anything except dig coal and they're lucky to be doing that, but this Jameson is a rabble-rouser. I'd toss him in jail, but I don't want to gain sympathy for him with the men. I'd rather tolerate his rumblings unless he gets too boisterous."

"And how will you handle it if he does?" Elizabeth asked.

Langdon's gaze was piercing. "You let me worry about that, young lady. Don't bother your head with things that don't concern you," Langdon replied abruptly. He appeared to regret saying as much as he had.

In any event, it was clear that the discussion was ended.

They ate in silence for a while, and by the time dessert arrived, Elizabeth was wishing she could go up to her room. Her father's attitude about his workers was vaguely discomfiting; it was true that she knew almost nothing about his business, but something must be wrong. Maura's brother had seemed almost desperate.

Elizabeth waited until Mrs. Tamm had removed her untouched cake and then said, "I'd like to be excused, Father. I'm very tired from the trip and want to get to bed early."

It was a flimsy explanation, but her father didn't examine it too closely. He nodded and reached for his box of cigars on the table.

Elizabeth fled, passing an unfamiliar maid on the stairs and nodding to her. When she reached her room, she found that Maura had set out one of her nightgowns and turned down the bed before leaving for the night. Elizabeth thought again about the girl and her brother, wondering what their home was like, suspecting that she would not be happy if she saw it.

She began to undress, thinking that already her life in Langdon was more complicated than she had expected it to be.

* * *

Sean glanced around at the torches flickering in the abandoned mine shaft, casting shadows on the faces of the assembled men. They were only a handful, but it was a start.

"I say sabotage is the only way," Jim Kelly insisted in his thick Kerry brogue. "Hit Langdon in the pocketbook—that will make him pay attention right enough. Blow the railway or interrupt the shipments to the wholesalers. That's the ticket."

Sean shook his head as a rumble of agreement went through the group. "No, no, that would be playing right into Langdon's hands."

"You've tried talking to him, man. How many times?" Kelly demanded. "Your tactics are getting us nowhere."

"You don't understand. Any violence and he'd make us look like a bunch of hooligans, to the newspapers, the cops. The law would be on his side. Destruction of property, public endangerment, creating a nuisance. The police would be lining up to help him."

"You talk like a lawyer!" Kelly snorted.

"We have to think like lawyers and not like a gang of thugs!" Sean responded heatedly. "We need a strike, a work stoppage, something that would hurt Langdon but not turn us into criminals he can prosecute with all the weight of the authorities behind him."

"Maybe he's right," Tim Shorter said.

Kelly threw up his hands.

"Will you just listen to me, just let me outline what I have in mind? Then we can discuss it," Sean said reasonably.

Kelly shrugged and looked away.

Sean studied the rest of the faces in the circle. They were all looking at him expectantly.

"All right," he said calmly. "This is what I propose to do."

Elizabeth passed the next month fitting into the routine of her father's house and getting reacquainted with neighbors she had not seen for a long time. She dutifully attended church suppers and other social gatherings. October came and the leaves fell from the trees, tumbling and swirling to the ground, where they made a russet carpet on the withering grass. Maura attended to her every need, but as often as she saw the girl, Elizabeth still could not penetrate the pleasant reserve the Irish girl wore like invisible armor.

One evening in the middle of the month, Elizabeth was awakened in the night by a thunderous blast that shook the floor. She stumbled, barefoot and half-asleep, to the window overlooking the valley. What she saw as she pushed her hair out of her eyes made her gasp.

Smoke was pouring from the mouth of number three, and there were flames shooting up in the background, illuminating the night sky. Panicked figures were scurrying everywhere, and more people streamed across the flatlands as whistles sounded in the distance, announcing the disaster.

Elizabeth turned from the window abruptly. Not even stopping for a robe, she thrust her feet into her slippers and ran from the room.

Chapter Two

Elizabeth flew down the back stairs and through the kitchen, emerging onto the rear lawn. Frost from the grass dampened her slippers and the hem of her gown as she ran. The air filled with drifting ash as she skirted the house and stumbled down the hill, coming closer to the mouth of the mine. In the distance she could see a flood of women, most of them dressed in nightclothes and hastily gathered shawls, running from the shanties toward the coalfields. It was a scene of alarm and confusion, cries of fear and anguish mixing with the shrieking whistles to form a hellish cacophony that made her want to cover her ears.

Elizabeth could see that some of the people staggering around in the chaos were injured, and she dodged as one of the men, running backward, almost crashed into her.

He turned and glared down at her, blood running into his eyes from a gash on his forehead.

"What are you doing out here in the middle of this?" he yelled, taking in her nightgown and tousled hair. "Get yourself home!"

Elizabeth stared. It was Maura's brother, the miner who had confronted Todd at her house on the day she'd returned home. Even with the coal dust and gore smearing his face, she recognized him.

"Did you not hear me?" he barked. "Take yourself off before you get hurt!" He turned away, dismissing her, and focused on another man who was rushing up to him. They had a hurried conversation, which Elizabeth couldn't hear over the din, and then the second man ran off into the crowd. Other people gathered around Jameson, and Elizabeth watched as he shouted and gesticulated, issuing orders, organizing the men in the face of the sudden chaos. Everyone did what he said, as if by instinct. It was some time before he looked around distractedly and saw that Elizabeth was still standing behind him.

"Did you not hear me?" he bellowed. "This is no place for you!"

"What ha-happened?" she stammered, her voice almost lost in the surrounding noise.

"Gas pocket in number three," he answered, turning away from her as a woman running past him grabbed his arm. Elizabeth waited, almost choking on the smoke, her eyes tearing painfully. When he looked back at her she was in the same spot, her feet planted stubbornly.

The exasperated look on his face said that he was about to toss her over his shoulder and carry her off himself.

"I can help," she said quickly.

He looked dubious at this piece of information.

"I had a nursing course in school," she told him loudly, trying to make herself heard. "I can treat and bandage cuts, I know how to use the latest disinfectants..."

He didn't wait for the rest of it, grabbing her hand and pulling her along after him. Either he believed her or he was just too anxious to get to the wounded and didn't want to leave her alone to be run down in the midst of the melee.

Elizabeth staggered along in his furious wake, her small hand lost in his callused one. As they slipped and slid down the hill toward the lip of number three, the fire brigade from Pottstown arrived, horses' hooves pounding and clarion bell clanging.

A tattered and bleeding group of men were scattered on the withered grass at the mouth of the shaft, some of the local women tending them. The crowd parted for Jameson as he arrived, and he pushed ahead, turning to point to Elizabeth and say, "Get started there."

The assembled people barely glanced at Elizabeth as she seized a length of sheeting from one of the women and began to make bandages.

"Margaret, do as she says," Jameson instructed a sandy-haired woman in her forties. "She has some schooling."

Margaret nodded and moved to Elizabeth's side, where she remained, silently following Elizabeth's directions. Jameson melted into the crowd but Elizabeth could hear his lilting voice behind her, calming and authoritative, bringing order to the chaos surrounding them.

The carnage was overwhelming. One man's leg had been crushed so badly by a fallen beam that Elizabeth was sure it would have to be amputated. Another had a gash in his arm so deep that it had slashed through the layers of skin to reveal the muscle beneath. Elizabeth moved as rapidly as possible, cleaning wounds, applying tourniquets, helping to carry the immobilized injured to makeshift litters. She was dimly aware of the firemen in the background dropping a hose into the well at the base of the hill and setting up a pump. The fire was internal, deep inside the mine, but every few minutes the shaft belched smoke, which billowed out into the air. The thick haze only increased as the firemen began to douse the blaze. The drifting ash settled on Elizabeth's skin and hair, turning the snowy linen of her nightgown to sooty gray. Oblivious to her running nose and streaming eyes, she labored on, tending the wounded alongside village women she didn't know, who were equally unaware of her identity.

Elizabeth lost track of Jameson as time passed and the firemen got the blaze under control. Once the debris was cleared, some of the men went inside the shaft to look for survivors. The worst cases were loaded into coal wagons to be taken to the hospital at Reading. For the first time in several hours there was a lull in the action, and she had a chance to look around her.

The night was cold with a clear sky littered with stars, but the smoke haze still hanging in the air partially obscured them. A few of the wounded were still lying on the ground but most had been carried off on pallets. The women who worked beside her had grime-streaked faces, and she realized she must look the same. The wind picked up and Elizabeth shivered, aware for the first time that she was badly chilled.

"Better have this," Jameson said behind her. She turned as he dropped his corduroy jacket over her shoulders.

He was looking down at her, his expression intent. He removed a folded handkerchief from his pocket and handed it to her. It was coarse but clean. When Elizabeth stood motionless with the handkerchief in her hand, he realized the extent of her exhaustion and took it back, gently wiping her face.

"Come and sit down," he said quietly, leading her by the arm to an overturned packing crate that had served as a rest station during the emergency. Elizabeth dropped onto it bonelessly, now fully conscious of the extent of her fatigue. She was also shaking, a delayed reaction to the shock of the tragedy.

"Easy there," Sean said. "You came through like a champion—don't give out now. Take a sip of this." He extracted a flask from his back pocket, unscrewed the cap and tipped the bottle to her lips. Elizabeth took a swallow and then pushed the flask away, coughing.

"What is that?" she gasped.

"Brandy. Best thing for you."

"I doubt it," Elizabeth said, grimacing.

Sean knelt on the ground next to her. "Yes, indeed. It will warm you right up and settle those shakes." He tucked his jacket closer about her shoulders and rubbed her upper arms through the ribbed material. "How do you feel now?" he asked, holding her gaze with his.

"I'm all right," Elizabeth replied unconvincingly, looking up into his green eyes.

"Oh, I can tell," Sean observed dryly.

"Have all the injured been seen?" she asked anxiously, looking back toward the mine.

"They have," he answered reassuringly. "Don't fret yourself."

"What about you?" she asked. "That's a nasty cut on your forehead."

Sean touched the mass of congealed blood as if he'd forgotten the injury. "Caught a splinter there," he murmured.

"Looks like it was more than a splinter. Were you in the mine when it blew?"

He nodded. "On my way up for a car, and that saved me. Others down below weren't so lucky."

Elizabeth refrained from commenting that none of them seemed very lucky to her.

"The explosion should never have happened," Sean said bitterly. "If Langdon would let the mine shut down for an inspection once in great while, we'd be able to tell that the gas was building up in there. But he won't stop production even for an hour. Miserable thief, I hope he's happy with this night's work!"

Elizabeth felt her stomach tighten. Was her father really responsible for this calamity?

Sean's eyes narrowed. "How is it I haven't seen you before tonight?" he asked. "Have you just come to Langdon?"

"I—I've just returned," Elizabeth said carefully.

"You were away, then?" he asked.

"Yes. At school."

"What's your name?"

She swallowed, unable to look away from him. Her heart was pounding.

"Elizabeth," she said.

A frown creased his forehead. The name, favored by the British aristocracy, was not exactly in vogue among the immigrant coal miners.

"Sean!" a voice exploded behind them. "Come on over here!" They turned to see one of the colliers gesturing wildly with a heavily bandaged hand.

"Stay right there," Sean said to her. "I'll be back."

Elizabeth watched as he strode over to join the man who'd summoned him, admiring the lean grace of his back in his homespun shirt. She was waiting for him, trying to get warm, when she spotted a familiar face among the dispersing throng. She stood abruptly, trying to slip away unnoticed, but it was too late.

"Elizabeth!"

She heard her name and froze.

"What are you doing out here?"

She turned slowly to face the music. The speaker was Chief Anson of the Pottstown Fire Department, a close friend of her father's.

"Does Arthur know about this?" the chief demanded, aghast.

Elizabeth sighed. "I heard the siren and saw the fire. I thought maybe I could help."

Chief Anson seized her arm in an iron grip and practically levitated her back toward the main house.

"Come along with me," he announced unnecessarily, since she had little choice. "Your father would not want you to see this."

Elizabeth was certain he was right about that.

"How did the fire start?" she asked, looking over her shoulder for Sean as the chief dragged her away.

"Don't you concern yourself about that," Anson said briefly. "These things happen every once in a while around here. You'll get used to it."

"But can't such accidents be prevented?" Elizabeth asked. "By routine inspections, I mean?"

Anson stopped walking and looked down at her. "Who have you been talking with, Elizabeth?" he asked sharply. "These miners are riffraff. Don't pay any attention to their incessant complaining. It really isn't your place to meddle in your father's affairs, you know.''

Elizabeth bit her lip as Anson started forward again, urging her up the rise toward the Langdon mansion. She had expected that the lamps would be blazing by now, but all the windows were dark.

''Is no one awake at the house?'' she asked, puzzled.

''Your father doesn't get up for these incidents,'' Anson replied flatly. ''He'll handle the situation during business hours in the morning, as he always does.''

Although she was relieved that she would not have to deal with a confrontation, Elizabeth was shocked at the implied indifference to the suffering she had just witnessed. How could her father sleep through such a scene? Did these accidents happen so often that he'd become completely inured to them?

''Now go right inside,'' Anson said sternly. ''I'll wait here until I see you in the upstairs window.''

Elizabeth nodded agreement and slipped into the silent house. It was amazing; everyone was sleeping! It was as if the drama down at shaft number three had never taken place. Then, as she mounted the stairs in the darkness, she heard a door close softly in the servants' quarters and saw the glow of a coal oil lamp snuffed out quickly. So, maybe not *everyone* was sleeping, but it was clear nobody was going to defy her father by expressing interest in the miners' plight.

She ascended to the second floor and signaled Anson from her window. She waited until he had slipped beneath the brow of the hill, and then she turned wearily away, dropping the curtain. She knew she should bathe and change her gown, which was stained with blood and gore, but that would call attention to her nocturnal wanderings. Better to wait until morning. She moved to her bed, stretching out on top of the coverlet she'd left disturbed hours earlier.

Sunrise could be only a short time away, but once she was prone Elizabeth discovered she couldn't sleep. Her mind was racing, reliving what she had experienced that night. It was clear to her now that she'd been living in a dreamworld at school, with no more idea of what was happening here in Langdon than in far-off czarist Russia. She had never thought of her father as a particularly benevolent figure, but the image of him that had emerged since her return to town was singularly disturbing.

Elizabeth turned her head restlessly against the feather pillow and realized that she was still wearing Sean Jameson's jacket. She sat up and took it off, folding the sleeves carefully. She held the bundle in her lap, finally raising it and pressing her cheek to the well-worn material. His musky masculine scent clung to it, and she closed her eyes, remembering his steady gaze, the strength of his hands when he'd draped the jacket around her. It was a poor man's threadbare garment, and for some reason his giving it to her made her want to cry.

Elizabeth shook her head abruptly, blinking, and tossed the jacket to the foot of her bed. She was tired, that was all. She would feel better after a little rest.

She must try to get some sleep.

When Sean finished his conversation, the girl was gone. He returned to the spot where he'd left her and she'd vanished as completely as if he'd imagined her. His disappointment was acute. He asked some of the women she'd been working with that evening who she was but no one knew, which meant that she had to be a very recent arrival. She was well-spoken, with an educated accent; maybe she was the schoolteacher who'd been promised by the board of education for some time.

Well, it was a small town. He would find her.

Elizabeth slept for a couple of hours and woke at first light. Maura usually came to her room at seven-thirty, so Elizabeth had plenty of time to change to a clean nightgown and dispose of the old one before the servant arrived to get her ready for the day. Sean's jacket was buried at the bottom of the wardrobe, where Maura would have no reason to look.

Elizabeth wanted an excuse to see Sean again, and the coat would provide the perfect reason for a meeting.

When Maura arrived with a tray, her eyes were downcast and Elizabeth could not tell from her expression that anything unusual had happened the previous night.

"Good morning, miss," Maura said impassively.

"Good morning," Elizabeth replied.

"Mrs. Tamm said to say that breakfast will be delayed about ten minutes from the usual," Maura informed her. "Will you have your tea first or shall I prepare your bath?"

"The tea," Elizabeth said.

Maura removed the cozy from the pot and put the leaves in the strainer. Elizabeth watched for a moment and then asked neutrally, "Do you know how many men were injured in the explosion last night?"

Maura looked up briefly and then down again. "No, miss."

"You heard nothing about it?"

"Nothing as to numbers," Maura replied.

"Any dead?"

"Somebody always dies. That's the way of it."

"Mining is a dangerous business."

Maura didn't answer.

"Some people say that it doesn't have to be as dangerous as it is," Elizabeth offered provocatively.

"Some do," Maura murmured, rattling china.

"Sean is one of those who hold that opinion," Elizabeth added.

Maura refolded a linen napkin nervously.

"Well?"

"Sean is never one to keep silent about what he thinks, miss," Maura finally said.

"Do you agree with him?" Elizabeth asked.

"I know nothing about what it's like in the pit," Maura said. "Sean goes his way and I go mine."

"But surely you think there are too many accidents?" Elizabeth prodded.

Maura sighed heavily and looked at Elizabeth with grim forbearance. She reminded the other women very strongly of her brother at that moment.

"Maura, I'm not trying to get you into trouble," Elizabeth said gently. "Or Sean, either, for that matter. I haven't spent much time here until now, and I've seen a lot of things that bother me. I'm trying to figure out what's going on, and I'm asking you to help me."

Maura waited a long moment and then lifted one shoulder in a half shrug. "Sean says there's a powerful lot could be done to make the pits safer, but the bosses like your father won't bear the cost of it."

"Yes, I know. Could I talk to him about it?"

Maura's mouth fell open comically. "To Sean?"

"Yes."

"Your father would have a fit, miss," she said in hushed tones, her eyes round.

"My father wouldn't have to know about it."

Maura shook her head warningly. "Mr. Langdon gets into some towering rages. If he was ever to find out—"

"Could you arrange it? Ask your brother to meet me, somewhere we wouldn't be seen?"

Maura kneaded her fingers worriedly.

Elizabeth took a step forward and touched the other girl's arm. "Maura, I was out there last night. I saw what happened. I want to help."

Maura stared at her, stunned. "You were out at the pit?"

"Yes. I heard the explosion and saw the fire. I ran down the hill to see what I could do."

"Your father?" Maura asked, swallowing.

"He thinks I was in bed all night. Apparently it's his custom to sleep through these things. As if anyone could."

"Did you see Sean?"

Elizabeth nodded. "I helped with the wounded. He didn't know who I was. He still doesn't."

There was a knock at the door.

"Come in," Elizabeth said.

Bess, another parlor maid, bobbed a curtsy and said, "Excuse me, miss, but Mrs. Tamm wants to see Maura in the kitchen."

Maura looked to Elizabeth for approval. "By your leave, miss," she said quietly.

Elizabeth nodded, frustrated that they couldn't continue their conversation but unwilling to get Maura into trouble. "Go ahead. I can finish here by myself."

Half an hour later Elizabeth joined her father in the dining room for breakfast. She would have liked to avoid sharing the meal with him, but he demanded her presence at his table and would have sent for her later if she remained in her room. It was better to preserve the appearance of normalcy.

He looked up from his copy of the *Philadelphia Bulletin* to greet her.

"Good morning, my dear," he said.

"Good morning, Father."

He spooned sugar into his coffee and went back to his paper. Mrs. Tamm bustled in with the porridge as Elizabeth fiddled with the salt-cellar beside her plate.

"What else would you like, Miss Elizabeth?" Mrs. Tamm asked, as Bess entered with a covered tray of kippers and deposited it in front of Arthur Langdon. He still clung to the customs of his forebears and insisted on a full British breakfast every morning.

"I'm fine, Mrs. Tamm," Elizabeth said. "I'm not very hungry." She selected a roll from the silver wire basket on the table and broke it into pieces. Her father went on reading.

He was clearly not going to mention the events of the previous night.

"I was very disturbed by the explosion at the mine," Elizabeth said, plunging into the subject.

Her father folded his paper down and peered at her over the top of it. "I'm sorry you lost sleep, my dear," he observed neutrally.

"That's not what I meant. I understand there were several serious injuries."

He resumed his examination of the paper. "It would be wise not to involve yourself with matters that don't concern you, Elizabeth. I hope you haven't been discussing my business affairs with the staff."

He was assuming that the servants would be her only source of knowledge. "It's not just a business affair, Father. Aren't you concerned about the welfare of the people who work for you?"

"The miners know the risk when they take the job," Langdon said, rattling pages. "No one forces them into their occupation, and I cannot be held responsible for the decisions of others."

Elizabeth sat forward earnestly. "But Father, you know that many of them are immigrants and that mining is the only job they can get. They would starve otherwise, which hardly makes working for you a 'decision.' Surely there is something that can be done—"

Arthur Langdon put down his newspaper with a thud. "That's enough, Elizabeth. I can see I made a mistake sending you to that progressive school your aunt recommended. I will not be lectured on this subject, or any other, by my daughter. I advise you to turn your attention to finding yourself a husband, an interest much more suited to a young lady of your age and station."

Mrs. Tamm entered the dining room again, and they both waited while she presented Arthur Langdon with a silver tray containing an embossed card.

"Frederick Anson," Langdon murmured to himself. He looked up at Mrs. Tamm. "Is he in the drawing room?"

"No, sir. He sent a messenger asking if you would be at home to receive him at two this afternoon. The boy is waiting for your reply." She kept her gaze averted, sensing the tension in the room.

"You may tell Chief Anson that I will see him at two," Langdon said. Mrs. Tamm glanced at Elizabeth, smiled encouragingly, then disappeared with a rustle of serge, trailing the scent of lemon verbena.

Elizabeth looked down at her hands with a sinking heart. She was certain that her presence at the mine would be one of the subjects Chief Anson wished to discuss.

"Father, I have something to tell you," she began.

"Elizabeth, enough," her father said brusquely. "I am weary of this talk. I have work to do and whatever you have to say can wait. If you don't plan to eat anything, I suggest you retire."

Elizabeth fell silent, conceding defeat. She pushed back her chair and left the dining room as Langdon returned to his paper.

Mrs. Tamm met her in the hall.

"I can send something up to your room later if you get hungry," the housekeeper said sympathetically.

Elizabeth shook her head.

"Try to understand your father, dear," the older woman said. "He has a lot of worries just now."

"You mean the explosion last night?" Elizabeth asked.

Mrs. Tamm sighed and looked away.

"Oh, I see you don't want to talk about it, either," Elizabeth said in irritation.

"Your father would prefer it," Mrs. Tamm said. "He instructed me to that effect."

"I don't see how I can ignore what's happening right under my nose," Elizabeth protested.

"You have enough to occupy you, my dear," the housekeeper said. "I believe you have several letters to write, and there's plenty of work left on the clothes cover you're embroidering for the church fair."

Elizabeth took her cue.

"I'll be in my room," she said wearily, and turned toward the staircase as Mrs. Tamm glided off to the kitchen.

Elizabeth was at her desk, writing a letter to her Aunt Dorrie, when shouts from below roused her from her task. She flung her door open and paused in the hallway, listening.

"I'm calling you, Langdon. Get out here and face me like a man!"

Elizabeth recognized the voice and the lilting accent. Her pulse began to race.

It was Sean.

Elizabeth crept to the landing and peered over the stairwell. Sean was standing in the lower hall, his sleeves rolled to the elbows, his hands on his hips. He was much cleaner than when she last saw him, free of sweat and coal dust, but his intent expression was the same. As she watched, the dining room door slid open and her father emerged.

"How did you get in here, Jameson?" Langdon demanded.

''Your watchdog was missing from the front door,'' Sean replied flatly. ''I've been here before, trying to get you to listen to what I have to say. Didn't the accident last night teach you anything?''

''I have nothing to learn from a ruffian like you,'' Langdon replied. He turned to Mrs. Tamm, who came into view behind him. ''Find Todd and send him down to the Coal Police. He's to tell Sergeant Rees there's an intruder in my house and I want him removed.''

Mrs. Tamm hurried out of sight as Elizabeth frowned deeply. The Coal Police were members of the company security force, which functioned like her father's private army; Sean would surely be arrested.

''Throwing me out won't prevent another explosion like the one you just had,'' Sean stated.

Elizabeth turned as Maura crept up behind her, drawn by the sound of her brother's voice. Elizabeth held her finger to her lips as Maura gnawed her knuckle anxiously.

''I've a good mind to fire you!'' Langdon said furiously.

Sean shook his head wearily. ''I'm the best powderman in Pennsylvania. Nobody knows your shafts the way I do. I've been down in those mines since I was twelve. You need me as much as I need the job, and well you know it.''

''I can see that your arrogance remains undimmed,'' Langdon said sarcastically.

''I'm aware of what I'm worth to you,'' Sean replied simply.

"I wish I *could* find another blaster," Langdon said between clenched teeth. "You'd be gone inside of five minutes."

"Until then we're stuck with each other, Langdon. There's nothing else I can do, and you can't find anybody else to do it. I know you've been running adverts in the Philadelphia papers, even sent a man to Cardiff to search the coal towns there. Came up empty. I guess you didn't know they don't use blasting powder on the other side."

Langdon's anger was dangerously obvious. Elizabeth took a step forward, wondering if she should intervene.

"That doesn't mean I have to put up with your insolence," Langdon said. "My houseman has told me you've been coming around here, imposing yourself and annoying the staff. You do your job and collect your wages. Beyond that we have no relationship and I have nothing to say to you."

"Why are you so afraid to talk to me?" Sean asked. "What can you lose by listening for half an hour?"

"Yes, that's right," Elizabeth said, descending the staircase. "What can you lose by listening?"

Maura moaned and reached out convulsively, then stuffed her fist in her mouth, shrinking back into the upper hallway.

Both men turned to look up at Elizabeth. Under other circumstances their expressions would have been comical.

"Elizabeth, stay out of this," Langdon said firmly.

"You!" Sean said in astonishment.

Langdon looked at him, then at his daughter. "You know this man?"

"What are you doing here?" Sean demanded.

They were both talking at once.

"Yes, Father, I know him," Elizabeth said.

"Father!" Sean burst out, dumbfounded. "This can't be your father!"

"How dare you speak to my daughter in that fashion!" Langdon demanded.

Elizabeth could see that she was not exactly accomplishing her objective. She opened her mouth to speak again, but her father cut her off rudely.

"Go back upstairs," he said curtly. "You have no business here."

"But Father—"

"You heard me! I will not repeat myself to you."

Sean stood rooted by the interchange, still reeling from the revelation that last night's nurse was this morning's heiress.

Elizabeth hesitated on the stairs, unsure what to do, as the front door burst open and Sergeant Rees arrived with two of his men, trailed closely by an irate Mr. Todd.

"Come along with me, Sean," Rees said in a musical accent, his billy club in his hand. "Stop making trouble now—this won't help your cause at all."

"Well, taffy, have you come to restore law and order?" Sean sneered at the new arrival. "You're Langdon's lapdog, no better than this one here." He jerked his head toward Todd, who glared back at him.

Rees was about the same age as Sean, a tall blond in the gray-blue double-breasted uniform of the Coal Police. He had full authority to detain Sean and turn him over to the constable in Pottstown.

"Father, don't do this," Elizabeth pleaded. "What good can come of it?"

"I'll have some peace in my own house, that's what good can come of it," Langdon replied. "Take him away, Rees."

"Will you be filing charges, sir?" Rees asked as his men came to stand on either side of Sean.

"Hold him overnight in the CIP cell," Langdon said roughly. "I'll be down to do the paperwork when I'm free."

"I'm scheduled to lay the powder for the north face in number five tonight on the four to twelve," Sean said as the two burly guards seized his arms. "You'll be holding up your own operation by throwing me in the cooler."

"I'll take that chance," Langdon said.

Sean looked up at Elizabeth for a long moment, his eyes locked with hers. Then he erupted into activity, shrugging off one guard and punching the other in the jaw. As the second man fell, Sean charged past Rees, shoving him out of the way. Sean would have made it through the door had not Todd blocked his path, holding him up for the split second necessary for Rees to recover and club the miner on the back of the head.

Sean went down like a sack of meal.

Elizabeth cried out and ran down the stairs.

Langdon blocked her path as the men lugged Sean's deadweight through the door, his feet dragging across the tile.

Elizabeth stared at her father, her eyes huge.

"I'm sorry you had to see that," Langdon said quietly as the door closed behind the men, "but I told you to go upstairs."

"Is that all you're going to say? That man came here, alone, to talk to you about conditions in the mines, and you set your hired thugs upon him as if he were making off with the family silver!"

"Force is the only thing that element understands."

"They knocked him unconscious, Father."

"He'll come around shortly. That boy has too hard a head to stay down for long."

"But what about the reason he came? I saw for myself the men who were hurt in the accident last night, and if anything can be done to avoid something like that happening again, you should listen to him."

"What do you mean you saw for yourself?" Langdon demanded, his eyes narrowing.

"I went down to the shaft when the whistle blew to see if I could help," Elizabeth said boldly, aware that he would find out anyway as soon as Chief Anson arrived.

"To see if you could help...." Langdon repeated incredulously. "Are you out of your mind? If I ever hear of your doing such a thing again, I will have you in a coach on your way back to your Aunt Dorothea's the same day!''

"Aunt Dorrie is touring Europe for four months," Elizabeth said calmly.

"Then I'll find another school for you, preferably in the Indian colony! Do you think I brought you back here to instruct me in the conduct of my business?"

"Jameson says that regular inspections would make the mines safer for everyone," Elizabeth said, ignoring him. "Why won't you consider the idea?"

"Do you know how long I would have to shut down operations for the kind of inspection he wants?" Langdon shouted. "Days at a time, for each shaft, costing me hundreds an hour in lost production. And that's not all! He wants paid health coverage, pensions, all coming straight out of my pocket. He would lay every case of black lung in the entire district at my door! You've had no trouble all these years accepting the benefits of my hard work, young lady. Have you thought what your existence would be if people like Jameson got their way?"

"There must be some middle ground, Father. It can't be right that these miners have to risk their lives every time they go to work."

"And what would you know about it? You've never worked a day in your life, and thanks to me you'll never have to do so. Now I'm about to lose patience with this nonsense, Elizabeth. I suggest you take my earlier advice and retire to your room."

Elizabeth knew she had pushed him as far as she dared and relented. She went back upstairs to find Maura quietly weeping in the hall.

"Maura, come with me," Elizabeth said quickly, taking the girl into her bedroom and shutting the door behind them.

Maura wiped her cheeks with her apron, sniffling.

"I really think Sean will be all right, Maura," Elizabeth said kindly. "He'll probably just have a bad headache when he comes out of it."

Maura shook her head. "That's not it, miss."

"Are you worried about the cut he received in the accident? I know it bled a lot, but it was minor."

Maura shook her head. "The last time he was locked up in Pottstown he was worked over pretty good."

"Worked over?"

"Beat up, you know."

"Why?"

Maura looked at her almost sadly, as if her ignorance were pitiable. "They're not fond of paddies down there, miss," she explained.

"Paddies? Oh, the Irish."

"Yes, miss. They don't like the new people taking jobs. They put up signs in the shops—No Irish Need Apply. And with Sean talking the way he does..."

"And I suppose there's no hope of him keeping his mouth shut," Elizabeth said dryly.

Maura smiled weakly.

"Don't worry about it, Maura. I promise you that Sean will not be going to the Pottstown jail."

Maura looked at her warily. "What are you fixing to do?"

"I'll get him released."

Maura shook her head. "Oh, miss, your father will chew you up and spit out the feathers."

"Not if it's his idea."

Maura blinked, nonplussed.

"Just leave it to me," Elizabeth said, trying to sound more confident than she felt. She went to her desk, capped the inkwell she'd been using when writing earlier and stacked the foolscap pages of her letter together. "Maura, why did Sean call Sergeant Rees 'taffy' when he arrived?"

"Rees is Welsh," Maura said, smoothing her apron back down over her skirt.

"And?"

"Taffy means Welsh, like paddy for Irish."

"Is it derogatory?"

"Please?"

"A bad name, a word used in a fight."

Maura shrugged, then nodded.

"Is there bad feeling between the Welsh and Irish workers?" Elizabeth asked, trying to understand.

"Some. The Welsh are the real miners, see. There's lashings of coalfields all over Wales, and they learned the trade in the old country."

"And Ireland has no mines?"

"None to tell. The Irish are just willing to take on anything in order to work, and going down into the mines is . . ." She stopped.

"A job no one else wants," Elizabeth finished for her.

Maura nodded unhappily.

"So the Welsh view the Irish as interlopers."

Maura looked blank.

"Upstarts," Elizabeth explained.

"Yes, miss. And the Irish don't like the Welsh working in the Coal Police. It's a job no Irishman would take."

"Why not? There are Irishmen on the police force in every major city nowadays. Since the War Between the States their numbers have been increasing all the time."

"City police, yes," Maura said slowly. "But your da's security force, well, they see it as working as..."

"Lackeys?" Elizabeth supplied.

Maura said nothing.

"I'm beginning to understand how your brother's mind works," Elizabeth observed thoughtfully.

"Good luck to you," Maura said morosely. "I'm here to tell you it's a thankless task."

"All right, Maura, I don't want to keep you in here too long. Don't worry about Sean, I'll take care of it."

Maura looked doubtful, but she bobbed a curtsy and left.

Sean looked up as Tom Rees unlocked the grate into his cell and slid a tray through the opening.

"Dinner," Rees announced.

"When are you moving me to Pottstown?" Sean demanded, ignoring the food.

"Not until Langdon files his complaint," Rees replied, walking back to his desk.

"Don't you ever get tired of taking orders from that man?" Sean asked wearily. He was stretched out on the cot in his cell with his hands folded behind his head, which was throbbing painfully.

"Don't you?" Rees countered. He unhooked a round of keys from his belt and tossed them into a drawer.

Sean sat up and winced. "What do you mean by that?"

"You work for him, don't you?"

"Not as his private peeler," Sean said nastily, using old country slang for cop.

"We both take his money," Rees replied mildly.

"There's an ocean of difference between the two of us," Sean observed with finality.

"I suppose it comforts you to think so," Rees observed. He lifted his booted heels to the desk and opened his book, Mrs. Stowe's *Uncle Tom's Cabin.* He was trying hard to become an American, and he'd been told this book had a lot to do with the last war.

Sean rolled over on his cot and faced the wall. There was no talking to some people. He closed his eyes and the image of Langdon's daughter rose before him.

She had looked a picture as she came down the stairs of the big house, her hair all loose about her shoulders, ready to do battle with the old buzzard.

Sean couldn't believe they were related.

Well, there went his chances with her. He might have had some hope with a schoolteacher—not much, maybe, but some. Arthur Langdon's daughter, on the other hand, was out of the question.

He felt worse about that than he cared to admit. He'd been counting on finding the girl he'd met at the mine accident, and now she had moved as far out of his reach as if she were on the moon.

Sean shifted on the cot, easing his weight off his bad hip. He'd taken a musket ball during the battle of Gettysburg while serving with the Fifth Pennsylvania Volunteers in the summer of '63. He was eighteen at the time and had gone back to the mines as soon as he was discharged. The dampness in the shafts had ensured that the joint remained stiff; it acted up a little when he was tired, and he was certainly tired now.

The pounding in his head subsided slightly, and he drifted off to sleep, dreaming of Elizabeth Langdon and her long sable hair.

Elizabeth entered the dining room and slipped into her chair as noiselessly as possible.

Her father nodded glacially when she caught his eye.

Elizabeth folded her hands. "Father, I want to say that I'm very sorry about interfering in your affairs earlier. I'm just having a difficult adjustment with my return to Langdon, and sometimes I overstep my bounds. I promise you it won't happen again."

Langdon eyed her suspiciously. Elizabeth was saying the right words but she wasn't sure he was accepting the apology.

"I realized afterward how much trouble I caused," she said humbly. "My maid, Maura, is very upset that her brother is in jail, and I know that if I hadn't barged in it wouldn't have ended as badly as it did."

Langdon's expression softened slightly.

Encouraged, Elizabeth said, "Is it really necessary to send Jameson down to Pottstown? I think he's learned his lesson. I doubt if he'll come back to the house. He knows where it will land him if he does."

"He's a hard man to teach," Langdon said gruffly.

"It will hold up your blasting operation in number five if he's not available to lay the charges tonight as planned," Elizabeth pointed out to him.

"So now you're only thinking of me, is that it?" Langdon asked with a faint smile.

Sensing that she was overdoing it, Elizabeth backed off rapidly, murmuring, "Maura's a good girl. I hate to see her so unhappy."

Langdon sighed as Mrs. Tamm arrived with a platter of biscuits. "All right, I'll send word to release Jameson and let him work the night shift," he said.

"Thank you," Elizabeth said quietly. Then, hurrying on lest he change his mind, she added brightly, "I don't think I've told you that I accepted Charles Brandon's invitation to tea with his family this Sunday."

Her father nodded benignly. Charles was high on his list of approved suitors for Elizabeth's hand.

Elizabeth shot a glance at the housekeeper, who was fussing about the table. "Mrs. Tamm said she would help me bake an apple cake to bring with me."

"Fine, fine," Langdon agreed, unfolding his napkin as Mrs. Tamm beamed approvingly.

Elizabeth, who had no more intention of marrying Charles Brandon than she had of joining a convent, smiled to herself and daintily picked up her fork.

That night Elizabeth undressed for bed with Maura's assistance and then lay resting after the servant had been dismissed. She listened to the nocturnal sounds of the household retiring; gradually they faded into silence. When she heard the midnight whistle blow, signaling the change of shifts at the mine, she rose and discarded her nightgown quickly.

After dressing by the light of the moon, which shone in through her window in full harvest glory, she tamped down the dying fire in the grate and straightened her bed. She waited a few minutes longer, giving the miners time to return home and clear the streets. Then she picked up Sean's jacket from the foot of her bed, tiptoed out of her room, closing the door behind her, and hurried down the hall.

Todd's flat above the carriage house looked out over the front courtyard, and the old man was a light sleeper. To make sure she wasn't seen, Elizabeth went out through the kitchen and followed the same path she had taken the night of the mine explosion.

Once away from the house, Elizabeth relaxed. She scurried over the brow of the hill and then circled the breastworks of the mine as she descended. Coal dust swarmed over her shoes and fouled the hem of her skirt. The flooding moonlight was cold and clear, and frost had crystallized on the gray, blighted grass at the edge of the road. Dry leaves scuttled across her path, and the indefinable smell of poverty—a mixture of sour laundry and cheap boiled food—clung to the area like a miasma even at midnight.

Elizabeth turned down the main street of the coal patch. She could see two stragglers from the second shift in the distance. They parted at the end of the lane and entered their respective houses. Elizabeth waited until they were inside before proceeding; Maura had told her that the Jameson house was the third shanty on the left down from the Welsh church. They all looked the same.

Elizabeth hesitated when she saw one of the Coal and Iron Police come around the far corner, swinging his billy as he walked and trying the doors of the company store. She ducked down an alley until he passed, then stepped back into the street. Not much farther now. She gathered her woolen shawl closer about her as she stopped before the Jameson house. It was a wildly inappropriate time to pay a call, but if she came during the day she would surely be seen and her father informed.

She had abandoned her former plan to have Maura arrange a meeting with Sean. After the scene at her house that morning, she knew that he would not come.

There was a light inside the house on the ground floor, but the second level was dark. Sean should still be awake; the shift had ended only ten minutes earlier. She hoped the light was his.

Elizabeth mustered every ounce of courage at her command and mounted the sagging steps. A stained wooden washtub stood on the porch next to an empty milk bottle. A tattered lacy curtain, a sorry vestige of former finery stained gray with coal dust, covered the streaked and pitted window. She took a deep breath and rapped sharply on the faded door.

Sean pulled it open seconds later. He was stripped to the waist, his suspenders dangling down the front of his trousers. Firelight flickered over his torso, polishing the hard muscles of his arms and shoulders and bringing out the coppery sheen of his hair. He had a thin gray towel in his hand, and traces of soap still clung to his ears and chin.

He stared at her in shock, then recovered, the line of his jaw hardening perceptibly.

"What do you want?" he said curtly.

Chapter Three

"I'd like to speak to you, if I may," Elizabeth said, turning crimson and trying not to stare at his body. She felt the warm flush spreading over her face and wondered if he could see it in the uncertain light.

"You shouldn't be here," he said gruffly, his expression hostile. He grabbed her hand and yanked her, stumbling, into the house. He slammed the door after her.

"I won't stay long," she muttered in confusion.

"How did you get past the peeler?" he asked, walking beyond her to draw back the curtain and look through the window.

"I hid until he went by," Elizabeth replied.

"Why would you take such a chance?" he asked, turning back to eye her suspiciously.

"I really need to talk to you. Please don't send me away."

He considered her for long moment, thinking. Elizabeth gathered her shawl closer about her, gazing back at him steadily, restraining the urge to drop her eyes under his scrutiny.

"Wait a bit," he said shortly. He disappeared up the staircase and returned seconds later, shrugging into a clean shirt and thumbing his damp hair back from his forehead. He stepped aside, gesturing for her to leave the doorway and precede him into the room.

"It's an unlikely time to pay a visit," he observed dryly.

"I didn't want my father to know that I came here," Elizabeth answered.

"If he finds out you were larking about the coal patch in the middle of the night, he'll be mounting my head on his trophy-room wall," Sean said flatly.

"I'm not trying to get you into trouble," Elizabeth responded, twisting the ends of her shawl nervously. She stared miserably at the floor.

Sean relented. "All right," he said softly. "Don't take on so, I'll not bite you."

Elizabeth looked up and met his eyes.

He still examined her as if he couldn't credit his senses. Was she really in his house?

"Will you sit down?" he finally said.

Elizabeth sat in the rough-hewn chair he pulled out for her. There was a scattering of papers on the table next to a single coal oil lamp, and he gathered them up quickly, stacking them on a shelf next to the mantel-piece.

"Excuse my appearance," he said stiffly. "It's not possible to get all the grime off in the coal house. You

always need another wash at home no matter how hard
you try.''

He had evidently been washing when she arrived. A
tub of water, still steaming slightly, stood next to the
fire. A basket of coal bits, the ''burrs'' sold at a dis-
count because the pieces were so small, sat on the
hearth to feed the blaze. There was a rocking chair next
to the fireplace and a ragged hooked rug on the floor.
The staircase, which led to the second floor, had huge
splinters missing from a few of the steps.

''Will you have some tea?'' Sean asked, like one of
her aunt's friends hosting a Sunday social. Somehow
his quiet dignity prevented the question from sounding absurd, even considering the place and the hour.

Elizabeth nodded.

He removed a kettle from the hob and poured tea
into two chipped, stained mugs. The family's mis-
matched collection of crockery stood on a shelf next to
the mantel, and Elizabeth found herself comparing it
to her mother's Limoges.

A cross made of woven river rushes hung on a nail
on the wall above the shelf.

''What is that?'' she asked, pointing to the icon.

''Saint Brigid's Cross. It blesses the house.'' Sean set
a cup before her. ''No milk until the delivery tomorrow,'' he said briefly.

''That's all right, I like it this way,'' Elizabeth replied. His proud refusal to apologize for his circumstances was oddly touching.

He sat across from her and curled his hands around his cup. She noticed that his nails were cracked and, despite efforts with a brush that had left his knuckles raw, still stained with coal dust.

"Why didn't you tell me who you were last night at the mine fire?" he asked bluntly.

"Would you have let me help if you knew?" Elizabeth countered, raising her brows.

There was a sound from the stairs, and they both turned to see Maura belting a thin cotton wrapper around her waist. She stopped short when she saw Elizabeth sitting at the table with her brother.

"Miss Elizabeth!" she said in surprise. "Is there trouble up at the house?"

"Miss Langdon is here to see me," Sean said abruptly, indicating with a glance that Maura should not pursue it.

"At this hour?" Maura asked anyway.

"Should she have checked with you first?" Sean inquired testily, his expression annoyed.

Maura looked from one to the other and then dropped her eyes. "I'm sorry to interrupt," she said. "I heard voices and thought there might be something wrong."

"There's nothing wrong," her brother assured her. "Go back to sleep, Maureen."

Maura looked up at her employer's daughter. "Good night, Miss," she said.

"Good night," Elizabeth said.

Maura went back upstairs. Elizabeth waited until the sound of her movement faded and then said to Sean, "She's a lovely girl."

"Too lovely," he responded, taking a sip from his cup.

Elizabeth had to smile, despite her nervousness. "How can a person be too lovely?" she asked.

"Too nice, then. She has to toughen up a little to get by in this world."

"Oh, I'm sure she'll get some toughness along the way."

"But then she wouldn't be such a good servant, would she now?" Sean asked archly.

Elizabeth, nonplussed, didn't know what to say.

He stood. "I'm not much like her," he said, unnecessarily.

"I know," Elizabeth murmured.

He leaned against the wall of the shanty and folded his arms. "Miss Langdon, why are you here?"

"I brought you this," Elizabeth said, holding up his jacket, which had been bundled under her arm beneath her shawl when she arrived.

"You could have given that to Maura," Sean said.

"I also didn't like the way my father treated you today," she continued, "and I wanted to apologize."

He looked at her for a measuring moment and then said, "Did you speak up to get me released tonight?"

"Yes."

"I thought as much. And why did you do that?"

"I realized that my interference earlier today only made my father angrier, and he took it out on you."

"You didn't have to do anything to make your father angry at me. Odds are I would have wound up in the clink any road," Sean observed dryly. "Your da doesn't take too kindly to home visits from the lowly working classes."

"He doesn't take too kindly to much that isn't his own idea, I'm afraid," she said. "I've been discovering that lately."

"You don't know him very well, do you?" Sean said thoughtfully. "Why is that?"

Elizabeth looked down at the table, tracing the scars of long years of use with her fingernail. "I've lived with my aunt in Wynnewood since I was two, and I was away at school for a long time. I just got back to town a few weeks ago."

"Then you must take my word for it that what you saw today is not unusual at all."

"If you knew it was futile, why did you keep coming back to the house to talk to him?" she inquired.

"I wanted to meet him face-to-face just once, give him the chance to see reason," Sean said, "and I have. Now, whatever happens, it's on his head."

"What does that mean?" Elizabeth asked, looking up, alarmed. She didn't like the determined, resolute expression on his face. "What are you going to do?"

"I'll not live this way anymore without trying to change things, that much I'll tell you," he answered, indicating with a glance the barren hovel and the bleak street beyond it. He sat down suddenly, leaning forward urgently, the firelight casting half his face into shadow and turning the new scab on his forehead black as ink.

Elizabeth drew back slightly from the intensity of his gaze.

"Will you listen to some hard truths, even though you may not like what they reveal about your father?"

Elizabeth, pinned by his burning stare, nodded resignedly.

"Do you know how long a miner in this valley can expect to live?" he asked.

Elizabeth shook her head.

"To age forty-two. And coughing up coal dust long before that. A few years in the mines and the lungs are gone, men spitting up black phlegm like a choking heifer with foot-and-mouth disease."

"My father said you wanted to lay all the cases of black lung at his door," she murmured.

He slapped the table with his palm. "That's where they belong! Not to mention the accidents like the one you saw, which can kill and maim at any time. Your father and his cronies are getting rich while the people digging their coal for them are dying young and dying poor."

Elizabeth bit her lip, not meeting his eyes.

"Do you know what my wages were for last week?" he demanded. He got up and retrieved a slip of paper from the shelf near the fireplace. He read aloud. "Coal mined, 20 cars at 66 ¢ a car. Total, $13.20. Deduct 1 keg of powder, $2.50, 2 gallons of oil at 90 ¢ a gallon, repairs to my lantern, 1 dollar, new cap, 80 ¢. I took home $7.10. And that's paying no mind to my tab at the company store, which is enough to keep me in debt for the rest of my natural life. I give them a little each week to keep them doling out the goods, like everybody else, but the total is out of reach entirely."

Elizabeth, appalled, said nothing. Her boots cost more than his net wages for a week of backbreaking work.

"Well?" Sean demanded.

"I . . . it takes some getting used to, I think. I was little when I left. I was raised by my aunt. I had no idea . . ." she trailed off lamely.

"The most amazing thing to me is that nobody questions the way of things around here. Your father acts like I'm a raving madman, when all I want is to be treated fairly. We all thought that when we came to this country things would be different, but it's the same here as at home. The rich exploiting the poor—nothing ever changes."

"When did you come to this country?" Elizabeth asked quietly, still shaken by his accusations.

"When I was ten. The hunger had taken hold by then, and there was nothing at all to eat. My mother was working in the house of one of the local Tories, and she got part of the passage from him. My father sold everything we owned to get the rest. We came here with nothing to escape the famine."

"Famine?" Elizabeth said.

"The potato famine," he said, as if there had only been one in the history of the world.

"I'm afraid I don't know anything about it," Elizabeth said, ashamed of her ignorance.

He sighed. "I guess it wasn't big news in your house." He gestured vaguely. "Most of us who worked the fields lived on the Brit estates as tenants. We grew potatoes on our small plots and lived off them. But suddenly, when I was a mite, one year the potatoes failed. A couple of hours after they were dug out of the ground, they turned black and slimy, poison to eat. If you fed them to the cows, the cattle sickened. And it happened year after year once it started. The overlords did nothing to help, just let us starve. I remember the bodies piled too high to bury."

"And so you came here."

"We were told there was work. And so there was. Work in the mines, work no native-born Yankees wanted to do. But the trip over in steerage almost killed us, packed in like praties, no air to breathe, garbage to eat once a day, if that. One of my sisters died and my mother has never been the same. She's sickly yet."

"And your father?"

"He was killed in a blasting accident the year I was twelve. I went down the mines right after that."

"You've been working in them ever since?"

"Aye. Except for the war."

"You were in the war?" Elizabeth asked, surprised. "Were you drafted? Isn't that only for citizens?"

"I volunteered."

"Why?"

"I'm against slavery of any kind, the Africans in the South or the immigrants up here. It's all the same, isn't it?"

A child's cough sounded from the second floor.

"I'd better go," Elizabeth said, rising. "I'm afraid we're disturbing your family."

Sean rose with her. "I'll take you home."

"You can't come with me, Sean!" Elizabeth said. "What if we're caught?"

"We won't be caught," Sean replied, putting on the jacket she had brought to him. He blew out the lamp and glanced at the fire, which was almost dead.

"I can make it back alone, same way that I came," Elizabeth said. "I got here, didn't I?"

"The patch is no place for a woman to be walking about after dark. Have you never thought why your father has the CIPs on duty the whole night through?"

Elizabeth didn't answer as he opened the door.

"The men are unhappy, dissatisfied," Sean said. "That leads to drinking and then to fights. And what if these drunken brawlers were to see the daughter of the man they hold responsible for their sorry fate tripping down the street of *their* town, all alone, in the middle of the night? Do you ken what might happen if they'd had enough jars not to care at all about their own fate afterward? When the drink is in, the brains are out."

Elizabeth shivered as she considered what he'd said, but protested faintly. "I didn't see anyone but the coal policeman, and I'm sure he didn't see me."

He closed the door softly behind them. "Then you were lucky, but you might not be lucky twice. I'm coming with you and I'll hear no more about it."

They started off down the street, Sean striding quickly and Elizabeth hurrying to keep up with him. The moon had gone behind a bank of clouds and the sky had become very dark.

"What would your father do if he knew where you had been tonight?" Sean asked softly as they walked.

"Send me away, most likely."

"Where?"

"I don't know. He mentioned India."

"India!"

"Yes."

"Why did he bring you back here?"

"He wants me to get married."

"Aye, I thought so."

Elizabeth turned to look at him, and at that moment they heard steps approaching around a corner up ahead. Sean grabbed her and yanked her up a flight of steps and into a doorway with him, pressing her face into his shoulder. He drew her shawl up over her head as the footfalls came closer to them.

"Be still, now," he murmured in her ear.

Elizabeth's mouth went dry as dust as a voice called out, "Who goes there?"

She felt the rumble in Sean's chest as he said, "It's me, Clarkson."

The CIP's voice said, "Jameson?"

"The same."

Elizabeth could hear Sean's heart pounding beneath her ear. He wasn't as calm as he sounded.

"What are you doing out here? Not stirring up any more trouble, I hope."

"Not at all. Just seeing the lady home."

"Have you got a girl there?" the voice said, coming nearer. Elizabeth turned her head slightly. Out of the corner of her eye she could see the flicker of a torch being lit. Sean's fingers on the back of her neck returned her firmly to her former position. She closed her eyes tightly, waiting for the ax to fall, inhaling the clean scent of Sean's lye and tallow soap.

"I do, indeed," Sean said, "and we'd be the better off for a little privacy."

"Quite a fellow for the ladies, aren't you?" the cop asked, his tone suffused with amused tolerance.

"Well, you know how it is," Sean replied conspiratorially, in his best "broth of a boy" accent. If Elizabeth hadn't been quite so terrified, she might have been offended.

"All right, on your way," the CIP said, snuffing out the torch. They waited, frozen, until he had walked away.

"Damn, that was close," Sean said fervently, releasing her.

Elizabeth sagged against the porch railing. "'We won't be caught,'" she mimicked him in her best Irish brogue.

"Making fun of me, are you?" Sean asked, smiling slightly.

There was movement inside the house behind them, and Elizabeth looked at Sean in renewed panic.

He cursed vividly under his breath in a language she couldn't understand. When he saw that she wasn't reacting, he shoved her away from him.

"Go!" he whispered, pointing to the steps.

Elizabeth fled into the street and dashed out of sight.

Sean turned to face the irate woman who opened the door of the house. She was wearing a nightdress and frilled cap and holding a guttering candle.

"What's all this noise in my front yard?" she demanded in a heavy Ulster accent. "My man has to be up for the dawn shift and needs his kip in peace."

Sean stumbled against the wall of the porch and stared at her blearily.

"Mrs. McCarty?" he said thickly.

She put her free hand on her hip and surveyed him with motherly disapproval.

"Sean Jameson, what do you mean by turning up at my door in this condition?"

"Wrong house," Sean mumbled apologetically, burping loudly and lurching forward unsteadily.

Mrs. McCarty shook her head disgustedly. "I'm not surprised you couldn't find your own door, dithering about as loaded as a tick. I should soak your head to bring you out of it, so I should.''

Sean backed up out of her reach. ''Sorry to wake you,'' he muttered hastily.

''Go sleep it off, Seaneen. And I'll be talking to Father Murphy about you taking the pledge!'' She banged her door closed.

Sean rattled down the steps and joined Elizabeth where she had been hiding.

''You make a very convincing drunk,'' she observed.

''I've been there a few times,'' he said. He glanced ahead as the moon came out to lighten the dark street. ''Shall we continue, or maybe we could attract a bit more attention if we hired a brass band.''

Elizabeth started to laugh and found she couldn't stop. She put her hands over her mouth to stifle the sound, but her whole body shook.

''I expect President Grant will be arriving shortly to see if we're enjoying our stroll,'' Sean added dryly.

''This seemed like such a good idea when I was back in my room,'' Elizabeth gasped.

Sean grinned, his teeth very white.

''Do you think I'll ever get back home?'' she asked, wiping her eyes with a corner of her shawl.

''I'll see to it. Come along.''

He hustled her up the street at such a brisk rate she was soon running to keep up with him.

''I didn't mean for you to turn this into a footrace,'' she complained.

"I see a light on in your house," he observed, squinting into the distance.

Elizabeth stopped abruptly. "Oh, no."

"Who might it be?"

"Is it on the second floor, at the front?"

"Aye."

"Todd."

"Him. What would he be doing?"

"He's a light sleeper. He's always prowling around at night."

"Maybe his conscience keeps him awake," Sean said darkly.

"Not everyone has your zeal for reform, Sean."

"More's the pity," he replied bitterly.

They came to the incline that led upward to the mansion. All was in darkness except for the pinpoint of light moving through Todd's rooms. He was carrying a lantern.

"I can make it from here," Elizabeth said.

"You certainly cannot—I'll take you to the door."

Elizabeth stopped and turned to gaze up at him earnestly. His broad shoulders formed a bulky outline against the backdrop of the moon.

"It's too dangerous for you," she said.

"And I suppose it's not dangerous for you to be wandering up the hill alone?"

"For heaven's sake, Sean, what can happen? I'm within shouting distance of the house. Let me go."

"You are a stubborn woman."

"My father would agree with you," she answered teasingly.

"Well, I would hate to find myself on his side of any argument," Sean said lightly.

A silence formed and grew between them. Neither one wanted to move away first.

"I'm glad I came to see you," Elizabeth said seriously. "I feel better since I talked to you."

"It's not many young ladies of your station who would care about the likes of me," he said softly.

"I care about anyone who I feel is being mistreated."

"You're a rare one. I fear you'll not last long in these coalfields in that state of mind."

"I hope you're wrong."

"I'll say goodbye now, then," Sean murmured. "I'll not be talking to you again."

"Why not?"

"Oh, Elizabeth," he said, using her name for the first time, "you know why not."

"If you see me, you won't speak to me?"

"I won't."

"Then I'll speak to you."

"You'll be the worse for it."

"I'll take that chance."

He reached for her hand suddenly and held it to his lips. Elizabeth felt his touch like a brand.

"Excuse the familiarity," he said huskily, "but I

read in books that this is the way to say farewell to a great lady.''

He dropped her hand, turned on his heel and disappeared into the enveloping night.

Chapter Four

Elizabeth didn't breathe easily until she was back in the safety of her bedroom. Todd hadn't noticed her passage around to the back garden, and the house had been quiet as she climbed the stairs. Now, with the moonlight pooling on her bed, she undressed down to her chemise and flung herself across the goose-down coverlet.

Sleep was a long time coming. The imprint of Sean's body against hers was as palpable as the kiss he'd pressed on her hand. She kept replaying the same scene in her mind: the instant when Mrs. McCarty had come to the door and Sean had swept Elizabeth into his arms. She remembered the feel of his corduroy jacket against her cheek, the movement of the muscles of his shoulder, the soap and warm skin smell of him.

It was enough to keep any woman awake, but for Elizabeth, who'd led a sheltered life among women in ladies' schools, the experience was overwhelming.

And for the second night in a row, it was almost dawn before she slept.

* * *

The next evening, four men wearing grim expressions sat around the bare table in the Jamesons' front room. A half-empty bottle of whiskey was planted in the middle of it.

"Well now," Jim Kelly said acidly to Sean, "are you ready to admit it's time for a strike, at the very least?"

Sean met his stare levelly, saying nothing.

"You had to go up there to the house and make a fool of yourself, didn't you?" Kelly continued. "I hope you had a fine time, getting thrown in the clink for your trouble."

"I said I would keep trying until I saw Langdon. I saw him. There's an end to it."

"To your self-respect, you mean," Kelly said darkly. "Have you no pride, man?"

"Have you no sense?" Sean countered furiously, rising to his feet as he finally lost his temper. The discussion had been going on for some time, and he was tired of Kelly and his theatrics. His tune never changed, and Sean had seen how far Kelly's tactics got their compatriots in the old country.

"Guts is what you're lacking," Kelly said disgustedly.

"Oh, I know. It's your solution to toss sticks of dynamite at every problem."

Kelly snorted. "And you'll talk us to death, I suppose." He turned away in dismissal as the other two men looked on silently.

"No. I was just setting up the situation, and if you looked at anything but the racing form and the pictures in the *Irish Times,* you'd know a bit more about how things work in this country and what I was trying to do."

Kelly rolled his eyes, but Shane, one of the older men who'd been in the mines for thirty years, said, "Tell us, Sean. We're listening."

Sean favored Kelly with an annoyed glance before saying, "Well. First thing is, any violence and we're in the wrong from the start. We'll have no chance for a hearing, we'll be arrested, and our cause will die in the courts before it's even heard. Second, we all know that Langdon is as rich as Midas—"

"Who?" Kelly said.

"—and has a host of powerful friends," Sean went on, ignoring him. "The last thing we want to look like to these people is a bunch of thugs just off the boat and out to disrupt the coal supply to heat America's homes." Here he favored Kelly with a meaningful glance. Kelly glared back at him defiantly.

"Langdon has friends in the state and federal legislatures, he has friends everywhere," Sean continued. "He can get laws passed making strikes illegal, making striking a hanging offense. That's why striking is so dangerous for us. All he has to do is grease a few palms and the next thing you know we're facing not prison, not work gangs, but the gallows. It's happened before, in Britain and Australia, and the Constitution here is based on the U.K. common law."

"He's talking like a lawyer again," Kelly said to the ceiling.

"It's a sure improvement over talking like the village idiot," Sean snapped back at him.

"I've heard this before," Kelly said. "I'd rather face the gallows than work in those damned pits any longer, ankle-deep in freezing water, just waiting for the earth to cave in on me."

"I haven't heard it," said Shane, who had missed the last meeting, "so shut your gob, Jim Kelly, and let Jameson here have his full say."

Kelly folded his arms in annoyance, but subsided.

"I'm not saying we shouldn't strike, just that striking has to be a last resort," Sean continued. "It has to look like we tried every route before taking that one. That's why I've made such a display of trying to see Langdon. Everyone knows I've been going up there to the house—the servants, the people in the town, even Langdon's daughter. We shouldn't lack for witnesses if I have to show in court that I tried to reach a compromise and Langdon wouldn't listen."

There was a silence as the men considered this.

"You mean it was all a show?" Shane asked.

"Not at all," Sean replied. "I was hoping Langdon would talk to me. But I also knew that making a loud nuisance of myself would leave a trail to show I tried."

"You're really down the well if you think the old man's daughter is going to speak up for the likes of you if it comes to that," Kelly finally observed.

"There were other people around—the house-keeper, the coachmen, my sister, Maura."

"Your sister!" Kelly exclaimed. "There's an unbiased witness the courts would dearly love to hear."

"What about the others?"

"They're all Langdon's creatures!" Kelly said. "He'll scare them off or pay them off. You're dreaming."

"I laid the groundwork," Sean replied stubbornly. "I can't worry about what Langdon might do or might not do, I just have to be smart as I know how to be and as careful as I can. It won't help anything to go blundering around like a Nationalist thug blowing up a British Rail line in Londonderry."

"Ah, you're a talker! You've got more brains than balls," Kelly said contemptuously.

Sean favored him with a pitying glance. "All right, Kelly, you have it your way. You send as many coal cars as you can rig to blow at once to kingdom come. You'll have ten seconds of satisfaction, and you'll hurt Langdon about as much as a hangnail on his thumb. Then we can visit you in jail, that is if you don't get deported first! That will solve all our troubles, won't it?"

Faced with the inescapable logic of Sean's argument, Kelly burst out with, "Your way is taking too damn long! I'll be as gray as Shane here before we take any action."

"Not at all," Sean replied. "I'm setting the first slowdown for Wednesday the thirty-first."

"Why then?" Shane asked.

"The next shipment goes that Thursday morning. I'm thinking it will be a bit light."

"How will we accomplish that?"

"Everybody will be slashing production by half. A man who usually cuts eighteen cars a week will cut nine. We'll still be taking home some money, but Langdon's proceeds will decrease enough for him to take notice. If that gets us nowhere, we'll drop out for a shift—nobody shows for the four to twelve, say, when we lay the charges. And so on that way up to a full stoppage, if we have to go that far."

They digested that for a long moment before Shane said, "What about Langdon's company picnic on the twenty-eighth?"

"We participate as usual. Anything else will put Langdon onto the scent."

"Where have you been getting these tactics, son?" asked Bill Conran, speaking for the first time. He was the oldest of the group at fifty and had seniority over Shane by four years.

"I've been reading about them in some labor books I got at the library in Pottstown," Sean replied.

"Reading, can you credit it?" Kelly said, sneering.

"I can't read," Conran said to him. "Can you?"

Kelly's sneer faded, but he didn't reply.

"I like an educated man," Conran said with finality, standing.

"I'm hardly that," Sean interjected, abashed. "The parish priest back home taught me lettering in exchange for doing chores."

"Well, you can count me in, and I'll speak for you to the others," Shane agreed, rising to stand next to Conran.

"Kelly?" Sean asked.

"We'll see how it goes," Kelly said grudgingly.

"And when will you tell the men?" Conran inquired.

"Send word round that there'll be a meeting in the old shaft at nine tonight, same time as before. I'll lay out everything then. And tell the men to go one by one through the underground passage—no groups. And stagger their arrival time. We don't want anyone to be spotted."

"We'll need a code word to keep these goings-on from the ears of those who would betray us," Conran observed. "There's some who would turn us in for the price of a pint, and well you know it."

Sean thought for a moment, picturing the men gathered in the tunnel by the light of their homemade torches.

"Torchlight," he said.

Conran considered it, then nodded.

"Torchlight it is." He clapped the younger man on the shoulder and then walked past the table and out the door, Shane following him. Kelly hung back to have the last word.

"I'm not saying I'm agreeing with you, now," he informed Sean warningly.

"God forbid," Sean responded dryly.

"But I'm willing to give it a go."

"Big of you."

"I can see that we all have to act together. A bunch of us running around like plucked chickens going in different directions will do more harm than good. If this is what the majority wants when we vote, I'm for it."

Sean waited.

"But if I see your plan isn't working, I'll be after bashing Langdon before you can put a stop to it."

Sean restrained the urge to throttle the other man. He knew better than anyone how the long hours in the pit, chipping away at solid rock until your arms ached in the dampness and foul air, put a man in a killing mood. But Kelly was a hothead; he came from a nation of hotheads.

Sean was determined not to perpetuate that mistake.

"Wait it out, Jim," he said. "Give me a chance."

Kelly nodded slowly. "I will."

Sean extended his hand and Kelly shook it. Once.

Then he left Sean alone with his thoughts.

For several days Maura went about her business at the Langdon house without mentioning Elizabeth's nocturnal visit to her brother. Finally Elizabeth could stand it no longer and said to the girl, "Aren't you going to ask me what I was doing at your house the other night?''

Maura was changing the sheets on her mistress's bed while Elizabeth worked away on the project she'd promised for the fair at her father's church. Her needlework was not wonderful at the best of times, and today she'd pulled out more stitches than she'd set in place. The lilac blossom she was embroidering looked like a purple explosion, the outlines blurred and scraggly. Elizabeth sighed.

She would probably wind up submitting something of Mrs. Tamm's and cravenly passing it off as hers.

Maura continued to punch the pillows on the bed.

''Well?'' Elizabeth prodded.

''I ken that's between you and Sean,'' Maura replied finally.

''Aren't you interested?''

Maura looked at her mistress with wisdom beyond her years. ''The less I know of Sean's doings the better.''

''You were curious the other night when you came down the stairs, weren't you?''

''I was surprised to find you there. We don't usually get visitors from the main house in the patch.''

''I thought my father treated Sean very badly, and I went to see him to say so.''

Maura stopped patting the comforter into place and faced Elizabeth directly.

''All right. Since you're asking, miss, I think I should say that you butting in like you did was no help to Sean. Defiance only sets your father on edge. I've been working here longer than you've been home, and believe me, I know."

Taken aback, Elizabeth said, "I reacted emotionally to that situation. I certainly had no desire to get Sean into further trouble."

"He manages enough of that very well on his own," Maura said. "But if you seem to be taking up for Sean, it will just drive your father into a distraction."

"I thought I could do some good," Elizabeth murmured.

"You can't," Maura said firmly. She had lived too long, unprotected by finishing schools or doting aunts, in the world of powerful men to have Elizabeth's faith in fair play.

"How do you know that if you never try?" Elizabeth asked.

Maura shook her head and lowered her voice. "If you go on like this, you might as well put Sean in chains right now!" she whispered fiercely, clenching her fists. "Your da will stop at nothing if he thinks you're after my brother!"

"After him!" Elizabeth repeated, blushing to the roots of her hair. "What do you mean?"

"Your father is not going to believe that your interest in Sean is purely for the welfare of the miners," Maura replied bluntly, gathering the used linen into a bundle forcefully.

"And you don't believe it, either—is that what you're saying?" Elizabeth demanded angrily.

"I've got eyes, and so has your father. Sean is young and handsome, and you're a woman."

"I do think the mine workers are being mistreated. I do!" Elizabeth protested.

"They are indeed, and they'll be treated far worse if you keep carrying on this way!" Maura said strongly. "Do you know nothing about the man who sired you? He won't see reason. He'll take revenge!"

Elizabeth fell silent, listening.

Maura paused for a long moment, then added wearily, "Excuse me for speaking to you this way, miss, but I see bad days coming and I'm sore afraid. Whatever your private thoughts are, you must act with your father as if you've forgotten all about this trouble. Make him think it was a girlish idea of yours to mix in, a...a..." She gestured helplessly.

"Whim," Elizabeth murmured.

"Aye." Maura nodded eagerly. "Pretend that you're sorry now and you're busy with other things. Do you not see that anything else would be putting Sean in danger? No matter what, your father won't hurt you, but he'll not stop at—" She broke off, frowning.

"At what?" Elizabeth asked, riveted. "Maura, what are you talking about? What do you know?"

Maura shook her head. "I've only heard stories, and I'll say no more. But please, miss, pay good mind to what I'm asking." Maura turned on her heel.

"Maura, wait," Elizabeth called, standing. Her embroidery hoop tumbled to the floor.

Maura fled. Elizabeth pressed her hands to her cheeks and closed her eyes, sinking back into her chair.

Was Maura hinting that her father had harmed people in the past to protect his interests? After what Elizabeth had seen already, that shouldn't really have surprised her, but somehow the idea was still shocking.

Maura was right. Elizabeth had been acting as impulsively as a child, heedless of the consequences her actions might have for other people in less fortunate positions.

From now on she would take Maura's advice.

Maura ran down the stairs and almost crashed into Sergeant Rees at the bottom.

"Good morning, Miss Jameson," Rees said politely.

"Who are you arresting today, Rees?" Maura demanded tartly. While she always used caution in conversation with those of superior station, Maura had no trouble speaking up to her equals.

"I'm arresting no one, just here to pay a call."

"How nice that you don't always have to be slapping people in jail," she said, trying to pass him. "Let me by, if you please."

"I don't please," he answered.

"Are those the manners you learned in Cardiff?"

"I'm from Holyhead, myself."

"I don't care if you're from the Holy City, Mr. Rees, though I seriously doubt it. Right now you're in my way."

"I mean to be. Are you going to the company picnic on the twenty-eighth?"

"I've no earthly idea, Mr. Rees."

"None at all?"

"None. And I have a word of advice for you. If you spent less time keeping young ladies from their work, you'd have more time to kiss Mr. Langdon's feet. Is that not why you're here?"

"Keeping order for Mr. Langdon is my job," he said quietly, still blocking her path.

"Oh, aye, your job," she said, her voice dripping contempt.

"Just like it's your job to change those sheets you're carrying," he observed, deftly pointing out that they were both working for the same employer.

She didn't miss his point. "Switching linens is not the same as hounding innocent people."

The door from the kitchen opened, and Mrs. Tamm entered the hall. Maura seized the opportunity to dodge around Rees, who gazed after her longingly.

She sure was pretty, with that flaming red hair and white skin. She was like the women in the portraits by a Renaissance artist who had impressed Rees, some Italian named Titian. Rees had seen a book of reproductions once and had never forgotten it. The rich colors, the ambers and russets and golds, could be found decorating prosaic Langdon in the hues of Maura Jameson's hair.

"Sergeant Rees?" Mrs. Tamm said pleasantly, bringing him out of his reverie.

"Uh, good morning," Rees said.

"Mr. Langdon is expecting you in the library."

"Thank you."

He followed Mrs. Tamm, who made a clinking sound when she walked from the ring of house keys on her belt, across the carpeted hall the few steps to the paneled sliding doors of the study. The housekeeper pushed open one of the doors and announced, "Sergeant Rees is here to see you, sir."

Langdon's study was filled with books. There were floor-to-ceiling shelves crammed with them and stools and stepladders positioned around the floor for easy access to the higher levels. Rees, who had the Welsh love of literature hampered by inadequate access to it, felt a stab of envy. All this, and the old man took it for granted. Rees was lucky if once in a while he could save up enough to buy a discard from the Pottstown library, where the stock did not exactly rival Alexandria's.

"Ah, Tom," Langdon said. He was sitting behind a burled walnut desk, and he rose to cross the inlaid parquet floor. There was a large wooden globe mounted on a stand, with all the continents marked in antique script, next to a glass-fronted case displaying the Langdon collection of Indian arrowheads. Rees stopped in front of it and waited for the older man to reach him. The curved, sparkling surface reflected his tall, lean frame and lush blond hair.

Langdon shook hands with him and gestured to an armchair across from his desk.

"Sit down, sit down, and tell me how things are going," Langdon said, returning to his own leather chair.

"No trouble from Jameson since I released him," Rees reported, sitting with his booted feet planted on the Oriental rug that flowed out from under Langdon's desk. He spoke slowly, trying to minimize his accent, which he'd been working hard to lose.

"He's been showing up for his shifts with no rabble-rousing on the side?" Langdon asked.

"None that we've been able to detect."

"No gatherings at his house?"

Rees shrugged. "Sometimes a few of his cronies show up for a grog, but I wouldn't call that a meeting. The old geezers he hangs out with couldn't organize a crow fight."

"But Jameson could. Don't underestimate him."

"I don't. We're watching him."

"I'd like to run him out of town."

"You need him," Rees responded bluntly.

"Do I need him badly enough to risk the damage he could do?" Langdon asked rhetorically. "Can't we train somebody else to use powder the way he does?"

Rees sighed. "Not without wasting a lot of valuable time. Jameson has the touch, and you can't teach that. He can run his finger over the surface of a rock face and *feel* where the strata are. He can look at a wall and tell from the veining where to lay the charge. The granite just breaks apart when he raps it like the halves of an orange to reveal the stripes of coal. I've seen him do it myself."

"Nobody's indispensable," Langdon growled.

"I'm telling you the truth, sir," Rees said implacably. "Firing him would hurt production badly. And I'm not sure that it would stop the trouble. All the men are hot for battle. Jameson is the most vocal and probably the smartest of them, but if he were out of the picture, someone else would rise to take his place."

"Are you saying I should make concessions?" Langdon asked darkly.

"It would take some of the steam out of Jameson's act if you did," Rees responded reasonably.

Langdon slammed his fist down on the desk. "I will not be intimidated by a bunch of illiterate, unwashed hooligans who are lucky to be in this country and to have a job at all!" he said emphatically.

Rees bowed his head and said nothing, aware that in Langdon's estimation he was one step away from that group himself. God, the man was obstinate. If he would just give a little, he could gain a lot, maybe prevent the powder keg they were sitting on from going up like a torch. But he would go on grinding the noses of the miners in the dust, refusing to budge an inch, until the whole valley exploded in a sheet of flame.

"Well, Rees?" Langdon demanded.

"Just as you say, sir," Rees replied, standing.

"I'll expect regular reports," Langdon warned.

Rees nodded.

Langdon glanced at the grandfather clock in a corner of the room. "It's getting on toward lunch. Why don't you go into the kitchen and ask Mrs. Tamm to give you something? She'll be free for an hour before she's needed to serve in the dining room."

Rees would have liked to before she's needed to serve in the dining room."

Rees would have liked to decline, but he knew better than to turn down one of Langdon's rare bursts of generosity.

"Thank you, sir," he said, and strode out of the room.

The wide front hall was empty. Rees wended his way toward the back of the house, passing burnished furniture redolent of beeswax polish and the numerous displays of fresh flowers Langdon regarded as a necessity for gracious living. Every piece of glass, from the flutes on the chandelier to the vases and the crystal bibelots on display everywhere, shone like tinsel.

The swinging door to the kitchen was closed. Rees pushed through it and confronted Maura Jameson, who was standing at a wide oak table, chopping vegetables with a cleaver.

She looked up and said challengingly, "And what might you be doing in here, Sergeant?"

"I'm looking for Mrs. Tamm."

"She's not here."

"I can see that. Where is she?"

"She had Todd drive her down to the butcher's in Pottstown. He keeps sending up the wrong cuts of meat. She'll be back shortly."

Rees stood uncertainly, then started to back out of the room.

"What did you want with her?" Maura asked briskly.

"Mr. Langdon sent me in to get some lunch," Rees reported unhappily, continuing his exit.

"Oh, and you hadn't the salt to turn him down," Maura observed, noting her visitor's expression.

Rees eyed her murderously but said nothing.

"Don't look so fiery—everyone around here is afraid of him, too," Maura said flatly. She swept a pile of diced carrots into a bowl with the side of her hand and started hacking up an onion. "It's all right, sit you down. I'll feed you."

Rees hesitated, but the desire to get to know Maura better won, and he did as she directed, glancing around the room. A double-size walk-in fireplace was hung with all manner of pots and pans. A black iron range with something simmering on top of it was vented by a pipe through the roof. Glass-fronted cabinets along the walls contained crockery of every description. In one wall there was a door that led to a pantry and cold storage room.

"You can take off your coat and stay awhile," Maura said dryly, noticing the degree of his discomfort.

Rees unbuttoned his tunic obediently and draped it on the back of his chair.

"Chicken stew and biscuits?" Maura asked efficiently.

"Fine," he said. He cleared his throat nervously. "Could I talk to you?" he asked.

"I thought you were already doing that."

"I meant personally. Over here with me."

She shrugged and came toward him.

"Could you put the knife down?" he asked.

Maura had to smile. She moved back a step and dropped the knife onto the cutting table, holding her hands above her head in a gesture of surrender.

"Thank you," Rees said. He indicated the chair across from him, and Maura slipped into it. She folded her hands before her and gazed at him expectantly, like a bright child in school.

"I've an idea you're not too fond of me," he said directly.

"I've no feelings about you whatever," Maura replied.

"That's not true."

"Are you putting the liar's name on me?" Maura demanded.

"Miss Jameson, every time you see me you act like I've come to collect your taxes. Now why is that?"

"Maybe we're not too fond of peelers at my house."

"I see. I'm convicted before trial because I'm a member of the Coal Police."

"You're the ranking officer in this town, which is a little different now, isn't it? Anytime there's trouble it's your face showing up and slapping the irons on people."

Rees sat back in his chair and sighed. "I think you should know something. When I first came to this country, I went down into the pits like everybody else. I was a miner for three years when Mr. Langdon noticed me and gave me the chance to get out into the air and sunlight. I took the opportunity, and I think your brother or anyone else would take it, too."

"My brother would never be picked for such service. He doesn't have the proper—" she paused significantly "—attitude."

"I see. I'm a groveling bootlicker and your brother is a noble workingman."

Maura shrugged. "You draw your own conclusions, Sergeant." She stood abruptly.

Rees stood with her and grabbed her wrist. At the same moment, Mrs. Tamm hurried through the back door with a package wrapped in butcher's paper and tied with string under her arm.

"That man is an idiot—it's worth your life to talk to him," she grumbled, still bristling from her encounter with the butcher. She didn't notice the two young people until she turned to drop the package onto the table and saw them frozen in tableau, staring at her.

"What's this?" she demanded, her brow creasing in concern.

Rees released Maura, who stepped away from him nimbly.

"Nothing at all," Maura replied lightly. "Mr. Langdon sent the Sergeant in here for some lunch, and I was about to get it for him."

Mrs. Tamm's eyes moved from one to the other. She was not satisfied with the explanation but didn't have time to pursue the matter.

"You get into the dining room and set the table. Use the Brussels lace cloth and the rose china," she said to Maura briskly. "We're having Mr. Faison from the newspaper to lunch. I'll set a plate for Mr. Rees."

Maura obeyed, glad of the chance to escape. Rees looked after her and then turned to face the older woman.

"I believe I'll skip that lunch, Mrs. Tamm," he said uncomfortably. "You already have your hands full here, and I really have to get back to the CIP office."

"Nonsense," Mrs. Tamm replied, untying the ribbons of her spoon bonnet and removing the pin from its crown. She had a maternal side, rarely seen, and was also not averse to the company of a good-looking young man. "It will be no trouble."

Rees subsided, defeated, and sat again at the table.

Mrs. Tamm hung her hat on a maple stand by the pantry door and unbuttoned the embroidered shoulder cape she wore. She folded the woolen garment neatly and draped it next to the bonnet.

"Now then," she said, donning an apron and patting her chignon, "let's see what we can rustle up for you."

Rees resigned himself to his fate and realized that he was, after all, very hungry.

On Sunday, Elizabeth dressed carefully for her tea with Charles Brandon. When Maura arrived to help her, there was an awkward moment, with the Irish girl laying out Elizabeth's best afternoon dress in silence with downcast eyes.

"It's all right, Maura," Elizabeth finally said gently. "I'm not angry with you for what you said the other day."

"I spoke out of turn, miss," Maura replied, appearing distressed. "My wagging tongue will finish me yet."

"You were right in what you said, and I will remember it," Elizabeth told her. "Now let's see if I can get dressed on time or Todd will be up here to carry me down himself."

Maura smiled. "Right you are about that, miss."

Elizabeth's outfit had been purchased in Philadelphia. It was advertised as a copy of the latest thing from the House of Worth in Paris. It was sky-blue Lyons silk, designed with a full bustle in the back and a sweeping apron across the front, both banded and fringed with black silk, with matching black silk bows on the flaring sleeves. The full-length cape was of black wool lined with the blue silk of the dress. A gypsy bonnet of black straw trimmed with silk cornflowers around the flat crown and tied with blue ribbons completed the ensemble.

"You do look a picture, miss," Maura said approvingly when Elizabeth was dressed.

"I've never met Mrs. Brandon, and the idea is for me to make a good impression," Elizabeth said, adjusting the cameo ear bobs that had belonged to her mother.

"Mr. Charles is a fine-looking man," Maura observed, picking up Elizabeth's dressing gown from a chair.

"He's nice enough, I suppose," Elizabeth replied.

"His family owns the Brandon Mercantile. They have stores in Philadelphia, Boston, New York—all over the country, I think."

"That's why Charles is such a favorite of my father's," Elizabeth said with more harshness than she'd intended, fastening the button at the collar of her cloak.

"Don't you like him?" Maura asked.

"I hardly know him. I've met him a few times on social occasions since I've been back. I accepted his invitation to make my father happy and distract his attention from my behavior earlier this week."

One of the day maids tapped at the door.

"Mr. Todd is asking after you, miss," she said when Elizabeth bade her enter.

"Tell Mr. Todd I'll be right down," Elizabeth said.

The girl disappeared. Elizabeth picked up her reticule and said to Maura, ''I'll be back for supper. My father is out so you can tell Mrs. Tamm to keep it light. About eight will be fine.''

Maura nodded.

''And Maura, that bundle at the foot of the bed is for you. We're about the same size, and there are some things in there I can't use anymore. A vest and a fringed shawl, some silk chemises. You can take them if you like.''

''Thank you, miss,'' Maura said, and bobbed a curtsy. She started to hang Elizabeth's dressing gown in the wardrobe as her mistress left.

Todd was pacing up and down in front of the coach when Elizabeth emerged from the front entrance. He leaped to the door and held it open as Elizabeth climbed the portable steps and then settled herself inside the trap. Todd climbed into the driver's seat, took up the reins and waited for Elizabeth to tap the roof of the coach before urging the twin bays onto the road.

It was a glorious autumn afternoon, but Elizabeth soon tired of the colorful scenery as they traveled the six miles to the Brandon estate just outside of Pottstown. She settled back against the padded seat and closed her eyes, allowing the swaying of the coach to lull her into a reverie.

She had not seen Sean since the night of her visit and didn't expect to see him in the future. The thought didn't upset her, exactly, but rather filled her with a sort of looming hopelessness and despair that she couldn't dismiss.

She wanted to meet Sean again, talk to him, but she didn't know how to manage it. She just couldn't forget him.

Her thoughts kept her occupied, and they turned into the Brandon's tree-lined drive before she expected it. The neoclassical, southern-style mansion waited for them at the end of the road, with a sweeping front patio and fluted Doric columns supporting the tiled roof.

The Brandon residence made Arthur Langdon's house look like a summer cottage.

The houseman was waiting for Elizabeth when she descended from the coach. He opened the door for her, and in the front hall, with its marble floor and winding staircase, she was greeted by Priscilla Brandon, Charles's mother.

Priscilla, a comely woman in her mid-forties, was wearing an afternoon dress of dark brown Italian silk, draped up in the skirt to show a floral-patterned lining in apple green. There was also an underskirt of pale copper silk, complemented by the amber earrings she wore and the amber silk bow in her light brown hair. She looked like a magazine illustration and made Elizabeth, who was very nicely dressed, feel dowdy.

"My dear," Priscilla said, "you must be Elizabeth. Charles has been looking forward to your visit so very much."

The servant took Elizabeth's cloak, and Priscilla led her into an elaborately furnished drawing room, where a fire was burning cheerfully in a marble fireplace. Several Louis IV chairs were drawn up before the fire, and a low carved table had been cleared for the tea.

"I thought it would be fun for us to get to know each other a little bit before Charles joins us," his mother said, indicating where Elizabeth was to sit. Elizabeth recognized that this meant Priscilla was going to interrogate her and determine her suitability for the Brandon heir before the man himself arrived. She settled in to endure the chat.

Priscilla waved her hand to indicate that the maid who had suddenly appeared was to serve the tea. "Charles's father is away on business, and his sister, Emily, is visiting her uncle, my brother, in Hartford. The house seems so lonely and empty with just the two of us here. We've both been so longing for company."

The maid returned shortly with a chased silver service, which she placed on the table in front of Mrs. Brandon. That lady poured tea into thin porcelain cups as she said, "Charles tells me that you've just returned to Langdon from school."

"Yes. I've only been back a short time."

"What school did you attend?" Priscilla asked pleasantly.

Elizabeth answered questions and made polite conversation while the maid passed around plates of almond cakes, dripping scones and crustless sandwiches of cold capon and watercress. Priscilla took one slice of cake and then spent her time crumbling it in to pieces on her plate; she ate nothing. Elizabeth began to wish Charles would appear, before Priscilla asked to see a detailed graph of her family tree back to William the Conqueror.

"I went to Oldfields in Baltimore. My mother was from the South, and she felt there was no finishing school for a southern woman except that one," Priscilla was saying. "Of course, that was before the war. A lot of things are so changed now—it's not the same country anymore. Not the same world, I'm afraid."

Elizabeth, who was eleven when the war began and fifteen when it ended, and who had been shielded from the conflict, murmured sympathetically. She recognized that for anyone with southern ties the outcome of the conflict had been devastating. People like Priscilla's mother mourned a way of life that was gone forever.

"Elizabeth!" Charles said as he entered from the hall. "Don't you look lovely!"

Both women glanced up as Charles advanced into the room. He was wearing a dark gray, single-breasted coat with short rounded tails and lapels finished with black braid. His trousers were worsted wool of a lighter gray, matched with a sleeveless waistcoat of the same material. He looked exceptionally clean and perfectly turned out, just like his mother.

He bent over Elizabeth and took both her hands in his. "I hope my mother has told you that we're both thrilled to have you here."

"Yes, she has."

Charles was a study in sepia; his hair, mustache and eyes were all the same shade of brown. He sat across from Elizabeth and accepted the cup of tea his mother handed him, balancing it on his knee.

"How did you find the trip over here?" he asked.

"Oh, fine. Todd is a good driver."

"He is, indeed. If your father's not careful, we shall try to steal him away from you," Priscilla said. "He's a much better man with horseflesh than our coachman, Simpson."

"I doubt you'll succeed there," Elizabeth said, smiling. "Todd is very loyal. His family has been with mine a long time."

Priscilla nodded. "You don't see that kind of dedication much anymore," she observed.

"Oh, I don't know," Charles said. "I'm rather dedicated to the family business."

His mother laughed. "I wasn't talking about your plans to revolutionize retailing," she said.

"And what are they?" Elizabeth inquired.

Priscilla set down her cup and threw up her hands. "Don't get him started on that!" she said. "We shall be asleep in minutes."

"Not everyone finds business as boring as you do, Mother," Charles said archly.

"I'd like to hear," Elizabeth said.

"Very well," Priscilla said, shaking her head. She rose, taking that as her cue to exit. "You two young people go on without me. Charles, I'll be in the conservatory if you need me. Elizabeth, thank you so much for coming, and we'll hope to have you visit again soon.'' She smiled and lifted her hand in farewell, gliding from the room and leaving the scent of tuberoses in her wake.

''I think my mother likes you,'' Charles confided.

''I like her, too,'' Elizabeth replied, which was true as far as it went. She had always supposed that any prospective mother-in-law would be full of questions.

''So, where were we?'' Charles asked contentedly. From his point of view, this was going very well.

''Your business plans,'' Elizabeth supplied.

''Oh, yes. Well, as you know, I've been running the Philadelphia store for the past three years. I keep an apartment in the city and only come out to the house on the weekends.''

Elizabeth nodded.

''Since the end of the war, business has been booming. Imports especially have been in great demand. I'm doing a wonderful trade in European silks and wools.''

Elizabeth nodded again. As Charles went on enthusiastically, she realized that was all she was required to do: nod occasionally while he talked. She refilled his cup twice, the maid came and removed the plates, and Charles was still talking. Darkness fell, the servants lit the lamps, the fire was replenished by the houseman, and Charles was still talking. Finally Priscilla came back into the room and said, ''Shame on you, Charles. It's six o'clock. I can't believe you've kept Elizabeth this long. What will she think of us?''

"I'm sorry, Mother," Charles said, not sounding sorry at all. "Elizabeth is such a wonderful audience for my schemes that I just lost track of the time."

"Elizabeth, you must excuse him," Priscilla said charmingly. "I fear you have touched on his favorite subject, and there's just no stopping him until his listeners have collapsed from exhaustion."

"Not at all," Elizabeth murmured, but she stood, shaking out her skirt, and Charles jumped to his feet. Priscilla signaled for the houseman to fetch Elizabeth's wrap.

"I'm afraid I'm needed in the kitchen, so I must go," Priscilla said. "We're expecting Mr. Brandon to return this evening, and the cook is making a special late meal that requires my supervision. Let me repeat that we'll be looking forward to seeing you again in the near future, Elizabeth. Good night."

Charles stepped forward to take Elizabeth's wrap from the houseman as his mother left. Charles settled the cloak about her shoulders, keeping his hands in place a few moments longer than necessary.

"Did I tell you that your father invited me to his company picnic at the end of the month?" Charles said into her ear.

I could have predicted that, Elizabeth thought. Aloud she said, "Will you be attending?"

"I wouldn't miss it," Charles said softly. "I think I'll bring the whole family. I'll see you there?"

Elizabeth nodded, moving out of his grasp toward the door. Charles followed.

"The day after Thanksgiving my mother is having an open house in the afternoon and a dinner dance in the evening," Charles said as they walked into the hall. "She's opening up the second-floor ballroom for the occasion. May I count on you to come?"

"I...I'll have to ask my father," Elizabeth said, feeling that events were moving a bit too fast for her liking.

"Certainly. He's invited, too, of course. My man will bring the cards to your house when the time arrives." Charles paused under the French cut-glass chandelier, twice the size of the Langdons', which hung down two stories from the vaulted ceiling. Elizabeth fiddled with the button on her cloak, suddenly nervous.

"Elizabeth, I hope you won't think it presumptuous of me if I say that I am finding you very compatible and hope that we will become good friends."

Elizabeth smiled, unsure what to say.

"I realize I'm very grateful that you've returned to our valley and that you will be in residence indefinitely. It will give us the opportunity to spend some time together. May I call on you? I'll be asking your father's permission, of course, but I wanted to be sure my attentions would be welcome before I did."

Elizabeth hesitated. She didn't want to treat him unfairly, but if her father found out she was discouraging Charles, he would be furious.

"Certainly, Charles," she said quietly. "Certainly you may call."

Charles beamed.

Todd appeared outside and looked in from the doorway.

"There's your man," Charles said. "I must keep you no longer." He lifted Elizabeth's hand to his lips and kissed it. "Good night, Elizabeth. You'll be in my thoughts until we meet again."

"Good night, Charles." Elizabeth left the house and followed Todd down to the coach. She was settled in her seat and Todd had started down the drive before she realized she was rubbing the spot on her hand that Charles had touched with his mouth.

Unfortunately his kiss only reminded her of another one. One that she definitely preferred.

Maura was gone by the time Elizabeth returned home, and she had a solitary supper in the dining room, with Mrs. Tamm rustling in and out with the several courses she always insisted on serving. Elizabeth would have canceled the meal altogether since her father was not at home, but such orders usually led to health lectures from the housekeeper, who had a zealous belief in proper nutrition. Mrs. Tamm also felt a dogged determination to do her duty as she saw it, and that included elaborate meals whether Elizabeth wanted them or not. Elizabeth nibbled at the food for a couple of hours, preoccupied with her own thoughts, until Mrs. Tamm gave up, sighing, and cleared the table.

A wind was gathering, a gray autumn wind that rattled the windowpanes and whistled round the corners of the house. Elizabeth read for a while in the library before she retired to her room, carrying a taper into the darkened chamber, where she lit the lamp on her bed stand with it and then blew out the candle. As she stepped back from the table, a hand clamped over her mouth and Sean Jameson's voice said in her ear, "Don't make a sound, now. If you call out, I'm dead for sure."

Chapter Five

Elizabeth stiffened in reaction and began to squirm frantically. Sean held her firmly and said, "I'll not hurt you, settle down. If you promise you won't yell for the servants, I'll set you free."

Elizabeth stopped struggling.

"Promise?" he murmured, his breath warm against her ear.

Elizabeth nodded vigorously.

Sean's arms fell away from her. Elizabeth whirled and spat, "How dare you?"

Sean held his finger to his lips, his eyes widening.

"How dare you sneak into my house, into my *room* and scare me like that?" she demanded, lowering her voice. "It's the most ill-bred thing I ever heard of in my life!"

Sean lounged against the wall, his pale eyes throwing back the lamplight. "I'd never lay claim to breeding, and as for the other, are you saying I should have come to the door and called like a gentleman? It seems to me I've tried that once or twice. I'm thinking you'll remember the reception I got for my trouble."

"How did you get in here?" she whispered fiercely, her heart still pounding with the shock of finding him in her room.

"I hung around back until the coachman went to the barn to put the horses down, and I saw the house-keeper go up to her room. I guessed your man would be back to lock up the house, so I slipped into the pantry and waited for my chance to get up to the second floor. Then I had to hide down the hall in an empty bedroom while he laid the fire in your room, but when he left I came in here to wait for you."

"You certainly went to a lot of trouble. And how did you know which room was mine?"

"Maura told me. First on the left, that's what she said."

"You mean she knows you're here?" Elizabeth said, aghast.

"No, indeed. But she's the reason I'm here." He jerked his head toward a lump on the bed, dimly visible in the lamplight.

"What's that?" Elizabeth asked.

"The castoffs you gave her."

"She asked you to return them?" Elizabeth demanded in complete confusion.

"She wanted to keep them."

"Then what are you doing here?" Elizabeth moaned, ready to throttle him.

"Jamesons don't take charity," he said simply.

Elizabeth stared at him.

He looked back at her impassively.

Elizabeth blinked and swallowed. "Let me see if I'm correct about this," she finally said. "You broke into my house and hid in my room, for which my father would have you drawn and quartered, at the very least, if he—"

"I knew your da was away," he interrupted to say.

"How did you know that? Oh, wait...."

"Maura told me," he said, nodding.

Elizabeth held up her hand. "And you did this to return a bunch of old clothes you knew I didn't want in the first place?"

"I don't like you treating Maureen like your private Red Cross case," he said flatly.

Elizabeth eyed him for a long moment and then said thoughtfully, "That isn't the real reason you came here tonight, is it?"

He looked wary. "I don't take your meaning."

"You wanted to see me again," Elizabeth said with a sudden surge of insight.

Sean straightened, his eyes locked with hers.

"The other night when we said goodbye...you knew if other people were around we never could...and you wanted to be alone with me." She strung the thoughts together lamely. "The clothes were an excuse."

Sean was speechless, stunned by her candor. Of course she was right, but he wasn't used to directness from women. The village girls he knew learned coquetry as small children and employed it ruthlessly, one of the few tools they had that might enable them to escape their dismal surroundings.

She took a step closer to him, then another, lifting her hand to touch his cheek.

"For a few stolen minutes, you would take such a chance?" she murmured wonderingly.

Sean didn't move, spellbound by the feel of her slight, warm fingers against his face.

"How did you know I wouldn't call for help when I found it was you?" she asked, tilting her head back to look into his eyes.

"I didn't know," he said huskily. "I hoped...."

"Oh, Sean," Elizabeth whispered, her eyes moistening.

He stared down at her for a long moment, his lips parted, and then gathered her fiercely into his arms.

"I don't know what I'm about anymore. I couldn't stay away for saving my life. A raging flood wouldn't have kept me from you tonight," he muttered into her hair, inhaling its sweet fragrance.

"Sean," Elizabeth said again, dreamily, running her hands down the hard, serge-covered surface of his back. She felt the strength of his workman's body, the taut leanness of his waist. "What does it mean, your name?"

"John to you, that's what it means in English," he replied, holding her off to look at her searchingly. "Do you think we'll be talking in future, for you to be calling me anything at all?"

There was a gentle tapping at the door. They sprang apart as Elizabeth's throat tightened with fear. She pointed to the space behind the door, and Sean flattened himself against the wall as Elizabeth opened the door a crack.

Mrs. Tamm stood in the hall, wearing her wrapper and gauzy nightcap and carrying a candle.

"I was coming back from the kitchen—I had gone down for a sip of milk—and I thought I heard voices in here," Mrs. Tamm said, her thin face shadowed with concern.

"I had a nightmare and I was talking in my sleep," Elizabeth said quickly.

"But you're still dressed," the housekeeper said, taking in the traveling outfit Elizabeth had never discarded.

"I was so tired from the trip I didn't undress, just fell asleep across the bed."

"Well, then, let me come in and help you," Mrs. Tamm said, moving forward.

Elizabeth almost shut the door on her foot. "No, no, that won't be necessary at all," she babbled. "I'm fine, really. Thank you so much for asking. Good night." She slammed the door closed and then waited, breathlessly, for the sound of the housekeeper's retreating footsteps. When it finally came, she sagged with relief and Sean caught her against his chest.

"Aren't you the cunning little liar, then?" he said teasingly. "Who'd have thought you had such a talent, going all to waste inside that proper lady's dainty skull?''

"Sean, it isn't funny. You have to get out of here. I dread to think what would have happened if she'd found you in this room." Elizabeth picked up the bundle of clothes and thrust it at him.

"I'll not leave till I know when I'll see you again." He tucked the bundle under his arm.

Elizabeth thought frantically, desperate to get him to go. "The picnic. Everyone will be there—it won't seem like an arranged meeting."

He nodded. "I'll find a way."

"Don't take any foolish chances," Elizabeth whispered.

"Ah, like the one I took tonight?" he asked archly, smiling with that tender look in his eyes that took her breath away.

"Yes, just like that," she said, wringing her hands. "You are far too rash."

"Now, I would have thought you'd like an adventurous man," he said, leaning in closer to her.

"Don't try to mesmerize me, Sean. You're not staying here another minute." With that she turned away from him and opened the door cautiously, checking the hall. She stepped out onto the runner and crept to the railing, gazing down over it into the empty lower vestibule.

"See anybody?" Sean said behind her, and she jumped a foot. He dissolved in soundless laughter and she swatted at him ineffectually, almost in tears.

"All right, all right," he said, seeing her distress. "Calm yourself, I'm going. Who might be about the house?"

"Only Todd and Mrs. Tamm live here, the other servants all come in by day." Elizabeth inched toward the landing.

Sean closed in on her elbow.

"Stay behind me," Elizabeth whispered fiercely, and he obeyed, following her down the seemingly endless staircase and through the darkened hall.

"Don't bump into anything," she breathed over her shoulder, negotiating the furniture lining the passage from memory.

"I got upstairs on my own, did I not?" he countered.

"Shh!"

They finally reached the kitchen, where the outer door in the pantry was locked.

Only Mrs. Tamm and Todd had the house keys.

"Didn't you know it would be locked?" Sean asked. "That man Todd always—"

"I thought I'd try just in case," she said hastily, interrupting him. "But there's another key hidden in the base of the hat stand in the kitchen."

"The hat stand?" Sean repeated incredulously. They were facing each other in the dark, whispering ferociously.

"Mrs. Tamm is cautious—she tries to plan for everything." Together they went back into the kitchen, where Elizabeth crouched on the floor and felt under the hat stand for the spring that released the compartment door. When the drawer popped open, she seized the large metal key by its length of grosgrain ribbon and led Sean back to the pantry. She inserted the key into the lock, and they heard the tumblers give way.

They released their breath in unison.

"Now go!" Elizabeth said, shoving open the door and letting in a wave of chill night air.

"Not yet," Sean said, drawing her back into the house. He set Maura's bundle on the sideboard.

"Sean, please," Elizabeth begged, but he grabbed her and held her fast, his hands like iron bands on her shoulders.

"Elizabeth, I'm not playing with you," he said seriously, and for a moment she didn't understand what he meant.

"Playing?" she murmured.

"This is not a lark for me. I'm here because I could do no other. I can't get you out of my mind."

She stared up at him, unable to speak.

"Most young ladies of your class, they don't even see me, or if they do, it's as a convenience of their lives, like Todd is to your da. But from the first you treated me like a man, and when you came to my house, I knew you were different."

Elizabeth touched the rough, callused hand that lay against her neck, twining her fingers with his.

Sean pressed his lips together, his expression grim. "What I'm saying is, if we go on with this, there could be trouble ahead for both of us. In some ways worse for you than for me. Think on it. Are you willing to take that chance?''

She nodded.

''You don't need to consider it?''

She shook her head.

He bent slowly, and she stood on tiptoe to meet him. When his lips touched hers, she felt as if she were melting. Time stood still as his mouth moved on hers, his tongue probing delicately. Elizabeth clung to him and his arms came around her convulsively, backing her into the pantry wall as he pressed against her until she was drowning in sensation, but with no desire to come up for air.

Sean finally broke away, his breathing harsh and labored. He put his head back against the wall and closed his eyes.

''You're a dangerous woman,'' he said softly, when he could talk.

''More dangerous than you know if you stay here much longer,'' Elizabeth answered warningly.

''Until Sunday,'' he said.

''Sunday.''

He touched her mouth, still moist from his kiss, with his forefinger, then grabbed Maura's clothes and slipped through the door. Elizabeth watched until he had disappeared into the night, then turned back into the room, locking the door carefully with the key and replacing it in the stand. When she tried to walk back up to her room, however, she discovered that her knees were too weak to carry her. She sat at the kitchen table, her head swimming.

She had never been kissed in her life until that night, except for chaste pecks from her father and people like Charles Brandon. It was clear that Sean knew what he was doing and also that he'd been as affected by the embrace as she was.

Yes, there was definitely trouble ahead. But she couldn't stop now and avoid it.

She knew she couldn't, because she did not want to stop.

Sean walked home as if he were several inches off the ground. He was due to start the midnight shift shortly, and he barely had time to stop off at his house to pick up his equipment and lunch pail. He was so happy that he didn't even mind the headlong run to the mine entrance as the whistle blew.

Elizabeth filled his mind as he filed down into the shaft with the other men and lit the wick on the front of his helmet. His hands still retained the feel of her; his arms remembered the curves of her slender body. He was infatuated, besotted, in love. Her family represented everything he hated—undeserved wealth and privilege that of necessity subjugated others—but somehow that didn't matter any longer. Or maybe that was part of her attraction for him; Sean wasn't big on self-examination, and he couldn't hope to analyze feelings so powerful that they drove him without thought for his own safety or even Elizabeth's. That's what alarmed him the most—not what would happen to him if their budding relationship were revealed, but the idea that Langdon could send her away at any time to a faraway place where Sean could not find her. He selected a pick from the pile on the ground and attacked the rock face before him, his mouth a grim line.

He had to make sure they were never discovered.

The week passed as slowly as if it were a month. Elizabeth said nothing to Maura about her brother's visit, and Maura apparently didn't know about it. Sean must have returned the clothes to his house and said nothing to his sister, which was probably for the best. Maura was concerned enough about the situation as it was.

The morning of the picnic dawned cool and clear, a perfect fall day for outdoor activity. Elizabeth dressed in a peach-and-white striped poplin day dress. It featured the new style oval skirt gathered into a bustle topped with a peach taffeta bow; Elizabeth loved the effect. The tight bodice had a high ruff neckline and buttoned down the center front, extending to a point below the waist. Maura dressed Elizabeth's hair, drawing it up and back to display the pearls in her ears and combing it into curls across her forehead and ringlets on the sides.

A Gaelic football game was scheduled for ten o'clock between Langdon and Chatauqua, a rival mine some miles away. Elizabeth and her father were driven by Todd to an open field at the back of Langdon's property, where the game was to take place. A dais had been set up at the edge of the field for the owner's families, and Mr. and Mrs. Hampton, the Chatauqua owners, were already in place. As Elizabeth gathered her skirts to ascend the rough wooden steps, Charles arrived by carriage with his family, and Arthur Langdon invited all four Brandons to share the dais with them. Charles maneuvered his sister, Emily, who was wearing a sprigged muslin dress with a dimity bib and a straw sunbonnet, to the end chair so that he could sit next to Elizabeth. The teams were assembling on the field as they settled in to watch.

Elizabeth spotted Sean immediately; he was the captain of the Langdon team, standing in the center of the field with the Chatauqua captain, supposedly going over the rules with the referee. The Chatauqua captain was listening, but Sean was staring fixedly at Charles Brandon, shading his eyes with his hand to see. Elizabeth gave no sign to acknowledge Sean's presence, but Charles noticed that he was being observed.

"Who's that miner looking up here?" Charles asked, moving a couple of inches closer to her and dusting his seat fastidiously.

"The captain of our team," Elizabeth replied evasively.

"What is he staring at?" Charles said.

"I guess he never saw all of us together before," Elizabeth replied, praying that Sean would turn away. Finally, he did.

"Strapping fellow," Charles observed amiably, anticipating a good game.

The onlookers, most of them Langdon people out for the spectacle, gathered behind ropes set up by the Coal and Iron Police. Tom Rees and his men, attired in full uniform, patrolled the perimeters, aware of the potentially volatile situation and ready for anything. Both teams took their football seriously, and an armed truce existed between management and the miners on both sides, with the Langdon miners resolved to give no hint of their upcoming work slowdown.

Arthur Langdon gave the signal to begin, smiling benevolently. He was always in an expansive mood on the one day a year he allowed himself to mix socially with his workers.

Soon the players were scuffling on the field, flinging themselves on one another and raising a cloud of dust. The referee blew the tin whistle around his neck, shouting and pointing, while the men called to one another in some verbal shorthand and ran up and down like madmen being chased by demons. Elizabeth had no idea what it was all about; Charles had explained that it was ground game with ball handling permitted, but that meant little to her. When the home crowd cheered she did too, and soon the referee was marking points up on a blackboard at the edge of the field. When she was sure she could take no more, the referee called a rest period. The players sprawled in the shade of some elm trees that still had leaves, dousing themselves with water and drinking lager. The village women walked through the crowd of supine men, serving them, while those on the dais were given lemonade prepared by Mrs. Tamm and brought out in the coach by Todd.

"I declare," Emily Brandon said, leaning forward to address Elizabeth across her brother, "this sun is just ruining my skin. I'll have to spend days bleaching my freckles out with lemon water."

Charles smiled at Elizabeth as Emily, who had clearly spent time with her southern relatives, frowned at a spot on the back of her hand.

"Why don't you go up to the house, precious?" her mother said. "Mr. Langdon said the guest bedrooms were all prepared if any of the ladies wanted to take a rest. And there's a parasol on the floor of the trap. Would you like Simpson to get it for you?"

Mrs. Brandon and her daughter continued to discuss the latter's discomfort while the manservant ran to get Emily's parasol from the Brandon coach. Once she was armed with it in addition to her sunbonnet, it was unlikely that any stray rays would make it through the shields to abuse Emily's wraith-pale skin.

"Where are your gloves?" Mrs. Brandon said to her offspring.

Emily removed her gloves from her reticule while Elizabeth watched Sean pour a bucket of water over his head. A young lady bending over him supplied a handkerchief, with which he wiped his face. Then he stripped off the damp shirt he was wearing and mopped his sweating torso with it, an action that elicited a lot of interest from the village women. Maura came up behind him and handed him a clean shirt. Elizabeth tried to look away but couldn't; as he pulled the fresh shirt over his head, his gaze met hers.

It was as if the throng of people between them vanished. Sean froze in the act of slipping his arms into his sleeves, and when Elizabeth saw that he wasn't going to look away, she did so herself, turning her head to meet Charles's interested brown gaze.

"Do you know him?" Charles asked, nodding toward Sean in the distance.

"Who?"

"The Langdon captain. The one who was staring up at us before the game."

"I think his sister works for my father. She's a maid up at the house. Maura Jameson."

"Jameson? Isn't that the miner who's been giving your father all the trouble?"

Elizabeth shrugged, wishing she could change the subject without seeming too obvious.

"Well, he must be channeling those energies into the game today," Charles said, chuckling. "He's certainly trouncing Chatauqua."

"Oh, look, they're lining up to start again," Elizabeth said quickly, gazing out at the field.

Mrs. Brandon and Emily disappeared a few minutes into the second half, going up to the Langdon house. Elizabeth stuck it out until Langdon won and Sean was awarded the team trophy. Sweaty and begrimed, he ascended the steps of the platform and accepted the statuette from her father, shaking the older man's hand stiffly and unsmilingly, then turning and holding the trophy aloft for his team to see. They roared their approval and surged forward to carry him on their shoulders off the field.

He hadn't glanced Elizabeth's way once.

The crowd broke up, drifting toward the barn at the edge of the field, where the Langdon servants had set out a banquet. Mrs. Tamm had been cooking the whole week, and tables along the sides of the huge room were loaded with more good food than the miners would see for another year. Hams and roasts, joints of mutton and lamb, plates of salads and relishes and all kinds of cakes and pies for dessert. Beer and ale were poured from vats by beefy miners with a generous hand, and most of the assembly were well on their way to a roaring good time when Elizabeth entered with Charles and their respective fathers.

They were seated at the head table with the Hamptons. This was draped with a cloth as a concession to their status and faced the rows of sawhorses covered with planking and flanked by benches that had been set up for the miners and their families. Children scurried everywhere, running between the tables and scattering the sawdust on the floor. The youngest clutched at their mothers' long skirts as the adults ate their fill. Elizabeth picked at her food and nodded and smiled, feeling as though her face would crack from the strain. She searched the throng for Sean all the while but could not find him. She saw Tom Rees, his arms folded as he leaned against a cross beam, surveying the crowd with his inscrutable, all-seeing policeman's gaze.

The more the miners drank, the louder they got, and Elizabeth wished she could leave. The Langdons had put in their appearance, and she was sure the townspeople would have a better time if her father were not sitting watching them like a feudal overlord. She was about to rise and make her exit when a procession of musicians filed in through the half-open barn doors. They took their places on an elevated platform behind her, used by one of the previous owners for cattle auctions when livestock were still sold there. For the first time she noticed the piano set up at the side and realized that there was to be entertainment.

Too late. It would be rude to walk out now, so she settled in to see what came next.

Music, not surprisingly. The fiddler set to with a jig, the other musicians joined in, and the floor was cleared for dancing. Neither the Irish nor the Welsh were known for their inhibitions, and they were all soon pounding the floor rhythmically, shaking the walls with the vibrations from their stamping feet. Elizabeth found herself tapping the table in concert with the tunes and was actually sorry when the musicians took a break.

That didn't slow the revelers down much, however. One of the miners called out, "Let's have a song!" and others took up the cry. Before long a man detached himself from the crowd and ran up the steps to the makeshift stage. Elizabeth turned to watch as he swept the floor with a courtly bow, folded his hands before him and began to sing. The rest listened respectfully as he sang a sad song about a fair maiden and lost love. At its conclusion the hall thundered with applause.

"'Annie Laurie,'" another voice called out from the faceless throng. "Where's Sean?"

Elizabeth sat up straighter. Were there several Seans?

"Sean Jameson. Where are you, lad?"

Sean stood up in the rear of the hall, waving the suggestion away. He was wearing a dark blue suit Elizabeth had never seen with a crisp linen shirt. His hair was glistening, still wet from his bath after the game, and his face was bronzed from the sun on the playing field. Elizabeth's pulse responded. She thought him the handsomest man there.

"I can't sing alone," he said, laughing, his strong voice carrying to the front of the room where she sat. "I haven't the talent in me to sing alone. I need the help of the piano."

Elizabeth found herself on her feet before she realized that she intended to stand.

"I know that song," she announced. "I can play for you."

Sean stared at her, undone. Arthur Langdon, unwilling to make a scene at his own party, said nothing as his daughter hoisted her skirts ankle-high and climbed up onto the stage.

Sean had no choice but to follow. He sent her one long, measured glance before turning to face his audience. Elizabeth waited. He lifted his hand, not looking at her, and she began to play.

The song was a tender ballad, and he sung it in a true tenor, falling in with her playing as if they had rehearsed together. At the conclusion he turned and gave her a half bow, and Elizabeth was glad no one but she could see the expression on his face.

Sean started to leave the stage, and a voice called out, "Let's have another!"

Sean shook his head good-naturedly, but when the demand persisted, he raised his arms and said, "All right then, here's a chaser. And I'll need no help with this!"

He launched into a lively song in Gaelic, which his audience obviously knew, the chorus of which seemed to be, "O'Donnell, Aboo!" He would sing the verses, point to the crowd at the appropriate time, and they would chime in enthusiastically, fairly screaming the chorus. The song seemed to go on forever, and Elizabeth took the opportunity to slip from the stage. She sidled up to Maura, who now stood on the edge of the crowd, watching her brother perform.

"What is he singing?" Elizabeth asked, noting the almost hysterical response of the crowd.

"A song about the glories of rebellion against unfair landlords," Maura replied dryly. "If your father had the understanding of it, he wouldn't be sitting still for the likes of that."

Maura was wearing a yellow-and-white checked muslin dress with a fitted jacket. The large, round mother-of-pearl buttons down the center of the bodice matched the white linen collar and cuffs. Her vibrant hair was piled high on her head, and tiny copper circlets dangled from her ears.

"You look lovely," Elizabeth said. "You're a wonderful seamstress."

"Thank you. I bring in extra money with sewing now and then." She nodded toward her brother. "Will you look at him? There's nothing he loves better than an audience."

When Sean finally left the stage to uproarious applause, Jim Kelly jumped up to take his place.

"I'll be needing the piano, too," he said, grinning at Elizabeth from his height on the platform.

"Of course," Elizabeth said, and resumed her spot on the bench to more clapping from the audience.

"'Yankee Doodle,'" Jim announced.

Elizabeth banged out the melody as Jim sang a loud, if off-key rendition of the rallying song. Elizabeth thought that her old piano teacher, Miss Beauregarde, who had hailed from Alabama, was probably revolving in her grave, but her fingers found the keys by rote. Jim went on to a few more old favorites, and Elizabeth followed him until he tired of the game. He made a sweeping bow in her direction and then charged off the stage, fists raised in salute to the crowd.

Elizabeth wound up playing the piano for about half an hour, for a succession of performers, until the musicians returned. When they did, they launched into a series of waltzes as she resumed her seat by her father's side.

"You're quite a virtuoso on the piano, Elizabeth," Charles said pleasantly.

"Yes, my dear, thank you for your contribution," her father said grudgingly. Mrs. Hampton, at the other end of the table, nodded in agreement.

Elizabeth smiled to herself, enjoying her father's discomfiture. She knew he hadn't liked her spontaneous gesture, but he couldn't very well admit that and maintain his kindly facade.

They watched the dancers for a while, as Charles made small talk with his father and Mrs. Brandon and Emily returned to sit with them. Elizabeth was twisting her mother's ring on her finger, waiting for time to pass, when a shadow fell across her hands and she looked up to see Sean standing in front of her.

She widened her eyes, trying to warn him off silently, but saw immediately that he was determined.

"Mr. Langdon, I'm requesting permission to dance with your daughter," Sean said in what was, for him, a respectful tone. "In return for the playing, you understand."

Arthur Langdon's face froze, but he said neutrally, "That's up to Elizabeth."

"Certainly," Elizabeth said smoothly, rising to her feet and taking Sean's outstretched hand. She waited until he had led her out onto the floor and they were moving away from the head table before she hissed in his ear, "Sean, have you lost your mind? What on earth are you doing?"

"Have you never heard that hiding best is hiding in plain sight?" he countered, waltzing her behind a pillar. "Your father would never believe I'd have the brass to do this if anything were going on between us. Look at him. He thinks I'm just trying to irritate him."

"Aren't you?"

"Indeed." There was a smile in his voice. "And what were you trying to do by jumping up like a jackrabbit and pounding that piano? Make him happy?"

Elizabeth giggled into his shoulder.

"None of that, now," he said in mock reproval. "Don't look like you're having a good time. You're just enduring this dance with a ruffian for form's sake, don't you know."

"Yes, sir. I will bear it in mind. You're a wonderful dancer, by the way."

"Oh, aye, we can dance. We're long on singing and dancing." He led her easily, without effort. "Now isn't this a lovely sight, the way we're all getting along like bread and jam—your father sitting up there powerful as old King Henry, and us singing and dancing for his pleasure? You'd never guess to look at this room tonight that we're really at one another's throats."

"I'm glad you can forget all that, for one evening."

"Who says I've forgotten?" He looked up at the head table. "Who's the toff you've been sitting with today?" he demanded.

"Charles Brandon," she replied resignedly. She'd had a feeling that subject was going to come up.

"Him with the store in Philadelphia?"

"The same."

"Is he your father's choice for you?"

"Him, or somebody like him."

"He looks a proper poof."

Elizabeth struggled not to laugh. "A what?"

"A poof. One of those that likes men."

"Sean, take my word for it, Charles is not a poof."

Sean spun her around so hard she almost lost her footing. "Has he been after you, then?"

"He's indicated his interest. Sean, please, you can't be jealous of Charles Brandon."

"And why not? He has more money than Maximilian, I'm sure, and both your father and his parents would probably be speechless with joy at the marriage announcement."

"There isn't going to be any announcement. It might interest you to know that I spend most of my time with Charles remembering what it was like kissing you." She cast her eyes downward, blushing helplessly at her boldness. Why was it she felt she could say anything to him?

His grip on her waist tightened. "Then why are you going along with it?" Sean asked huskily.

"I have to make my father think I'm interested in Charles or else he'll wonder if I'm involved elsewhere."

"You are," he murmured. He looked down at the top of her head. "What's all that fuss with your hair?"

"Maura did it. Don't you like it?"

"I like it loose about your shoulders," he said throatily.

"Sean, I can't wear it down in company. Everyone will think I'm getting ready for bed." She bent her head farther.

"Stop staring at my shoes, girl," he said, chuckling. "Are you thinking I'll step on your feet?"

"I'm afraid that if I look into your face, everyone will see what I'm feeling."

He pulled her closer. "I have to see you tonight or I'll go mad for sure," he said savagely.

"What can we do?" Elizabeth moaned. They were nearing the end of the song and running out of time.

"I'll come to your house."

Elizabeth gasped. "After what happened last time?"

"Do you want to see me or not?" Sean demanded.

Elizabeth finally raised her head and gazed into his eyes. The reckless longing she saw there mirrored her own.

"Turn away," he said desperately. "If you look at me like that I'll not be responsible."

The music stopped.

"I'll come to your window late, at three, and throw stones. You go down to the kitchen and let me in," Sean said swiftly, leaning in toward her as he led her back to the table.

Elizabeth didn't have a chance to reply. She slipped back into her seat bonelessly, her legs trembling so badly she crossed her ankles to steady them.

"Thank you, sir," Sean said calmly to her father.

Arthur Langdon nodded glacially.

Elizabeth admired Sean's facility for dissimulation. She herself felt as if she were going to faint and was afraid she looked it.

"And thank you, Miss Langdon," Sean said.

"Not at all," Elizabeth murmured, feeling the heat creeping up into her face. Was she turning red?

"He's very well mannered, for a miner," Charles observed superciliously as Sean walked away.

"And so...brawny," Emily Brandon chimed in thoughtfully. "What's his name?"

"Trouble," Langdon said darkly, leaning back in his chair. "Trouble is his name."

"Hush, child," Priscilla Brandon said. "Elizabeth will think we've neglected your upbringing."

Elizabeth thought no such thing. She could easily understand Emily's appreciation of Sean's charms, since she shared it.

It would seem a long time until three in the morning.

"You just can't resist asking for it, can you?" Maura said to her brother as he came back to their table.

"Asking for what?" Sean replied, picking up his mug and draining it of foaming ale.

"Dancing with Miss Elizabeth," Maura said. "You really want to drive the old man to it, don't you?"

"I was just entering into the spirit of the evening, with all of us getting along so well," Sean said, smirking at her.

"Tell it to the Scots," Maura said scornfully, turning her back on him. Five-year-old Matthew dashed out from under the table, chasing one of the other village boys.

"Matthew," Maura called after him, "sit yourself down before I take a switch to you."

"Where's Ma?" Sean asked.

"She went back to the house. She was tired."

Sean said nothing. His mother was only forty-six and she was always tired.

Brother and sister both looked around as Tom Rees approached them and said, "Dance, Miss Jameson?"

"Bugger off, peeler," Sean said, looking away.

"What's that you were saying about the spirit of the evening?" Maura asked her brother airily.

Sean shot her a disgusted glance.

"I'd be honored," Maura said to a surprised Rees, who held out his arms. They drifted away.

"I thought I'd get more of an argument from you," Rees said wonderingly to Maura. "After the way we left things in the Langdon kitchen, I didn't know if you were speaking to me."

"I've a forgiving nature," Maura said mischievously. "Any road, 'twill be a cold day in hell when

Sean Almighty Jameson tells me what to do, especially with himself proceeding exactly as he pleases.''

"I see. I owe my good fortune to the fact that you're fighting with your brother.''

Maura had the good grace to smile.

"Ah, that's better,'' Rees said, twirling her in a circle. "I've noticed myself that Sean does have the habit of ordering all of you about like his own set of toy soldiers.''

"He can't help it, I suppose. He's been the head of the family since he was twelve, when my father died.''

"Twelve, you say?''

Maura nodded.

"Then what about Matthew?''

Maura looked up to meet his eyes directly. "He's not mine, if that's what you're asking,'' she said stiffly.

Rees flushed. "No, no, I'm sorry. I didn't mean to pry.''

Maura sighed. "Matthew is a by-blow. My mother's. Her last attempt at a new life for herself, gone wrong.''

Rees was uncomfortable, wishing he'd never raised the subject. "You don't have to tell me about it,'' he said quickly.

Maura shrugged. "I might as well—it's been village gossip since it happened. I'm surprised you haven't heard about it before this.''

"The patch people don't talk much to me,'' Rees said truthfully.

Maura let that pass. "My sister, Katie, died on the voyage over here from Ireland, and my ma died a little with her. Then after my father was killed, it seemed there was nothing left to keep Ma going, until she met Brendan Coyne. He was a drifter. Sean hated him, but my mother wouldn't listen. He was full of flattery and attention, a Wexford man."

"Yes, I know," Rees said soberly. The music stopped and they moved together to the edge of the floor.

"Brendan stopped here in Langdon, even got a job in the mines for a while," Maura went on, her pretty face a mask of sadness. "There was talk of marriage, and my mother was young again. When she got pregnant, she told him, thinking they would get married faster to legitimize the child. Brendan was gone the next day."

"I'm sorry to hear it," Rees murmured.

"Sean was wild, went absent from work and scoured three counties hereabouts for a scent of the man, but Brendan was nowhere to be found. Probably hopped a ship in Philadelphia. He'd vanished like a genie gone back into the bottle. Matthew was born seven months later."

Rees shook his head.

"So now you know our shameful story and why you rarely see our mother," Maura finished flatly. "She can't face the whispers, the stares. People with little else to enliven their days don't forget a story as rich as that one."

"It must be a hard thing."

"For a man as proud as Sean?" she snorted. "He got into more fights the year Ma carried that child. Anyone who snickered in public over his mother's big belly lived to rue it, that much I can tell you. But of course he couldn't quiet the talk behind closed doors. He'd just got back from the war and could hardly walk to begin with and—" She stopped short, suddenly realizing how much she was telling him.

"Yes?" Rees prompted.

"My mouth is running away with me. I'd better get back before Matthew destroys the place entirely."

Rees blocked her path.

"You've a bad habit of standing in front of me, Sergeant Rees," Maura said, but her tone was mild.

"I have the day off next Sunday," he said. "May I come to your house to call on you then?"

Maura hesitated.

"I'll speak to your brother first . . ." Rees began.

"Come for tea at four," Maura said abruptly. "And don't you worry, I'll handle Sean."

Rees smiled to himself as she walked back to her table. He bet she would do just that.

Elizabeth watched the clock as if she were waiting to be executed; it was the longest night of her life. She had dressed in her best *indienne*, a peignoir of the finest Indian cotton, fastened at the neck with a pink silk ribbon and trimmed at the collar, cuffs and hem with *broderie anglaise*. The long, full sleeves were of such delicate material that her arms were visible through them, and under the loose gown she wore a thin batiste camisole and panties trimmed with blond silk Chantilly lace. She felt naked without her corset, undressed, which suited her incautious mood. Her hair was freshly washed and loose about her shoulders, her body scented with essence of rosemary.

She was ready.

Elizabeth sat in the dark next to her window, the only illumination in her bedroom coming from the dying blaze in the grate. At a few minutes to three there was a shower of pebbles against the pane, followed shortly by another.

Elizabeth drew back the curtain, allowing herself to be seen by the light of the fire behind her. She could dimly make out a figure on the crushed stone drive, slightly paler than the blackness surrounding it.

She dropped the curtain, running headlong for the door. She negotiated the distance through the silent house on slippered feet, alert to any sound. She had already removed the key from the hat stand after Mrs. Tamm went to bed, and Elizabeth clutched it now. As soon as she reached the back door, she thrust the key into the lock with shaking fingers. She turned the knob and the door flew open to reveal Sean standing on the other side of it.

He took two steps and crushed her in his arms, lifting her off her feet and swinging her in a circle.

"Lizzie," he said hoarsely, his mouth pressed against the fragrant skin of her bare neck. "Lizzie, my girl."

Chapter Six

"My mother used to call me that," Elizabeth whispered, her eyes closed, her feet finding the ground as he set her down.

"You look grand," he said gently, touched by her efforts to appear attractive for him, "and you smell like a garden."

She took him by the hand and led him into the kitchen, where she lit a candle, shielding the flame with her hand so it couldn't be seen through the window.

"Are you afraid?" Sean asked, reading her expression in the feeble light.

Elizabeth paused, gazing up at him, and nodded.

"Do you want me to go?" he asked, holding his breath.

"No, no, I'll die if I can't be with you tonight," she answered, dropping the candle and flinging her arms around his neck. The taper rolled under a chair and snuffed out as she added, "It's just so dangerous for you to be here. I don't want anything bad to happen to you."

He held her tightly, his lips moving in her hair. "This is the only place we can meet. There's the chance of being seen anywhere else."

"I know," she murmured. "But my father's right upstairs, and if anyone wakes up in the night..."

"We have to get out of this town, Lizzie. That's the only answer. I feel like I'm suffocating here. All this creeping around is driving me daft. I want to walk with you in the sunlight. I want everyone to know about us. We have nothing to be ashamed of, and I'm weary of acting as if we do."

"Where can we go?" she asked, gazing up at him, his burnished hair and green eyes visible as bright glimmerings in the darkness.

"I don't know, I don't know. I have to think. Right now let's get out of this kitchen. We're sitting targets here."

Elizabeth felt for the candle on the floor and relit it, leading the way to her room. They slipped through the door and Elizabeth closed it behind them.

The fire was low and Sean added a couple of logs from the stand near the hearth. When he turned to face Elizabeth, she was standing behind him, the firelight flickering across her pale skin and bringing out the sheen in her sable hair.

"Are you all right?" he asked, reaching out to touch her cheek.

"I'm nervous," she said honestly.

"Of me?"

"Not of you. Just in general."

"Skittish?"

"I . . . I guess so. It's just . . . I don't do this sort of thing all the time. Bringing a man to my room is a little unusual."

He took both her hands and led her to sit next to him on the bed. "A little unusual?" he prompted.

"An unprecedented event," she admitted.

He smiled slightly.

"Can I ask you something?" Elizabeth said.

"Anything you like," he replied, tucking an errant strand of hair behind her ear.

"You've been with women before, haven't you?"

He hesitated, seemed about to say something, then nodded.

"A lot of women?" she asked.

He looked away from her, then shrugged.

"Were you in love with them?" Elizabeth asked.

"No." His voice was low.

"Never?"

He looked back at her. "Never till you. That's the truth of it."

Elizabeth twisted her fingers in her lap nervously.

"What is it, Lizzie? You can tell me—out with it now." His tone was gentle, persuasive.

"I hope you're not with me because you think it's the best way of taking revenge on my father," she blurted out.

He stared at her.

"Oh, don't look at me like that," she said miserably.

"I suppose I should have realized that idea would come to you," he said slowly.

"I know how much you hate him," she whispered.

"I hate what he does, what he stands for, but that has nothing to do with my feeling for you." He stood and walked over to the fireplace, leaning on the mantel and staring into the blaze.

"You're plotting against him, aren't you?" Elizabeth inquired resignedly. She got up and walked over to stand at his side.

"Don't ask me about that, Lizzie. I can't discuss it with you. And don't ask me to give it up. I won't." He continued to watch the flames with a set expression.

"Did you think I would make that a condition of our relationship?" she inquired, tugging on his arm until he turned and faced her.

He gazed down at her, his expression unreadable. "You must know by now that you'd be able to turn my course more than anyone. I gave you that power when I fell in love with you."

Elizabeth felt her throat closing with an unnamed emotion. How hard it must have been for him to admit that; he saw his feeling for her as a threat to his very soul.

"I wouldn't use your love to dissuade you from going against my father, Sean," she said quietly.

He gestured helplessly. "You may not agree with what he's doing—you've made that plain enough—but he's still your father, Elizabeth," Sean said. "I mean to bring him down, not just him but his whole way of life, and that can't be a source of happiness for you.''

"It isn't," Elizabeth said quietly. "But I know that what you're doing is very important."

"Not just to me, Lizzie, to this whole country. America is supposed to be the shining example of equality for the whole world, but it can never be that while one class exploits another this way."

"And I'm a member of the exploiting class. How that must hurt you," she said wretchedly.

He shook his head. "No. You've just followed the way of life you were born to, that's all. You can't be expected to know what it's costing me to feel this way about you. I'm betraying my background, my people, everything I've always believed in all of my life."

"That's why I was worried that striking back at my father was part of your interest in me," she said quietly.

He gazed at her steadily, studying her face. "Maybe there was some of that in the beginning. That and . . ."

"What?"

"Fascination with you because of who you were. The lady in the house on the hill, you know. You were so out of reach."

"You reached me."

"And you reached me. God knows I didn't want it, but it happened anyway."

"You sound unhappy about it," Elizabeth murmured, watching his expression.

"It makes me feel as if I've lost control," he said quietly, shaking his head.

"But Sean, I want you to be happy."

"Oh, Lizzie, I am." He took her by the shoulders and said, "It's gone beyond your father, your station, if that's where it began. It doesn't matter to me any longer who you are or where you came from—I just want you. Do you understand me, girl?"

"I understand," she said, her lower lip trembling.

"You know, it's just as hard for me to accept that you would choose me over the likes of Charles Brandon."

"You're the one I want, Sean. I think I have since the first moment I saw you."

He pulled her into his arms, and she rested her head on the broad expanse of his chest. "And when was that?"

"The day I arrived here. You showed up at the house, demanding to see my father, and had a fight with Todd."

"One of many."

"I thought you were very brave to defy my father. Few have tried, none successfully."

"Where were you?"

"Inside the house. I watched the whole thing from the vestibule with Mrs. Tamm."

"Ah, that's why I didn't see you. The first time I laid eyes on you was the night of the mine explosion."

"I remember."

"You were a vision, running around in your night-dress. You disappeared afterward and I didn't know who you were or where you had gone. I thought you might be a new schoolteacher."

"Schoolteacher!"

"From your posh way of talking."

"Oh, Sean." She nuzzled him and he tightened his grip.

"Well, it was plain to me you weren't from the village."

"Or you would have known who I was, right?" she replied teasingly. "I gather that there weren't many women under the age of forty that you missed."

"Who's been telling you tales? Maura?"

"You just told me yourself!"

"I said I'd been with women, not that I'd—"

Elizabeth clamped her hand over his mouth. "I don't care. I don't care about anything that happened before this night." She pulled open the collar of his shirt and pressed her lips to the pulse in his lean brown throat, standing on tiptoe and hooking her arms around his neck.

He groaned and threw his head back, closing his eyes and holding her against him. She kissed him repeatedly, her eager passion making up for lack of experience, until he pushed her away far enough to tear off his jacket, tossing it at the foot of the bed. Then he bent swiftly to slip an arm under her knees. He straightened with her in his arms and carried her to the bed.

They fell on it together, embracing full length. Elizabeth had never been held so intimately before, and when he raised up on one elbow to undo the tie at the neck of her dressing gown, she froze.

Sean felt her stiffen and dropped his hand. "Easy now," he said soothingly, lying next to her again and cradling her in his arms. "I'll not force you to do anything, Lizzie. It's all your choice. Tell me what you want."

"I want you," Elizabeth whispered, hiding her face in the crook of his arm. "I'm just..." She stopped and sighed. "Virgins are such a lot of trouble."

He began to shake and she realized that he was laughing. She sat up, incensed.

"Sean Jameson, I do believe you're enjoying this!"

"Oh, I am...I am, indeed," he answered, pulling her down again and kissing her cheek. "I'm enjoying this—" he moved his mouth to her neck "—and this—" he lowered his lips to her breast "—and this, as well."

Elizabeth closed her eyes as his mouth burned through the thin layers of cloth, searing the sensitive flesh as if she were wearing nothing. She bit her lip and held his hand against her, running her fingers through his thick, soft hair.

"I'll have this off," he said hoarsely, reaching again for the neckline of her gown.

This time she did not protest.

The gossamer gown slid off the bed and fell to the floor as Sean rolled Elizabeth, now clad only in her chemise and panties, under him and pinned her with his weight. He kissed her again, deeply, his tongue twining with hers as she felt him, hard and ready, against her thighs. When he moved his head to kiss her neck once more, she gasped, ''Take off your shirt.''

He obeyed, sitting up and unbuttoning it rapidly, sliding the shirt off his arms and tossing it in a corner of the room. His eyes, shining in the firelight, never left hers.

When he bent toward her again, she clasped him to her and pulled him down to the bed.

''Oh, Lizzie, if you knew how you feel to me . . .'' he moaned, marveling at the delicious sensation of her body next to his.

''I know how you feel to me,'' she answered, running her hands over the smooth surface of his back, the muscular ridges of his upper arms. ''Make love to me, Sean. The future doesn't matter that much right now, does it? All this talk, all these problems. Let's forget them and live for tonight. I don't care what happens to me tomorrow if we can be together, just this once.''

Her words did not have the effect she had anticipated. He removed her arms from his neck and sat up, heaving his legs over the side of the bed and propping his elbows on his thighs.

''Sean, what is it? What did I say?'' Elizabeth asked anxiously, putting her hand to her mouth.

''Lizzie, this isn't right. I knew it all along, but I just wanted you so much . . .'' He hung his head and thrust his hands through his hair. ''I feel like a scoundrel. It isn't decent to come into your house like a thief in the night, sneaking past your father to take you this way.''

"I want you to take me."

He shook his head. "I have nothing to offer, no money, no future. It's not an easy thing to stop, I admit. I'm used to taking what I want when I can get it, before it's snatched away. But this is different, Lizzie. You're diffcrent. I could hurt you, badly, and I couldn't stand the burning shame of that on my conscience."

"I don't care what you have or don't have or what your prospects are. All I want is you."

He turned and looked at her, his gaze compassionate but knowing. "That's because you've always had everything. You don't know what drivel you talk."

Elizabeth stared at him, hurt. "Sean!"

"I mean no unkindness, Lizzie, but it's the plain truth of the matter. Look at what you're wearing." He gestured at her handmade underthings, sewn by an order of nuns in a convent in the Auvergne. "Do you even know what it cost?"

Elizabeth made no reply. She didn't know.

Sean nodded. "I can tell you one thing for sure, weeks down in the pits wouldn't pay for what you've got on your back this minute." He gestured broadly, to include the room, the house. "Can you give all this up? Because I don't want just a night with you, and if we're to have more than that, you must make a choice."

Elizabeth moved forward to face him. "Sean, listen to me. I can't say I haven't enjoyed the fine things my father has provided, but I don't *need* them. Nobody needs silk underwear."

"Silk, is it?" he said, impressed.

"You're more important to me than articles of clothing or furniture or anything else that money can buy. Don't you see that?"

He was silent a long moment. Then he said, "I see that all this is new and exciting to you. You have the romantic feelings of a young, untouched girl, and you've fastened them on me. I just don't have the crust to take advantage of the situation. In a way I wish I did."

Elizabeth sat in chastened silence. Finally she said, "You don't think much of me, do you?"

"I think the world of you, Lizzie."

"No, you don't. According to Sean Jameson, dispenser of wisdom, you have the sincere, mature emotions of an experienced adult toward me, but I'm a goosey girl with a killer crush on the first dashing man who looked my way."

"Now, Lizzie," Sean said, looking alarmed, "I never said that."

"Yes, you did," Elizabeth replied, working up a head of steam. She vaulted out of the bed and confronted him, standing in her underwear, hands on slim hips, dark hair cascading over her shoulders. "I'll have you know, Mr. Jameson, that I could have Charles Brandon eating out of my hand this very minute if I chose to encourage him."

"I've no doubt of it," he said quietly.

"You give me no more credit than my father does. You both think I have to be managed and handled like a...a...colt that's being broken to the saddle!" She suddenly realized what she'd said and threw her hands up to her face, feeling it flood with heat.

Sean fell back on the bed and pulled the pillow over his head, stifling his laughter.

She jumped on top of him and pummeled his naked torso.

"You're laughing at me again!" she said fiercely, almost in tears.

He threw the pillow onto the floor and grabbed her hands, flipping her onto her back.

"Shush now," he said, "be still. You'll wake the whole house and have them in here with us."

"Do you believe I love you?" she demanded, her eyes filling.

"Oh, aye," he said with a sigh, worn down by her persistence, "I do. I'm not about to argue any further with so incurable a romantic as yourself."

She flung her arms around his neck, and he felt hot tears on his skin. "And what are you going to do about it?" she whispered thickly, sniffling.

He disentangled himself and sat up, wiping her wet cheeks with his thumb. "Nothing tonight, sweetheart. I meant that much. I want you to think and wait a bit, and then we'll see."

He moved to stand, and Elizabeth seized him from behind, wrapping her arms tightly around his waist.

"Think, think, think! I'm through with thinking. I've had twenty years to think."

"Now, Lizzie."

She licked the nape of his neck lightly, and he expelled a harsh breath between his teeth.

"Stay with me," Elizabeth crooned.

"Learning fast, aren't you?" he said.

"I hope so."

"You take the will right out of a man," he said huskily, leaning back into her caress.

"Don't go. We don't have to do anything, but please stay the night." She ran a row of kisses down his spine.

He arched his back in reaction, then turned to look at her. "It will be no easy thing lying next to you and not touching you."

She flung herself away from him and folded her hands primly. "I'll stay on my side of the bed," she said piously.

"Liar. You won't be able to resist me."

"Now who thinks no small beer of himself?" Elizabeth asked archly, imitating his brogue and using one of Maura's favorite expressions.

He shook his head warningly. "I think I'd better go. This is waltzing up to trouble and inviting it in for a drink."

Elizabeth inched closer to him. "Who knows when we'll be able to get together again, Sean?" she said seriously, looking into his eyes beseechingly.

He sighed and slumped visibly. He knew she was right.

"You'll stay?" she whispered.

He lay back on the bed and Elizabeth crawled next to him, putting her head on his shoulder.

"I thought you were keeping to your side of the bed," he said wearily, closing his eyes.

"You were right," she said contentedly. "I am a liar."

"Just as I thought." He put his arm around her, and she curled into his side.

"Your skin is so warm," she said dreamily.

"Let's have no talk of how warm I am—it's a bad subject to raise," he said dryly.

"May I say that I can feel the muscles in your leg?"

"You may not."

About thirty seconds passed.

"Sean?"

"I'm still here."

"Where can we go to be together? You said we had to get out of this town."

"I'm working on it."

"I have an idea."

"I'd be pleased to hear it."

"Philadelphia."

He was silent, thinking.

"I could say I was going in to see Aunt Dorrie."

"You said she was away until Christmas."

"Right. I could say I was going shopping then, take the train from Pottstown."

"Your father would never let you go alone. He'd send a chaperon with you. Mrs. Tamm, very likely."

"Oh, God," Elizabeth moaned.

"Is there anybody else?"

Elizabeth sat bolt upright. "Maura."

"I don't think your father would regard Maura as a suitable companion," Sean said, looking up at her.

"But suppose I could talk him into it?" Elizabeth said excitedly. "He likes Maura. He thinks she's . . ."

"Docile," Sean supplied.

"Yes."

"He's wrong."

"I know that. But do you think she would do it?"

"Maura speaks for herself."

"She would have to know about . . . us."

"I think she has an idea already."

Elizabeth nodded slowly. "I think she does, too."

Sean caught her chin in his hand and turned her to face him. "How is that?"

"When I was arguing for you with my father she told me to stop it. She thought it would look to him like . . . I was interested in you."

"Were you? Then?"

Elizabeth nodded.

"Nothing much is lost on Maura," Sean said.

"Could you get the time off? To go to Philadelphia, I mean?" Elizabeth said, returning to the original subject.

Sean shrugged. "I might fake an illness. An injury, maybe. But I'd have to take a different train. We couldn't be seen going in together."

"I could arrange to stay overnight in a hotel," Elizabeth murmured, her eyes lambent.

Sean groaned. "Ah, Lizzie, don't tempt me."

"No sneaking around, no prying eyes," she said, dropping next to him again. "And all night to be together."

"All right, we'll do it."

She fell on top of him, covering his face with kisses.

"Elizabeth?"

"Yes?"

"I have to go to work in three hours."

"You don't want to kiss me?"

"You devil, what you're lacking is a good spanking. Leave off me now or I'll give you what for."

"What for?" Elizabeth teased. "What is that, what for?"

"I'll teach you all about it in Philadelphia."

"Is that a promise?"

"It is."

"You'll get word to me?"

"I will."

Elizabeth subsided, taking comfort from his nearness. She was surprised at how tired she felt; just having Sean there should have kept her awake, but it had been a very long day. Her eyes closed almost against her will, and she was soon asleep.

She had forgotten to lock the door.

Maura tapped on Elizabeth's door. There was no response. She waited a long moment, then tapped again.

Silence. Elizabeth must still be sleeping. Well, she would have to be awakened. Her father wanted to see her at breakfast.

Maura opened the door and beheld her brother, naked to the waist, entwined on the bed with Elizabeth, who was wearing only a chemise and a pair of panties trimmed with lace. They were both fast asleep.

"Jesus, Mary and Joseph," Maura breathed, crossing herself. She slammed the door shut, locked it and then blocked it with her back.

"I knew it!" Maura said loudly. "I knew it all along."

Sean stirred, blinking, and then saw his sister. He leaped to his feet in confusion, dropping Elizabeth back onto the bed. She came awake in a rush, looking around wildly.

"You're lucky I was the first one in here," Maura said briskly to both of them, folding her arms like a stern headmistress who'd caught them in a prank.

"I forgot to lock the door," Elizabeth groaned.

"It's not the way it looks," Sean said quickly to his sister.

"Oh, indeed? And how is it?"

"Nothing happened. We just wanted to be together. It had to be in here, in secret, so no one would see us."

"And?"

"And then we fell asleep." He struck his forehead with the heel of his hand. "I slept right through the whistle at the change of shift."

"We both did," Elizabeth said, rising and retrieving her dressing gown from the floor.

"What time is it?" Sean demanded, looking around for his shirt. Elizabeth picked it up and handed it to him.

"Eight-thirty."

"I'm late for work," Sean said, buttoning his shirt.

"We've a worse problem than that," Maura said flatly. "How do you propose to get out of this house, with everyone abroad?"

Elizabeth and Sean exchanged glances.

"The old man is already downstairs in the dining room and he wants to see you, Elizabeth," Maura added darkly.

Elizabeth's heart sank.

"Mrs. Tamm is bustling back and forth like a freight train, and the maids are wiping and polishing. If you think we're going to hide something as big as him, you've got another thought coming."

Elizabeth ruminated desperately. "I'll just have to create a distraction," she announced.

They both looked at her.

She summoned up clues from every penny dreadful she'd ever read. "I'll go down, dressed like this, and tell my father I'm too ill to eat breakfast and that I'm going back to my room to rest."

"How does that get Sean out of the house?" Maura asked, her eyes narrowed.

"Then I'll...I'll pretend to faint. Everyone will come running, you shut the dining room door behind me, and Sean can sneak out through the kitchen."

Brother and sister stared at her in astonishment as if she'd lost her mind.

"Well? Do you have any better ideas?" Elizabeth challenged them. "Someone else is bound to show up here any minute. We've got to do something fast."

Sean saw the wisdom in that and shrugged into his jacket, smoothing his hair back with his hands.

"Go," he said. "I'll listen and wait for my chance."

Elizabeth threw her arms around his neck. "I have to have word from you or I'll go crazy."

"You'll have word," Sean said, bending to embrace her and then looking up to meet his sister's eyes.

"Hurry," Maura said urgently.

"And no matter what you hear of my doings this week, you remember that my feeling for you doesn't change, ever," he added.

Elizabeth nodded. He released her and pushed her gently toward the door.

"Go ahead," he said.

"I'm right behind you," Maura said.

Sean left the door ajar and put his ear to the crack.

Elizabeth straightened her hair as she descended the stairs, leaving her nightclothes somewhat disarrayed, as if she'd just risen.

Her father looked up from his newspaper as she appeared in the doorway of the dining room.

"Elizabeth!" he said in surprise. "What are you doing down here in your nightclothes?"

"I'm sorry, Father," she said, aware that she had violated one of his cardinal rules of etiquette: a lady never appeared improperly dressed. "But I knew you wanted to see me so I thought I'd tell you myself, not just send word with one of the servants."

"Tell me what?" he said as she stopped near his chair.

"I'm not feeling very well."

"Oh, I'm sorry to hear that."

"Yes, in fact, I haven't been feeling well for several days, and I thought it would be best if I spent the morning in bed."

"I see."

"There was something you wanted to discuss with me?"

"Yes. I've had a letter from your Aunt Dorothea, and she's returning from her trip earlier than expected."

"Oh." Elizabeth's mind raced. Perhaps an ally was about to make a reappearance.

"Didn't she write you about it?" her father asked.

"I haven't looked at my mail. There might be a letter there. When will she be back?"

"A month early. Two weeks before Christmas, so I imagine she'll be able to spend the holidays with us."

Maura coughed behind Elizabeth, who glanced around and saw the girl standing nervously near the door. Maura glanced meaningfully toward the staircase.

"Thank you for telling me, Father," Elizabeth said quickly. "I'll just go up now."

Langdon looked down at his paper once more.

Elizabeth moved along the wall and then slumped suddenly, catching the back of a chair as she fell. The chair tumbled with her.

"Oh, miss!" Maura yelled, turning her head so that her voice carried to the stairwell. "Mr. Langdon, she's fallen. Mrs. Tamm! Mrs. Tamm!"

Arthur Langdon bolted out of his chair as the housekeeper flew in from the hall, followed by two of the maids. Maura waited until everyone had flooded into the room and gathered around Elizabeth's prone form before she pulled on the door, leaving it open far enough to see Sean dart down the staircase. She waved him through the hall and watched him disappear into the kitchen before turning to join the concerned group, closing the door behind her.

Elizabeth's eyelids were fluttering as Maura knelt next to Mrs. Tamm, who was chafing Elizabeth's wrists.

"She's coming around," the housekeeper said as Elizabeth looked up into Maura's face.

Maura nodded, winking.

"I'm all right," Elizabeth announced, trying to sit up.

"Stop fussing over her. Give her some air," Langdon said as he helped Elizabeth to her feet and into a dining chair.

"I just felt dizzy, suddenly," Elizabeth said weakly.

"And no surprise, going without breakfast," her father said firmly. "Mrs. Tamm, help me get Elizabeth up to her room, and then send for Dr. Marks."

"I don't need a doctor," Elizabeth said, truthfully enough.

"Nonsense," her father said briskly.

"You should have an examination, my dear," Mrs. Tamm said. "Fainting can be an indication of something serious."

"You're to bring Elizabeth a tray," Arthur Langdon instructed Mrs. Tamm. "And I want to hear that you ate a substantial meal, Elizabeth, or I'll know the reason why."

Elizabeth left the room supported between her father and the housekeeper.

Maura stepped out of the way as they passed, then followed behind to settle her mistress in bed.

The slowdown in the mines started that Wednesday, Allhallow's Eve. The men showed up for work as usual, but they deliberately cut only about half their customary level of coal. This went on for a few days before the Langdon supervisors realized that the decrease was deliberate and not some freak of production or miscalculation of output. By Saturday, Arthur

Langdon was livid and called a meeting with CIP officers and the shift managers at his house.

Elizabeth, not surprisingly recovered from her mysterious illness, lingered in the library observing the men assemble until her father noticed she was there and asked her to leave. She stepped into the hall and encountered Maura, who was standing off to one side watching Tom Rees enter the library and close the door behind him.

"What is this all about?" Elizabeth asked.

"Part of Sean's 'doings,' I'll warrant," Maura replied. "Do you remember what he said when he was leaving your room the other morning?"

Elizabeth nodded. "Is it a strike?"

"It's something. Did you see the long faces on the people coming in here?"

"What do you think is going to happen?"

"Your father will take some measures against them. He's not one to sit still for any antics he doesn't like."

Maura was right. Inside the library Arthur Langdon was saying to one of his managers, "How much is the decrease?"

"Significant," the man replied.

"That's not an answer. How much will we be hurt by the end of the month?"

The manager looked as if he didn't want to answer the question but finally said, "We'll be down by more than half if nothing is done."

"Has there been any formal acknowledgment of this action by the miners?"

Tom Rees shook his head. "They're behaving normally, acting as if nothing is different."

Langdon stood abruptly. "Jameson. This sounds just like him. He's waiting for me to make a move."

"Maybe we should sit it out a little longer," Rees said hastily. "The miners are being hurt financially. Since they're paid by the car of coal, when production decreases they take home less money. If this drags on, they may not go to a full strike because they can't afford to. You can wait them out and see what happens."

"And let that paddy think he's got the best of me?" Langdon demanded angrily. "No. I'm going to run ads in all the papers and send men out to recruit on every dock in the East. I'll have replacements for every miner who isn't working up to snuff in a week."

Rees sighed inwardly. And so it begins, he thought. Langdon would bring in scabs and the lines of battle would be drawn.

Langdon was talking again, laying out his plans, but Rees wasn't listening.

On Sunday afternoon, Maura readied the Jameson shanty for a visit from Tom Rees while Sean bellowed in the background.

"I'll not have that peeler in this house!" Sean said.

"You have nothing to say about it," Maura replied crisply, setting the table with the best pieces of crockery she could find.

"I do, indeed."

"And how do you come by that opinion?" Maura asked.

"I'm keeping this family, and my judgment should be respected," he said pompously.

Maura threw him a dirty look. "Last time I looked I was still working," she said dryly.

Sean said nothing, his smoldering glance speaking volumes as he paced around the room.

"You've a nerve, I'll say that for you," Maura observed, slicing the golden cake she'd made herself with sugar saved for months.

"Don't give him all of that," Sean said, horrified, watching her carve up her masterpiece.

"I'll give him the work of my own hands if I so choose, thank you very much," Maura replied.

Sean grabbed a piece as she slapped his wrist. "What's this about the nerve I have?" he inquired, taking a bite of cake, unwilling to let the matter rest.

"You've a nerve dictating to me while you're carrying on with Miss Elizabeth right under her father's nose."

They both fell silent as their mother came down the stairs from the loft and fetched her sewing basket from a stool by the fire. They waited patiently until she had gone back to the second floor before resuming the argument.

"I am not carrying on with Elizabeth," Sean said vehemently.

"What do you call it?"

"It's not an affair."

"I guess you were holding a prayer meeting in her room when I found you there," Maura said sarcastically.

"Oh, why am I wasting breath talking to you? You wouldn't understand."

"I understand that you do as you damn well please while issuing orders to everybody else. Do you think I don't know you've been chasing every girl in the patch since you were old enough to notice they were wearing skirts? I like Miss Elizabeth a lot, and I'm more than a little worried about what's going to happen to her."

"Because of me?" Sean said, shocked.

"Because of no one else."

He set the rest of his cake down on the table and moved closer to his sister. "Maura, I'm not going to hurt her."

"You might do just that without meaning to at all." She bustled away from him and he followed her like a child.

"You mean because of her father?" Sean asked.

"You're a brilliant boyo, aren't you now? Her father, her family, the slowdown—do you need a list? You're not exactly the suitor the Langdons would choose for her in their fondest dreams."

Sean sighed deeply. "I've thought of all that. Endlessly. In fact, I've thought of little else. But I can't stop myself. I'm not trifling with Elizabeth. I need her with me for the rest of my life."

Maura paused in the act of placing a flatiron on the fire. "What are you saying, Sean?" she asked, turning to face him, concern in her voice and posture.

"I'm saying that I love her."

Maura searched his face, putting his words in the context of her knowledge of his life. "I hope you don't mean that you love her money, because she's bound to get little of it if she takes up with the likes of you."

Sean looked away from her, his temper rising. "Don't shame me, Maura."

She saw that he was serious and dropped the iron on the fireside bench. "Oh, Sean, I'm sorry." She put her arms around his neck, and he held her in an affectionate embrace.

"I'm scared, Maureen," he said above her head. "I've never felt this way before. It's like I'll do anything to be with her and take care of her. I'm going ahead with the slowdown, I won't give up my work, but I'm thinking about her all the time, worrying about her. I'm so distracted I'm not like myself at all."

Maura stepped back and looked up at him sympathetically. "You're in love, all right."

Sean combed his hair back from his forehead with his fingers. "And that's probably why I'm giving you a hard time about this visit from your taffy boyfriend."

"He's not my boyfriend. He's just coming for tea."

"Aye, I know." Sean sighed. "That's how it starts." He eyed her intently. "Maureen, I have to ask a favor."

"After the miserable time you've been giving me this day? Get off with you."

"I mean it."

"I'm listening."

"Elizabeth and I are going to try to get together in Philadelphia sometime soon."

"For a tryst?"

"I don't think that's the word I would choose."

"The choice of words aside, might I ask about my role in this grand plan?"

"She'll be needing a chaperon for the trip, and she told me she wants to ask you."

"Her father will insist on Mrs. Tamm or somebody else just as much a jailer."

"Maybe so, maybe not. But if she can get her father to agree, will you go?"

Maura was silent.

"You'd be doing me the good turn of my life."

"I'll think about it."

"You do that." He glanced around as if emerging from a trance. "Well, I ken I'd better take myself off if you're expecting a caller."

"How considerate of you."

"Where is Matthew, by the by?"

"Matthew is spending the afternoon at the Kellys' with Kevin. They're learning to toss darts from old man Kelly."

"A fine influence, that's just what Matt needs," Sean said darkly. "Kevin's father is one step away from lunacy, and we're sending Matt to sup with him."

"Matt won't be playing with Jim Kelly, he'll be playing with his son. I believe you said something about leaving?"

There was a knock at the door.

"Be still my heart," Sean said in a dramatic stage whisper, putting his hand to his chest.

"Sean, I'm warning you," Maura said between her teeth, her eyes shooting sparks.

"I'm off," Sean replied, grinning, removing his coat from a chair. He slung it over his shoulder and pulled open the door.

Tom Rees stood on the porch, wearing a tweed Norfolk jacket and carrying a box of candy purchased at the company store.

"Rees," Sean said civilly, nodding to him as he passed.

"Jameson," Rees replied, surprised that Maura's brother had acknowledged him at all.

"Come in," Maura said, appearing in the doorway. She was wearing the same dress she'd worn to the company picnic, obviously her best, with a crisp white apron.

"This is the first time I've seen you out of uniform," she added as he walked past her into the room.

"I feel undressed without it," he admitted.

They faced each other in front of the table.

"This is for you," he said, extending the candy box.

"Isn't that lovely. Thank you."

An uncomfortable silence fell between them.

"Well," Maura finally said. "Sit you down."

Chapter Seven

Rees took off his cap and sat awkwardly at the scrubbed table, stretching his long legs beneath it. He noted that it was already set, with slices of yellow cake displayed on a china plate and carefully ironed linen napkins.

"Handsome napery," he said.

"They're a discard from the Langdon house, too worn for use there, according to Mrs. Tamm. But not too worn for use here, that much I can tell you."

"I would have thought your brother wouldn't allow them in the house," Rees said lightly.

"Oh, he squawks and flaps a bit, but the practical side of things usually overcomes him before too long."

"Did he kick up a fuss about my visit today?"

"Well, you know Sean, but you seem to be here and the house is still standing."

"What did he say?"

"He said a great deal, but with Sean it's always more important what he doesn't say."

Rees watched her alertly. "What do you mean?"

"He suspects you're courting me to get close to the family, so you can spy on him for Langdon."

Rees was so startled that he didn't know what to say. After a protracted silence, during which Maura calmly sliced a lemon, he ventured, "Did he imply—"

"Not at all. He may seem like a lout to you, Mr. Rees, but where his kin is concerned my brother is as sensitive as a stringed instrument. He objects to you on other grounds, loudly and impressively, but I know what he thinks."

"And what do you think?"

Maura fixed him with a gimlet stare. "If I agreed with him, you and I would not be having this conversation," she said dryly.

"I'm relieved to hear it," Rees said, leaning back in his chair, glad that they could clear the air.

"I know you have your job to do, but I can't believe it would extend to chatting up women in order to spy on their relatives," Maura said, setting down the plate containing the lemon and wiping her fingers on her apron.

"You must have a higher opinion of me than your brother does," Rees said.

"Ah, Mr. Rees, that wouldn't be hard at all," Maura replied mischievously.

"Please call me Tom."

"I will. And take off your coat."

Rees unbuttoned his jacket and undid the top button of his crisply starched shirt.

"Why is it I'm always asking you to undress?" she added teasingly, her eyes laughing.

"An invitation I'll never refuse," he replied in the same vein. He looked around the room. "I saw Sean leaving, but where are Matt and your mother?"

"Matt is out for the afternoon, and my mother is upstairs, sewing. She won't be coming down."

"Then we're alone."

"Hardly. If I raise my voice to shouting level, you'll have a clutch of Irishmen with pitchforks standing on the porch in five minutes. We've walls as thin as rice paper here."

"My place is the same," Rees said, watching her examine the water in the teakettle before she put the pot on the hob.

"Something off with the water?" he asked.

"The well's been murky, but it smells fresh." She shrugged. "Have you been staying above the CIP office long?"

"Since I got the promotion to sergeant a year ago. The flat comes with the job."

"You've done well for yourself."

"You wouldn't think so if you saw the place."

"Bad, is it?"

"It's roomy as flats hereabouts go, but the last man who lived there smoked a pipe, and the walls are ribboned with the grime. They want a whitewashing in the worst way. And the fireplace flue is choked—it blows ash back into the house." He shook his head. "I never seem to have the time to redd the place up."

"Too busy arresting my brother, are you?" she asked archly. She was grinning.

"That, and a few other things."

"Chasing the ladies?"

"Only one," he replied, holding her gaze.

His serious tone made her nervous, and she got very busy rearranging dishes on the table.

"Why don't you stop playing with that crockery and sit down here with me," he said quietly.

Maura hesitated, then complied, sweeping her skirts up with one hand as she sat down across from him.

"I've been looking forward to this since we fixed the time," Rees said ingenuously.

Maura stared back at him, noting his clear blue eyes, the gossamer eyelashes of the natural blond. His stylish light brown mustache was a shade darker than his fair hair. Sean alone of the Langdon young men disdained the fad for facial hair, and Maura thought that her companion's finely molded mouth was flattered by the fashion.

"I have, as well," she admitted.

"Truly?"

She nodded.

"My job doesn't bother you any longer?"

Her lips twitched. "I can't say that. You don't suppose you could take up another line of work?"

He sighed and looked away from her, not smiling. "When I came to this country, I was good for nothing. There was nothing I could do, except the mining I had hoped to leave behind in Wales. I've tried to make the best of a bad job.''

"Why did you leave Wales?''

"Same as your people. To find a better life.''

"Not exactly the same. We had no choice—we were starving in Ireland.''

"It leads to the same result when you can't earn a living wage. I'll never get rich working for the CIP, and if my plans work out, I won't be with them much longer, but I've got a sound roof over my head and the glimmer of a future. That's a lot more than I had at home.''

"Can't you understand that Sean only wants that very thing for himself and the rest of the miners?''

Rees looked down at his hands. "We're in the same boat, but on opposite sides of it.''

"It seems a pity,'' Maura whispered.

Rees nodded wordlessly.

"What was your home like?'' Maura asked quietly.

"Oh, smashing, if you're talking about scenery,'' he said, shrugging. "Holyhead's an island, you know, off the west coast of Anglesey in the north. It's a seaport, lots of shipping and fishing, but the jobs were all sewed up by the commercial firms. You had to go inland, to the south, to get work in the mines, and it paid less than here.''

"That's hard to picture. Do you still have family there?''

"My father and brother—they live together in the family house. My mother is dead.''

"Do you miss it?"

His throat worked slightly. "I do."

"What do you miss most?"

He laced his fingers together on the table before him. "The language, I think. We mostly speak Cymric at home, you know. It's not like Ireland, where the change to English was forced. And even English sounds different here. I can't get used to it. The way of talking in this country is so... flat."

Maura smiled in agreement. It sounded flat to her, too.

"I've tried to lose the accent—didn't want to sound like I just got off the boat—but it's not easy."

"Sean won't lose his. He says he wants everyone to know where he came from."

"That sounds like Sean."

"He could do it, too. He's such a mimic, he could lose it in a minute. He's just too stubborn."

There was a sound from the second floor, and they looked up simultaneously.

"That's my ma," Maura said, rising. "I'll go and check on her. Wait a bit. I'll be right back."

Rees waited, thinking that Maura and Sean both treated their mother as if she were an invalid although there didn't seem to be anything physically wrong with her.

"Is she all right?" Rees asked when Maura returned.

Maura nodded. "She fell asleep and tipped her basket onto the floor. She'll be fine."

"Maura?"

She looked at him over her shoulder as she fixed the tea.

"What's wrong with your mother, exactly? I know you told me her story, but...is she sick? Now, I mean?"

"Not in the body," Maura replied, returning to the table with the pot, which she place on a crocheted pad. "But she's given up. Have you ever known anyone who's done that? She's sort of vague and not responsible. She couldn't raise Matthew any more than she could an elephant. She can do small chores, so we keep her busy and don't ask too much of her. We get by."

"She's broken," Rees said.

"Aye, and I know what broke her."

"What's that?"

"Life."

"It doesn't have to be that way," Rees said gently.

"And who's going to make it different?"

"I could. For you."

Maura dropped the tin of tea she was holding onto the table with a bang. "Oh, aye. My mother heard that song often enough, and look where it got her."

Rees jumped up from his chair and grabbed Maura by her elbows, spinning her around to face him.

"Are you saying I'm like that blackguard who took advantage of your mother?" he demanded hotly.

"I don't know what you are!" she answered, tears rising. "You come here with your candy and your pretty face, telling pretty stories of home—I don't know what to think at all.'' She covered her face with her hands.

He pulled her hands away and made her look at him. ''You must have thought there was something in me, or you wouldn't have crossed your brother to have me here.''

''I thought . . .'' she began.

''Yes?''

''I thought that I wanted you,'' she said, so low he could hardly hear it, but he did, and then he kissed her.

He'd been thinking about doing it for a long time, so he wasted no time with preliminaries. Within seconds Maura was hanging on to him, too weak to stand, and Rees was pressing his advantage, too hungry to be polite.

''Tom, I can't,'' Maura finally protested, struggling away from him, her eyes wet.

''Let's leave, then,'' he said. ''My place . . .''

''No, no,'' Maura moaned, shaking her head. ''I can't get involved with you, 'tis not fair. There's Matt and my ma . . .''

''Don't worry about them—we'll manage somehow. Just tell me there's a chance, tell me that I can hope.''

Maura was silent, torn.

''Oh, Maura, don't you deserve a life for yourself? Does it have to be all work and family and nothing else at all?''

Matthew chose this inopportune moment to burst through the door. He stopped short when he saw his sister and the CIP man talking so close together, Maura obviously upset.

"What's amiss?" he said, his brow knitting, his expression a miniature imitation of his half brother's.

"Nothing, nothing at all," Maura replied, wiping her eyes. "You're home early. Did you wear out your welcome?"

"I had a fight with Kevin."

"Grand. What did you do?"

"I did nothing. He wants to be chief all the time and his ma takes up for him." Matt grabbed a slice of cake and jerked his head toward Rees. "What's he doing here?"

"Matthew Jameson, mind your manners!" Maura said sharply.

Matt shrugged and headed upstairs, munching busily.

"A few more years and he'll be starting down the mines as a breaker boy," Maura said after the child had disappeared into the second floor. "Or a mule driver to be crushed in a shaft, or a nipper waiting at the air door a quarter mile underground to be crushed by a coal car or overcome by the firedamp if he falls asleep. Oh, I can't bear it."

"Then let's get out of here. Together. We'll take him with us, and your mother, too."

"You're dreaming, man."

"Why am I dreaming? Staying in this place there's no chance at all, with a future written out for us like a sad play. What can we lose by trying to change things?''

"As easy as that, is it? Then why aren't we all doing it, I wonder? Why are so many poor fools hereabouts marching down into the bowels of the earth every day? Why don't we all take off into the wide world and make our fortunes like the princes in fairy tales?'' She threw up her hands in a gesture of abandonment.

"If you never try, you'll never know,'' Rees said quietly, immune to her sarcasm.

"And you're the man to try with, are you?''

"I'd like to be. There's work out west. The railroads have expanded beyond Chicago all the way to the Pacific coast. All you need is a strong back and a strong will to get work. I've got both.''

"I have to think,'' Maura said distractedly, shaking her head.

"I wasn't suggesting we go tonight,'' Rees said dryly.

Maura looked at him longingly, and her conflicting desires were mirrored in her eyes.

"I'm going, Maura,'' Rees said flatly. "I want to take you with me, but if you choose to stay, I'll go anyway. Depend upon it. I'll not waste my life here.''

"Are you setting me a time limit?'' she demanded tartly, with some of her old fire.

Rees smiled, glad to see her usual feistiness returning. "I can wait. But not forever.'' He looked around them. "Wasn't I invited here for tea?'' he asked.

"You'll get your tea,'' Maura said, resuming her preparations with alacrity.

Matthew clomped back down the stairs, eyeing his sister and then the set table hopefully.

"Would there be any more cake?" he asked.

"Sit yourself down and have some," his sister said, setting out a cup for him on the table. "You can join us if you've a mind to it. Is Ma still asleep?"

"She is. Why is the sergeant here, then?"

"He's here to visit me, if it's any of your business, which I very much doubt."

"Does my brother know?" Matt asked.

Maura looked at Rees.

"He saw me coming in as he was leaving," Rees said.

"Sean won't like it," Matt said, shrugging.

"Sean has a tongue in his head to talk for himself, little man, so why don't you stop speaking for him and eat your cake. I'll not repeat that," Maura said sternly.

Matthew said no more, looking from one to the other of his companions with his mother's deep blue eyes.

Maura poured the tea and they all sipped in increasingly uncomfortable silence, the child sitting like a sentry between the two adults.

"Good tea," Rees observed, draining his cup.

"There's no trick to making tea," Maura replied neutrally.

"You're wrong there. You have to get the proportions right, and you've added a sprig of mint, unless I'm mistaken."

"You're not."

Rees waited a socially acceptable amount of time, making a few further pleasantries, and then rose to his full height, the top of his head barely clearing the ceiling beam.

"Well, I'm off, and I thank you very much for the hospitality," he said to Maura.

"You're welcome."

"Matt, goodbye."

Matt looked at him, then looked away.

"Maura, I'll call again, and bear in mind what I said."

"I will do that," she replied, watching him don his coat and cap and then leave, glancing over his shoulder at her meaningfully as he went through the door.

Maura turned on Matthew immediately. "I'm ashamed of you," she said flatly.

"Why is that peeler in my house?" he retorted.

"Saints bless me, if you don't sound like a perfect parrot of your brother. When someone is a guest in this house, which is *our* house, you'll behave respectfully or I'll know the reason why."

"He's one of those works for Langdon."

"I know what his job is," Maura replied, marveling that at five he already knew the sides being taken in the town and where he belonged in the fight. Of course, he would have to be deaf not to be influenced by Sean, whom he adored.

Matthew sulked, examining the candy box from a safe distance, trying to determine its contents.

"Are they for us?" he finally asked, pointing.

"They're for me," Maura responded, teasing.

"May I have one?" Matt asked in his best altar boy manner, eyes downcast, voice low.

"You may have two, and there's an end to it. You'll spoil your dinner after that cake."

Matt attacked the box as Maura watched, thinking how much she loved him and wondering if she really could keep him out of the mines if she married Rees.

To be with someone she wanted desperately and help her small brother at the same time—it was a solution, wasn't it?

But she had never known a life outside Langdon, and she was afraid. She wished she had Sean's brass, but he seemed to have gotten all the mettle in the family. Or was it there, inside her, waiting to be mined?

"Have a candy, Maureen," Matt said, chewing noisily. "They're a treat for sure."

Maura moved to join him, her mind on other things.

That evening the workingmen of Langdon assembled in the abandoned mine shaft, torches flaring from the niches in the walls, to hear what Sean Jameson had to say.

"Langdon's said not a word so far," Sean announced, "but it's coming. He's tallied the production losses and has got men out hiring scabs and getting them ready to take over for us at any time."

"Then I say go to full strike," Jim Kelly interjected. "Might as well be hung for a sheep as a lamb."

"Not yet. We'll cut out the four to twelve shift first," Sean replied. "There'll be no charges laid, that'll cause trouble right enough, but he won't be able to cry strike to the newspapers. That man from the *Tribune,* Faison, is in Langdon's pocket, you know."

"Along with the governor and a passel of other politicians," Kelly replied.

"Let's go out entirely and put an end to it," a man called from the rear. "These half measures are driving me daft."

"I'm for that," Kelly added.

Sean shook his head.

"Why not? This is getting us nowhere, fast," Kelly said.

"We've only been doing it a few days!" Sean countered. "Can't you wait a bit, have a little patience? Maybe Langdon will deal. Are there many of us here who could bear the losses of no work at all?"

The men were silent, thinking that with no money coming in they'd be close to starvation in no time.

"Let's hurt him a little, to show him we could possibly hurt him a lot. We want to seem reasonable. Going wild is not the answer in this country, boys. There are other ways."

Conran and Shane, the two older men sitting together, were silent.

"There'll be time enough for further measures if they become necessary," Sean added.

"What will you tell him if he calls on you about the slowdown?" Shane asked.

"I'll tell him that we want to be reasonable, and if he reacts the same, we can reach an agreement."

"And if he brings in the scabs?" Conran demanded.

"He won't do that unless we go to full strike," Sean said.

"How do you know?" Kelly asked.

"He'll look like he's overreacting otherwise. I know the man. He's very conscious of his image with the politicians and the press."

"I hope you're right," Kelly said.

"We're all hanging on your planning, son," Shane said.

"I know that," Sean replied, subdued but firm. He looked around the group, at the men jammed three-deep into the confined space.

"Anyone else want a voice?" he asked.

He was met with silence.

"Right, then, let's plan the dropout of the midnight shift," he said, and the men leaned in to listen.

Elizabeth eavesdropped carefully at her bedroom door, waiting for Maura to enter. When she heard the Irish girl's voice on the stairs, she backed away just far enough for the door to swing inward from the hall. When Maura came in she almost crashed into her.

"Well?" Elizabeth demanded.

"A bit anxious, are we?" Maura said dryly, placing a stack of clean linen in Elizabeth's wardrobe.

"What did Sean say?"

"He said to set the trip for this Thursday."

"Thursday. What will he do to get off work?"

"He didn't confide in me. You may have noticed that he tells me as little as possible at all times." Maura shut the drawer and turned, facing Elizabeth.

"The train leaves at ten in the morning and three in the afternoon. It only goes into Philadelphia twice a day," Elizabeth said.

"The station manager, Mr. Thurston, is your father's spy. He reports everybody who goes and comes, so he'll be sure to notice if you and Sean both travel to Philadelphia on the same day," Maura said.

Elizabeth groaned.

"Sean will have to go over to Mauch Chunk or one of the other Schuylkill stations and travel into the city from there," Maura said. "Let's hope nobody connects the fact that he misses work and you take your trip at the same time."

"My father's preoccupied with his labor troubles. I'm hoping he's so distracted that he'd notice only the most obvious bungling," Elizabeth offered.

"Lord grant we won't be obvious," Maura said fervently.

"Amen."

"How will you get your father to agree to taking me with you?" Maura asked.

"I've had an idea."

Maura waited.

"I don't have a ball gown to wear to the Brandon's party the day after Thanksgiving," Elizabeth said.

Maura looked doubtful. "In all those clothes?" she said, gesturing at Elizabeth's well-stocked closets.

"Of course I do, but I'm going to tell my father I don't," Elizabeth went on impatiently, wondering if Maura was having a sudden attack of density. "He has no idea what I've got up here. I could have Grand Army of the Republic uniforms in the closets. He just expects me to present myself suitably dressed."

Maura nodded.

"I'll tell him that I want to go to the city to purchase material and a pattern for a gown, and I want to take you with me because you're going to make it," Elizabeth stated triumphantly.

Maura stared at her.

"You told me you made your own clothes. You're an excellent seamstress. You could do it."

"Wouldn't it just be much easier to buy one that's ready-made?" Maura asked.

"Maura, what's the matter with you today? If I bought one ready-made, I wouldn't need you to go with me, would I? I'll tell my father I want something unique. And your making the dress would give us time to talk together, time Mrs. Tamm would have to give you away from your other duties." Elizabeth was so pleased with her cleverness that she grinned.

"There's one problem with all of this, speaking of Mrs. Tamm," Maura observed.

"What's that?"

"Your father may decide to send Mrs. Tamm with *both* of us."

"I've already thought of that."

Maura waited patiently, certain she was going to hear all about it shortly.

Elizabeth leaned closer conspiratorially.

"Mrs. Tamm's daughter is coming down to visit from Buffalo on Wednesday. She's staying for a week in the guest room. Guess who gave her the idea for the trip?"

Maura looked at the ceiling.

"I sent her a message and asked her to come, in gratitude for all Mrs. Tamm has done for us," Elizabeth went on. "Now my father wouldn't send Mrs. Tamm off on a two-day jaunt while her daughter is visiting from out of town, would he?"

"Two-day?" Maura said warily.

"I'm planning on staying overnight in a hotel."

"With Sean?"

"Well, not with General Sherman."

"And what am I supposed to do with myself?" Maura asked, holding out her hands, palms up.

"I'll book a room for you."

"Are you fooling yourself that your father won't notice that he's paying for two rooms instead of one?"

"I have some money my father doesn't know about, enough to pay for the extra room."

Maura merely looked at her, saying nothing.

"From my Aunt Dorothea," Elizabeth explained.

Maura sighed. "Are you sure about this?"

"Yes. I know it seems risky and headstrong."

Maura snorted at the understatement.

"But I have to do it. I can't think about *not* doing it. Can you understand that?"

"Unfortunately, I can. Sean seems to be in the same condition. When are you going to talk to your father?"

"Tonight, at dinner."

"Good luck."

"You'll help us, then? For sure?"

Maura nodded.

Elizabeth smiled and threw her arms around the other girl, hugging her tightly.

"I was afraid you'd try to talk us out of it," she said.

"I know a grand passion when I see one," Maura replied wryly, resignation in her tone.

They both looked toward the hall as Mrs. Tamm's voice sounded in the passage below them.

"I'd best be off. She'll be after me to do the rest of the ironing," Maura said, and slipped from the room.

Elizabeth sat at her desk to plan her strategy for the evening.

At dinner Elizabeth waited until the main course had been cleared before saying conversationally, "Did you receive the invitation to the Brandon ball, Father?"

He looked up from the napkin he was refolding. "Not yet. I expect to shortly. Why?"

"I would really like to look my best," she said. "All the cream of the county will be there, the fine people from miles around, and I really don't have a suitable dress."

"Somehow I doubt that, Elizabeth," her father said, aware of what was coming.

"It's true. I didn't attend any evening parties at school, you know, and my old things are out of style since the bustle came in and—"

"All right," Langdon said tolerantly. "You want a new dress. I suppose that could be arranged."

"I'd like to go to Philadelphia for the materials—all the best samples are there. Pottstown only has one furnishings shop and Reading is really almost as long a trip."

Mrs. Tamm came into the room and served the *bombe glacé,* handing them the porcelain dishes in silence.

"I can take the train," Elizabeth added.

"Mrs. Tamm," Langdon said, "it appears Elizabeth will be taking a trip into Philadelphia. I'd like you to accompany her, after your daughter leaves, of course."

"Father, it can't wait that long," Elizabeth interjected quickly. "I want something unique, and Maura promised to make it for me. We barely have enough time as it is. I have to go in this week."

Langdon looked at her in exasperation.

"Maura can go with me," she said.

"Elizabeth, a servant is not a fit chaperon for a young lady of your station," Langdon said firmly.

"Maura is a good girl," Mrs. Tamm offered, eager to preserve her time with her daughter.

"Father, I traveled all the way from school alone," Elizabeth pointed out.

"Todd met you at the station," her father countered.

"That would still be the case. Todd could take us to and from the station, and we could arrange for a hansom to meet us in Philadelphia. Oh, please, Father, I want so much to look nice for Charles," she said, abandoning all scruples and concluding with a shameless lie.

"All right, Elizabeth, I don't have time for any more debate about this. I have a meeting in fifteen minutes." He dug into his dessert and added dismissively, "Tell Mrs. Tamm the details when you've made your plans. I'll arrange for a bank draft to cover your expenses. Is there anything else on your mind?"

"No, thank you, Father. May I be excused?"

Her father nodded, and Elizabeth rose, leaving the dining room before he could change his mind.

Chapter Eight

Elizabeth packed three times for her trip to Philadelphia, filling and then emptying two shagreen leather traveling bags until Maura was fit to be tied.

"It doesn't matter what you wear, Sean just wants to see *you*," she finally said, when Elizabeth had changed the contents of the larger bag for the last time.

"I want to look nice," Elizabeth said petulantly.

"How could you not?" Maura asked in exasperation.

"I wish I didn't have to wear that plaid cloak," Elizabeth muttered, not listening. "It makes me look like I'm marching in the Scots guards, and the fringe on the shoulder cape is too long."

"Aren't we fussy?" Maura said archly. She had finally stopped addressing Elizabeth as "miss," except in the presence of others. "There's many who'd be glad of a nice wool cloak like that one of a cold winter's day."

"Oh, I know I'm being a brat," Elizabeth said apologetically. "It's just that I'm so nervous, everything that I want to take with me seems to be lost. My Aunt Dorrie gave me that plaid cloak, and I never liked it. Do you want it?''

Maura gazed at her in puzzlement. ''You're giving it to me? Just like that, because you don't like the fringe?''

''Yes, take it, take it. I know I have a short blue cloak somewhere,'' Elizabeth mumbled, riffling through the stock of garments hanging in the wardrobe. ''I like it much better than the plaid one, but I can't find it. Have you seen it? It has bell sleeves trimmed with black braid, and a matching muff.''

Maura walked across the room, pushed aside a dark green dress finished with alençon lace and extracted the blue cloak from the depths of the closet. She handed it to Elizabeth wordlessly.

Elizabeth took it, abashed, and then sank to the edge of her bed, her hands in her lap.

''I'm not doing very well, am I?'' she asked rhetorically.

''If it's going to upset you this much, maybe you shouldn't go,'' Maura advised.

''Oh, no, I want to go with all my heart. I'm just afraid for Sean. I can't imagine what my father would do to him if he found that I was meeting him there.''

''Or to me,'' Maura added dryly.

''If we're caught, I'll tell my father that I pressed you in to it, and you were afraid you'd lose your job if you refused to go along with me,'' Elizabeth said.

''What about Sean?'' Maura asked.

Elizabeth rose briskly and dropped the cloak onto the bed. "I'm not going to think about that because it's not going to happen," she said firmly. "There's no reason for my father to believe that this trip is anything but what I said it was. Now let's get this room put to rights so there's a place for me to sleep tonight."

Maura started to put things away obediently.

"Maybe I should wear the gray *paletot*," Elizabeth said thoughtfully. "It's not as warm as the woolen coat, but it's really not that cold yet, is it?"

"I thought we just settled this," Maura said in what was a tolerant and reasonable tone under the circumstances.

"Do you know where it is?" Elizabeth asked.

"With the claret velvet bands and buttons?"

"Yes."

"Mrs. Tamm took it to resew a button that was loose."

"Good. I think that fitted style is much more flattering to me, don't you?"

Maura, who found all the items of Elizabeth's wardrobe staggeringly luxurious, merely rolled her eyes.

"And under the coat I'll wear the black silk dress with the mauve ruching and the black kid slippers and the black silk reticule trimmed with the jet beads. And those marcasite earrings with the jet drops. What do you think?"

"I think Sean would prefer to see you naked, if you want the pure truth," Maura burst out in exasperation, her supply of patience coming to an end.

Elizabeth stared at her, then blushed furiously. Both women started to laugh at the same time. They continued to laugh helplessly, releasing tension, until they both fell on the littered bed, weak and drained by an excess of merriment.

"Forgive me, Maura, I know I've been driving you crazy," Elizabeth said when she could speak. She wiped her eyes. "You'd better go. Mrs. Tamm will wonder what we're doing in here."

Maura stood, shaking out her skirt.

"Take the plaid cloak with you. I'll get the *paletot* back from Mrs. Tamm. And remember, I've ordered Todd to have the coach ready for nine-thirty sharp. I don't want to miss the train."

"I'm on duty here at seven," Maura reminded her gently. "I'll be here before you're awake."

"I know, I know. Be sure to bring your overnight bag with you. And I hope you have some ideas for a dress, because we'll actually have to make one when we get back."

"The furnishings shops sell the patterns as well as the materials, don't they?" Maura asked. She had never sewn anything from a dressmaker's plans before; her ideas came from magazine illustrations and her own head.

Elizabeth nodded. "I cut a pattern from *Harper's Weekly,* maybe we can use that, but Dunstan's on Re-

vere Lane has design sketches from Worth and Gage-
lin, Doucet, the other Paris houses. Velvet would be
nice, or double-faced silk, but just use your judgment.
You'll be doing the buying. I assume I'll be occupied . . . elsewhere.''

''Indeed,'' Maura said.

''All right, then, you'd better go,'' Elizabeth said.

Maura nodded. ''Good luck to us,'' she said.

''Luck,'' Elizabeth echoed as Maura took her leave.

In the morning Elizabeth was dressed and ready long
before breakfast and nervous as a cat. Her bags were
waiting in the front hall by the door for Todd to put in
the carriage. As she left the dining room, where her
father lingered over his last cup of coffee and his
newspapers, she donned the cloak and gloves lying on
the hall table.

''I've made a snack for you,'' Mrs. Tamm said in the
hall, handing Elizabeth a wrapped package.

''Oh, thank you, but that wasn't necessary. There's
a dining car on the train.''

''I'm aware of that, but you never know what that
food will be like,'' Mrs. Tamm sniffed.

Maura entered the hall from the kitchen, wearing the
cloak Elizabeth had given her and carrying a tapestry
carpetbag bound with hemp. Her hair picked up the
rust in the busy plaid, and the greens and blues en-
hanced her eyes.

"You look better in that than I ever did," Elizabeth said sincerely. "It's much more suited to your coloring."

"You'd better not let your aunt know you gave that away," Mrs. Tamm said to Elizabeth in an undertone.

Elizabeth made a dismissive gesture, much more intent on starting her journey than worrying about trifles.

"Ready when you are, miss," Todd said from the entry, his cap in his hand.

"You can take the bags out now, Todd," Elizabeth said to him. She gestured for Maura to add hers to the two waiting by the door. Todd's face expressed his disapproval but he dared not cross his mistress. He picked up all three bags, muttering to himself.

Mrs. Tamm hugged Elizabeth, then nodded to Maura. "Have a safe trip," she said.

The two young women followed Todd out to the coach, where he assisted them inside and then climbed onto the box. Elizabeth spread the lap robe over them to guard against the early November chill, using the gesture as an excuse to lean in close to Maura.

"Just talk nonsense until we're out of the trap," she whispered. "I'm not sure how much he can hear up there."

"Nosy old coot," Maura whispered back. "It's no wonder that Sean hates him."

Elizabeth widened her eyes warningly.

Maura nodded and began to natter about pleasantries as Todd clicked to the horses and they started off down the lane. Elizabeth answered her in kind, watching the coal patch disappear into the background. It gave way to the open autumn countryside, blazing leaves and dying grass changing before her eyes into the bleached, sere landscape of winter.

The train station was a faded clapboard structure set atop a sagging wooden platform. A sign with the town's name was nailed above the door and visible from the tracks. As Todd unloaded their bags from the coach, Mr. Thurston, the station manager, came out of the office to greet them effusively.

"Miss Langdon, I hope you have a pleasant journey," he said, gesturing for a lackey to move their bags to the platform. "Your father arranged everything for you. It looks like you and your girl here will be the only travelers going into the city this morning."

Elizabeth made light conversation with Thurston until the belching steam engine hissed into the station, and she didn't relax until she and Maura were installed in their seats and the train had pulled away from the depot.

"Saints preserve us, I'm a gibbering wreck," Maura said anxiously, adjusting her bonnet. "I kept expecting that man Thurston to pull out a pistol and arrest us on the spot."

"For what? Taking a trip to Philadelphia?"

"For what we were contemplating. I felt like he could see inside my head and read my mind."

"My father set him onto us to smooth our way, that's all. If he really suspected anything, we wouldn't have gotten this far, believe me."

They settled in as the train sped through the Pennsylvania countryside at twenty miles an hour, following the path of the Schuylkill River on the Reading spur down to the great port city. They weren't due to arrive until midafternoon, so they explored the Pullman cars, walking through the parlor and the smoking salon—all male—to the dining car, where they had a fine lunch—oxtail soup and broiled bluefish—attended by uniformed waiters. By the time the train glided into the Philadelphia station, the two young ladies were relaxed enough to enjoy the sights and sounds of the big city.

And what sights and sounds they were! Philadelphia was in its heyday, the focal point of shipping and trade for much of the East Coast. The station was bedlam: the bell clanging in the depot cupola to herald their arrival, the travelers' mingled conversations, the whistles of the cabbies, the shushing of the idling steam engine all contributed to the noise. Porters were lined up under hotel signs to take possession of luggage, and equipages of every description crowded the street outside, which was bordered on either curb by giant elms. Fringed surreys, slender buckboards, basket phaetons drawn by hackneys, dogcarts with booted grooms, a heavy victoria with a monogrammed harness and two liveried coachmen on the box all converged on the station with one intent: to pick up passengers disgorged by the train.

Elizabeth and Maura looked at each other in bewilderment and wondered which of these myriad carriages was their transportation.

Suddenly, bearing down on the lesser vehicles, came a four-in-hand, which was brought with a pounding flourish to their very feet. Two grooms leaped from the back to hold the horses steady, and the driver jumped down to the ground, sweeping his top hat from his head and bowing dramatically.

"Miss Elizabeth Langdon?" he said.

"Yes," Elizabeth replied somewhat breathlessly.

"I have been directed by your father to take you and your companion to the Union Hotel on Broad Street. Is that correct?"

Elizabeth nodded.

"Allow me," he said, offering his hand.

He assisted Elizabeth and Maura into the carriage and then got their bags. He drove them the several blocks to the hotel at a steady pace, allowing them the time and opportunity to look at the shops and passing traffic. Elizabeth had been to Philadelphia before, but Maura gaped with undisguised curiosity at the bustling scene.

"I have to say one thing for your father," Maura finally observed to Elizabeth, "he knows how to get things done."

Elizabeth had been thinking the same thing. She had many quarrels with her father, but she would hate to be left at the mercy of the big city without his intervention.

The Union Hotel was a three-story brick structure with a marble-tiled lobby dominated by several cut-glass chandeliers. The driver carried their bags in to the registration desk and then tipped his hat, disappearing into the crowd flooding the first floor. Elizabeth tapped the bell with the flat of her hand, looking around as she waited for the clerk to attend her.

She'd been to the hotel a couple of times as a child but was too young then to have a clear memory of the place. A black walnut main staircase at the rear of the lobby swept down on either side from a central platform. The stairs were fitted with a thick, flowered carpet. A steam-powered Otis elevator with a wrought iron grille carried guests who did not wish to make the climb from floor to floor.

The reception desk, where Elizabeth stood, was carved of the same black walnut as the staircase, and there were gas jets shielded by Tiffany shades on the walls behind it. A billiard room for gentlemen only ran off to the left of the lobby with a ladies' parlor—powder room—on the right. A ballroom tiled with the lobby's white marble was also on the right. Its most commanding feature was an eighteen-by-thirty-foot portrait that covered the entire west wall, depicting the *Spirit of America* as a Rubenesque beauty dispensing gifts from a horn of plenty. Below was a basement, which Elizabeth's father had said was devoted to a well-stocked wine cellar and meat locker.

"I can't believe my eyes," Maura murmured at Elizabeth's elbow. "We might be in Europe, in Paris or Venice."

"This is where my father always stays when he's in town," Elizabeth replied dryly.

"Sean is going to fit in here like a tart in a nunnery," Maura said. "I wonder how he's planning to get up to your room."

"I can't imagine," Elizabeth replied nervously. "But he usually knows what he's doing, doesn't he?"

The desk clerk arrived and registered them, assigning them the accommodations Elizabeth's father had reserved. While Elizabeth was signing the book, Maura wandered over to the dining salon. She was staring through the glass doors at the round, linen-covered tables when Elizabeth joined her.

"It can seat four hundred," Elizabeth said to her. "The *Tribune* says that it serves the best hotel fare in Philadelphia."

"The *Tribune* should know. Mr. Faison has graced Mrs. Tamm's table often enough to judge."

That day's luncheon menu was still posted under glass on the wall next to the double doors. Luncheon featured entrées of local squab *jardinière,* calf's tongue with sauce *piquante,* stewed breast of lamb and softshell crabs *Piedmontaise.* Dessert—divided into pastry, sweet and cheese courses—ranged from whortleberry pie to *crème de nougât* and *pastilles à la rose.*

"Look at that," Maura said, pointing to the massive brass light fixture that hung from a plaster medallion in the frescoed ceiling. "It must have seventy arms."

"We've no time to count," Elizabeth replied, grabbing her hand and dragging her back to the desk.

They followed the bellboy carrying their bags into the elevator, watching in fascination as he closed the grille across the front of it. They ascended unsteadily, the uncertain steam power providing a jerky ride. The bellboy was unlocking a solid oak door as they walked down the hall. Elizabeth took the key from him as she passed.

"You can summon the chambermaid to unpack for you whenever you like," he said politely, setting their bags on the rug.

Elizabeth fished in her reticule for a tip.

"That's not necessary, Miss Langdon," the bellboy said, waving his hand dismissively. "Your father has already covered all gratuities. Please enjoy your stay with us." He left, closing the door behind him.

Elizabeth's father had also made it unnecessary for her to use her own money to accommodate Maura; he had booked one of six "cottage suites" available in the hotel. These suites featured a parlor, several bedrooms and a private bath.

"Cold running water," Maura announced from the latter, fiddling with the tap above the marble washstand.

"Hot water has to be ordered and is brought by a chambermaid in a covered container," Elizabeth announced, gesturing to a notice posted on the wall.

The notice also said that visitors were announced by card, and that all meals could be delivered to the occupants, to be served in the parlor or on a private veranda that overlooked an enclosed garden at the back of the hotel.

Elizabeth opened a set of French doors and stepped out onto the veranda. "I'm glad I don't have to clean this place," Maura said fervently, moving up to stand behind her.

The two young women went back inside the suite, dropping their cloaks onto the brocade sofa in the parlor, which had elaborately carved walnut furniture of the same style as that in the lobby. A figured carpet with a pattern of intertwining green leaves against a blue background ran through all the rooms. Thick, cream-colored Brussels lace curtains graced the tall windows. A tasseled bellpull hung alongside the marble-faced fireplace. Elizabeth walked over to the mantelpiece and picked up a card framed like a daguerreotype.

"Listen to this," she said to Maura, reading aloud. "'Previous occupants of this suite include General Robert E. Lee, commander in chief of the southern Confederacy, and the distinguished actor Edwin Booth, who lodged in these rooms while appearing in William Shakespeare's *Hamlet* at the Market Street Playhouse.'"

"Is that the brother of President Lincoln's assassin?" Maura asked, aghast.

"Must be," Elizabeth replied. She remembered reading that the darkly handsome Booth, forced into retirement by his brother's infamy, had resurrected his career again in the late 1860s. Pressed by debts and driven back onto the stage, he had won new acclaim and removed himself from the shadow of his brother's crime.

"I don't know if I'd advertise his presence," Maura said stiffly. She had been a great admirer of the late president's.

"Why not? Mr. Booth is a successful celebrity. He's not responsible for John Wilkes's behavior. Anyone can have a crazy brother."

"I know that much," Maura said dryly, and Elizabeth smiled.

"Let's look at the bedrooms," she suggested.

There were three, similarly outfitted with carved bedsteads, gas jets jutting from the walls on either side of the beds and fireplaces that were smaller versions of the one in the parlor. The master bedroom, the largest of the three, had a coromandel changing screen and a canopied bed draped with gauzy hangings. They stood in the doorway and gazed at it.

"I'm starting to get a little scared," Elizabeth said.

"Starting?" Maura said. "A little?"

"You have no idea where Sean was beginning the train trip?" Elizabeth asked anxiously.

"He wouldn't tell me—you know how he is. It had to be someplace he could walk to easily if he was taking the later train."

"Was he?"

"Of course. He couldn't be on ours and he couldn't leave from the same station."

"Then he won't get here until this evening. What am I supposed to do? Sit downstairs in the lobby waiting for him like a lady of easy virtue looking for a sponsor?"

"You know you can't risk being seen with him. He said he would find you, and he will."

Elizabeth sighed. "All right. I guess I'll just have to wait. I'm going to ring for some tea."

She summoned the maid, who presently appeared with a pot of tea accompanied by an assortment of meringue tarts, *biscuits à la reine* and toast points with port wine jelly.

"Mrs. Tamm should see this," Maura said, biting into a peach meringue tart.

"The hotel stole their pastry chef away from the Prince of Wales," Elizabeth replied.

"How?"

"They paid him more."

"Than Queen Victoria's son?" Maura asked in amazement.

"He's young yet. He'll have more money when he ascends the throne," Elizabeth said jokingly.

"What kind of tea is this?" Maura asked.

Elizabeth glanced down at the room service menu. "Orange pekoe, it says."

"What's that? From India? Ceylon?"

Elizabeth shrugged.

"It tastes funny."

"Oh, you Irish. Everything has to taste like that black brew you make. You can stand on it."

"Fine hotel like this, can't make a proper cup of tea," Maura grumbled to herself.

"They have French coffee," Elizabeth offered, tapping the menu with her forefinger.

"That's worse than Irish tea."

"How do you know?"

"I had it once. Bitter."

"Mrs. Tamm buys coffee imported all the way from Colombia for my father."

"Well, we can't expect your father to deny himself much, can we now?" Maura said flatly.

Elizabeth watched the other girl as Maura spread a piece of toast with jam the color of a pigeon's blood ruby.

"Maura, do you remember when you hinted that my father had hurt some people who opposed him?"

Maura put her knife down, not meeting Elizabeth's eyes.

"Do you remember it?" Elizabeth persisted.

Maura nodded.

"What were you talking about that day?"

Maura sighed. "It's just stories, rumors, you understand."

"I understand. Tell me."

"The word is that a while ago, before the war, another man was organizing the miners like Sean is now."

"And?"

"He disappeared. Not long after that his family left town, pensioned off, the tale goes, by your father."

"Do you believe it?"

"I believe your father is capable of something like it. Don't you, Elizabeth?"

"And you think Sean is in the same danger?"

"I don't think your father could get rid of Sean so easily. He's been smarter, more careful and a lot more vocal, if you follow me. Your da would be afraid to pull the same thing twice, especially with someone as visible as Sean. The other man was just getting started when he vanished. Sean's efforts are much further along. And your father must have realized by now that he just can't keep stamping out the random flames— sooner or later the fire's going to blaze."

"Oh, what does that mean?" Elizabeth demanded. Sometimes Maura could be as wordy and obscure as her brother. "Do you think that Sean is in danger?"

"I think Sean's too loud a creaking wheel to knock over the head and dump in the Schuylkill. But there are other ways, and your father knows, or can buy, all of them."

"Political?" Elizabeth asked, the tea she had just drunk roiling in her stomach. She knew her father well enough to guess that if strong-arm tactics hadn't worked, his next move would be more subtle, if no less effective.

"Do you know about the governor's power to declare a state of emergency?" Maura asked, dropping her untouched slice of toast onto her plate.

Elizabeth shook her head. Her education had included one inadequate civics course, and her ignorance on the subject was appalling.

"Sean's been telling me about it," Maura said. "He's always reading—you know that. He's a powerful one for those books he gets out of the library."

Elizabeth nodded.

"It seems that if there's a strike, all your father has to do is convince the governor that the interruption of the coal supply would be a health or safety hazard, and the governor could send in troops, declaring the strike illegal as against the public interest. I don't think the governor would want much convincing from Arthur Langdon, do you?"

Elizabeth shook her head sadly. "My father had dinner at the governor's mansion two weeks ago."

"And the newspapers?"

"Mr. Faison is my father's chess partner. You know how often he comes to the house. And the *Tribune* has the largest circulation. The other papers follow its lead."

Maura nodded. "And if the strike were declared illegal, any miners participating would then be criminals, subject to arrest and imprisonment. Any loss of life associated with the strike would make them murderers and lead straight to the gallows."

Elizabeth stared at her, horrified. "You've thought all this out, haven't you? No wonder you're worried."

"I do know one thing. Sean's not a hooligan, no matter how wild he looks on the surface. He lays things out like a clock maker assembling the works. That's why he's taking this strike in stages, trying not to seem irresponsible or violent. That's exactly the picture your father would like to present.''

"It's a setup, isn't it? Everything's leveraged against Sean, but still he tries.''

"That's his nature. He has to try, he can do no other. But I don't know how much longer the men will listen to him—they're getting terrible restless. They're tired of it all—the low wages, the accidents, the lung diseases. They want action.''

Elizabeth watched the other girl thoughtfully, almost jealous that Sean had shared so much of his soul, his plans and aspirations, with his sister.

Maura looked down at the abundance of untouched food on the tray. "What a waste.'' She sighed. "Matthew would go half-crazy if he saw all of this.''

"Did you leave him at home with your mother?''

Maura shook her head. "He's staying with the Kellys. My mother's too . . . forgetful to watch him.''

"Won't that alert people that both you and Sean are away?'' Elizabeth asked worriedly.

"No. Matt stays there a lot. He and the Kelly boy are great mates, though they fight like Punch and Judy.''

The chambermaid knocked, then entered on Elizabeth's command to come in and clear away the tray. She glanced at the bags sitting on the parlor floor and said, "Will you need me to unpack for you, miss?''

"No, thank you,'' Elizabeth said. "We'll take care of it.''

The maid curtsied and disappeared with the tray.

"Speak for yourself," Maura said when the girl was gone. She was grinning wickedly. "I'd enjoy being waited on like a great lady for once. It would give me something to remember for my old age."

"Wait until we have dinner in the dining room. Captains, waiters, French crystal glasses, Meissen china."

"Dinner? After that tea?"

"Oh, you can't miss it, even if you eat nothing. It's a spectacle. My father took my Aunt Dorrie to dinner here once when I was at school, and she never stopped talking about it. Let's do it up right. We'll order one of everything and I'll ask the sommelier for the best champagne."

"Som-al-what?"

"Wine steward."

"Aren't we fancy, now?"

"Yes, we are. Did you ever taste champagne?"

"Never in my life. Guinness is about as tony as we get in the coal patch."

"Is that the liver-colored stuff the miners are always drinking? Looks like diluted blood, foams like beer?"

"The very same. And you'd better get used to it, my lady fair, because Sean loves it."

Elizabeth glanced down at the watch pinned to her bodice. "Let's get changed. Dinner is at seven."

"Elizabeth, I truly couldn't eat another thing."

"Oh, come on. It will take my mind off Sean and how he's going to get here."

They both got up and headed for the cluster of bags standing on the floor.

Elizabeth and Maura emerged from their separate bedrooms twenty minutes later and examined each other critically.

"Oh, how pretty you look!" Elizabeth said, taking in Maura's lilac cambric dress. "What a lovely frock."

"You should like it, considering that it used to be yours. You gave it to me."

Elizabeth narrowed her eyes. "Did you alter it?"

"Yes. I took it in at the waist."

"Thank you . . ."

"And I changed the neckline, lowered it and put on the lace trim. Oh, and I added the apron overskirt and redraped the bustle."

"In other words, you redid the whole dress. No wonder I didn't recognize it. Maura, you're a sorceress with a needle. You should have no trouble making my gown for the Brandon ball," Elizabeth stated with evident satisfaction.

"It's honored I am that you have such faith in me," Maura said wryly. "Though I'm thinking you won't be too happy if you wind up there at the big house, with all the gentry from miles around, looking like Harlequin escaped from an Italian comedy."

"That certainly won't happen. Whose sewing machine have you been using?"

"Mrs. Tamm has been letting me use her new straight needle Singer. My mother has an old Howe lockstitch machine, but the Singer is a dream. You can support the material on a table, and that makes the seams so much easier."

Elizabeth nodded enthusiastically. She had never sewn anything except embroidery in her life—and that badly—so she didn't know what Maura was talking about but trusted her ability.

"How does this black silk look?" she asked Maura, pirouetting.

"Same as it did yesterday in your room," Maura answered.

"Oh, for heaven's sake, Maura, will you humor me? I'm one breath away from the vapors right now."

"The black silk looks glorious, fit for the Princess Royal herself. Does that suit you?"

"Let's go down to the dining salon," Elizabeth muttered, and Maura followed her out of the room.

"Well, what do you think?" Elizabeth asked, watching Maura take her first sip of champagne.

Maura wrinkled her nose. "Vinegar. Vinegar with bubbles."

"Vinegar! That stuff is the best in the house."

"Aye, well, I'm a peasant, I know." She put her crystal flute down, murmuring, "I'm afraid I'm going to break that thing. It weighs no more than a feather."

Elizabeth glanced up at the octagonal stained glass window behind their table. "That must be beautiful in the morning light, with the sun streaming through it," she said dreamily.

"It's bright as daylight in here right now," Maura replied, nodding to the blazing gas jets in the brass chandelier over their heads. She turned her butter plate over and said, "What's this word?"

"Dresden."

She glanced up inquiringly.

"Germany," Elizabeth clarified.

Maura nodded. "I knew it wasn't Pottsville."

"What's this picture on the front of it?"

"Venus rising from the sea. The design is copied from a famous painting."

"Venus looks as if she might be catching a chill, right enough," Maura observed, replacing the dish on the table.

The sommelier, as nattily attired as any dandy, with the gold medallion signifying his trade draped around his neck, arrived and asked Elizabeth in French if the wine was satisfactory.

"Mais oui," Elizabeth said, "but I'd prefer to speak English, if you please."

"As you wish, *mademoiselle,"* he replied smoothly, bowing slightly from the waist.

"I believe we're ready to order. Would you tell the captain to send our waiter to the table now?"

"Certainly." He left and was replaced almost instantly by the waiter, dressed slightly less formally but with linen as white as rice, neat waistcoat and trousers crisply pleated. He bowed and waited.

"I think we'll have the gumbo filet *Bresilienne* to start, and the cold *consommé.*"

He inclined his head, scribbling on his pad.

"And then the veal *Fricandeau* for my friend, and the frogs' legs *Cardinal* for me."

Maura made a disgusted face.

"And let's see, you choose the vegetables...."

"Very good, *mademoiselle,*" the waiter said.

"Potatoes," Maura interjected.

"Boiled, mashed, *au gratin,* lyonnaise?" the waiter inquired.

"Mashed," Maura said decisively, on firm ground there.

"And we'll have the Roman punch and...oh, I'll choose the dessert later, I think," Elizabeth concluded.

The waiter bowed and took off for the kitchen, crossing the acres of embroidered rug like a ship bound for a harbor.

"Frogs' legs?" Maura said.

"They taste like chicken."

"I'll take the chicken. You certainly know how to handle these people. You were firing orders like Colonel Jim Fisk."

"They recognize the name Langdon, that's all. My father made the reservation himself, and he's a valued customer. He brings in a lot of business. He warned everyone ahead of time that we were coming, two unescorted young ladies alone in the hotel, so they're being extra careful with us."

When the food came, Maura had to admit it was delicious—including the frogs' legs—but when Elizabeth mentioned dessert, Maura groaned and dropped her head onto her folded arms.

"Coffee *éclairs*, chocolate *Africaines*, coconut drops, *Génoise glacé?*" Elizabeth recited, reading from the menu.

Maura groaned again.

"Tutti-frutti pudding with Kümmel sauce? Figs, bananas, plums? Roquefort, cottage or Edam cheese?"

"I can't get up from this chair," Maura said feebly.

"Nothing more now, we'll have coffee in our suite," Elizabeth said to the waiter when he approached again.

"*You* can have coffee," Maura said, raising her head slowly. "I'm going to die."

"Maura."

"What?"

"You're not going to die. I need you. It's eight o'clock and Sean isn't here yet."

Elizabeth signed the tab when the waiter presented it, and they left the dining salon a little more slowly than they had entered it.

The elevator was occupied so they negotiated the stairs to the second floor, also slowly. Maura, who hadn't liked the champagne but had two glasses of Roman punch, found that she was a little unsteady on her feet. Elizabeth unlocked the door of their suite, and they entered to find the room empty.

"Maura, where is he?" Elizabeth inquired fretfully, locking the door behind them.

"If you say that once more I'm going to belt you," Maura replied. She stepped on the hem of her dress and crashed into one of the upholstered chairs.

"For heaven's sake, are you drunk?" Elizabeth demanded.

"Of course not," Maura said indignantly.

"Then what's wrong with you?"

"I . . . I need some fresh air." She moved over to the balcony and gasped loudly.

"What is it?" Elizabeth hissed.

"Lord, maybe I am drunk, or else I'm seeing things."

"What are you babbling about?"

"He's on the balcony!"

Elizabeth hurried to Maura's side and peered through the glass at the darkness of night.

"Lord above, will you open the door?" Maura said. "Sean is out there on the porch."

Chapter Nine

Elizabeth lunged for the latch on the French doors and yanked them open, letting in a blast of cold air.

"Well, it's glad I am to see you girls," Sean said, stepping over the threshold into the parlor. "Getting a bit nippy out there." He grinned as he opened his arms and Elizabeth ran into them.

"Oh, Sean, where have you been?" she murmured into his collar. "We were so worried."

"Well, for the last couple of hours I've been lurking out there on the veranda getting a frostbite. I had to hide behind the portieres when the maid came in to tidy the rooms and light the fires," he said, holding Elizabeth off at arm's length to examine her.

"We were at dinner the whole time," Elizabeth lamented.

"Oh, and did you enjoy yourselves?"

Elizabeth looked at Maura, who burped.

Sean peered at his sister. "What the devil ails Maura?" he asked, narrowing his eyes. He released Elizabeth and shrugged out of his jacket, dropping it onto a chair. He unwound a green woolen scarf from his neck, and it fell in a pile on top of the coat.

"She had two glasses of Roman punch," Elizabeth explained, somewhat uncomfortably.

"I can speak for myself," Maura protested, glassy eyed.

Sean chuckled delightedly. "Holy Hannah on a horse, Maureen is drunk," he said.

"Am not," Maura said as she sank bonelessly into a chair.

Sean crossed the room to kneel in front of his sister, taking her chin in his hand.

"Yes, you are, darlin'. You're skunked," he said gently. "Come along with me, now, and Lizzie and I will get you to bed."

Maura rose without protest and allowed herself to be led into the second bedroom, where Sean and Elizabeth undressed her down to her chemise and panties and then tucked her into bed. She was snoring lightly as soon as her head hit the pillow.

"How did this happen?" Sean whispered as Elizabeth hung up Maura's dress. "Maura thinks that booze is the curse of the Irish. She never drinks."

"That's why it happened. It's my fault. The punch tastes just like fruit juice, and I didn't notice she was drinking so much of it until it was too late."

"Ah, don't take on so about it. She may have a bad head in the morning, but after that she'll be as good as new." He held his finger to his lips and they both tiptoed out into the parlor. Sean closed the door behind them quietly.

He walked to the fire and held his hands out to the blaze. "Feeling is coming back into the fingers," he announced.

"I'm sorry you had to wait outside so long. And it wasn't this cold earlier today, was it?"

"Temperature dropped fifteen degrees late this afternoon. I know this because they have a big thermometer hanging outside every train station. I made careful note of the drop each time we passed one, since I knew I was going to be walking hard in the open air at the other end of the trip."

Elizabeth laughed. "I'll ring for some hot chocolate. That will warm you up."

"Shall I hide in the bedroom when the maid comes?" Sean asked. He sidled close to the door and said in the deep, dramatic voice of a house detective, "Miss Langdon, do you have a man in there?"

Elizabeth giggled. "You're in a good mood."

He was at her side in two steps and scooped her up into his arms. "I'm always in a good mood when I see you."

"Put me down, Sean. I have to ring for the maid."

"How much did you eat at dinner? Seems like you're putting on a little weight there, Lizzie."

"Oh, for heaven's sake, Sean, put me down."

He bent his head and explored the base of her throat with his tongue. "What's this?" he said. "Lizzie's pulse? Beating fast, there, Lizzie. Jumping like a jack-rabbit.''

Elizabeth tipped her head back against his shoulder, opening up a farther expanse of skin to his touch.

''It's not slowing down at all,'' he murmured.

''And it won't, if you keep on doing that.''

His lips traveled up her throat and then found hers, lingering until she surrendered completely and her arms reached out helplessly to encircle his neck.

''What was that about chocolate?'' he said against her mouth.

''Are you hungry?''

''Not for food.''

She drew back and looked at him.

''When was the last time you ate something?'' Elizabeth asked.

He sighed and put her down. ''Yesterday.''

''Yesterday!''

''I spent most of my money on the train ticket, and then I had to bribe the desk clerk to tell me where your room was.''

''Maura told you the number of the room we reserved before we left Langdon,'' Elizabeth said.

''She told me the number, but I didn't know where in the building it was. This is a big place. I had to dope out the location and then scale the wall to get up here.''

''Aren't you the clever boyo, then?'' Elizabeth said, walking over to the bellpull and giving it a tug.

''Are you making fun of my way of talking, Miss Lizzie?'' he asked archly.

"I love your way of talking, and well you know it. I was thinking of developing a brogue myself."

"Your father would disown you. He'd shoot you first, then he'd disown you."

"It may come to that, anyway," Elizabeth said seriously.

"What? Shooting you?"

"Disowning me."

Sean looked at her searchingly, then nodded.

There was a light tap at the door.

Elizabeth jerked her head toward the master bedroom, and Sean slipped into it.

The crisply dressed maid looked at Elizabeth inquiringly when she opened the door.

"I was wondering if I could have a pot of hot chocolate," Elizabeth said. "And a plate of sandwiches. Oh, and some of the meringue tarts we were served at tea."

The maid gazed at her strangely but said, "Yes, miss." She curtsied and left.

"Well?" Sean said, emerging from the bedroom as he heard the outer door close.

"She took the order, but she knows Maura and I went down to dinner more than an hour ago. Dinner here is a bacchanalia. She must think I'm the victim of a wasting disease."

"Elizabeth?"

"Yes?"

"What's a bacchanalia?"

"Big party."

"Oh, a donnybrook."

"Is that a big party?"

"A big party with fights."

He chuckled, then sobered as he sat on the sofa, sliding down on the base of his spine and stretching his legs.

"What is it?" Elizabeth asked, noticing his abrupt change of expression.

"I wonder what your old man would say if he knew I was taking advantage of his hospitality."

Elizabeth didn't answer.

"It's funny to think that when you ring the bell back at your house, Maura answers the call."

Elizabeth sat next to him and took both his hands in hers. "Let's not think about any of that tonight, Sean, all right? Not Langdon, not my father, not the strike, not any of it."

He closed his eyes and nodded. "Done."

When the food came Sean devoured it, leaving not a crumb on his plate.

"Best tuck I ever had," he said, draining his cup of chocolate.

"I'm **not** surprised."

"No wonder your da has that gut on him, chowing down like this every meal."

"Well, I don't think Mrs. Tamm is exactly up to this standard on a daily basis," Elizabeth observed dryly.

Sean sighed and put his head back against the brocade sofa.

"Tired?" Elizabeth asked.

He shrugged dismissively, which meant that he was exhausted. She had never seen him admit to fatigue.

"Why don't you go in and lie down on the bed? I'll join you in a minute."

He stood and ambled toward the bedroom, too worn out to protest her suggestion.

Elizabeth stacked the dishes and banked the fire in the parlor, unwilling to ring for the maid again. By the time she walked into the bedroom, Sean was sprawled atop the spread, his heavy brogues on the floor and his shirt unbuttoned to his waist. He looked fast asleep.

Elizabeth turned down the gas jets and undressed in the semidark, taking off everything and then slipping on a thin cotton dressing gown. She added some wood to the fire and then knelt next to Sean on the bed, studying him.

The firelight played across his relaxed face, emphasizing his high cheekbones and the jutting line of his jaw. His face was lean, too lean really, the result of hard physical labor and inadequate food. But nothing could detract from the simple beauty in the firm column of his neck, the breadth of his shoulders, the strong young body that made Elizabeth feel weak and hungry with longing. She touched his lower lip with a tentative forefinger and was startled when his mouth returned the pressure and he kissed her hand.

"Didn't think I was sleeping, did you?" he asked lazily, his eyes opening.

"Faker," Elizabeth said.

"Come here to me," he growled, reaching up to pull her down into his arms.

"I suppose you were watching me undress," she said.

"I was trying with all my might," he replied. "You cut the light so much I was going blind with squinting."

"You are such a devil," Elizabeth said with a sigh, settling against him luxuriously.

"So everyone's been telling you," he reminded her.

"Not your sister."

"Ah, well, she's a loyal lass." He buried his face in the curve of her neck, tugging at the collar of her gown. "What's all this?" he said.

"It's a nightgown, Sean. I assumed you were out for the night, and I couldn't very well sleep naked."

"And why not?" he demanded. He undid the ribbon at her throat. "I can't believe you thought I'd fall asleep with you waiting for me in this little bit of nothing."

"You were pretty tired. The train trip, all that walking, and then climbing the balcony..."

"I'm never that tired." She sat up as he slid the sheer sleeves down her arms. "I'll have this off, if you please."

Elizabeth arched her back as he pulled the flimsy garment down to her waist, leaving her torso bare. His eyes moved over her in the uncertain light, his lips parted, his throat working.

"Until this night I never thought myself a lucky man," he finally whispered.

"Sean, let me turn off the light completely," Elizabeth said, trembling with nervousness.

"I will not."

"But I'm shy, Sean, I truly am."

He answered her by leaning forward and taking her nipple in his mouth, tonguing it until it turned pebble hard. Elizabeth forgot about the light and moved into his arms again, holding his head against her and running her fingers through his hair. He kissed her everywhere he could reach, his lips leaving a trail of fire along the surface of her skin.

"Lizzie, soon there'll be no stopping me," he said huskily. "Are you certain this is what you want?"

"Yes," Elizabeth moaned, gasping as he dragged the wisp of flimsy material from her limbs and left her naked on the bed. He lay next to her and clasped her to him, as Elizabeth, slim and shivering in his arms, hid her head against his shoulder.

"Easy now, don't shake so. I'll not force you," Sean said quietly.

"But you just said..." Elizabeth murmured, breathing in the warm, musky smell of his skin.

"It was just a manner of speaking, Lizzie. Did you think I would take you against your will?" he said, moving his lips in her hair. He drew the heavy brocade spread over her and rocked her gently.

"It wouldn't be against my will, Sean—you know that. I would never have gone to so much trouble to arrange this trip if I didn't want just what's happening right now. I'm just . . . oh, I'm scared,'' she concluded lamely.

"And so you should be. This isn't what you expected from your life at all. You thought you'd be married to some natty young swell like Charles Brandon. . . ."

"Oh, please," Elizabeth mumbled, nudging aside the collar of his shirt and rubbing her cheek against the satiny surface of his shoulder.

"And Charles would be... What would he be doing? Adding up a column of figures in a ledger, most likely."

Elizabeth dragged her tongue along the edge of his collarbone, closing her eyes.

"Keep on with that and we'll have no more conversation," Sean said abruptly.

"Fine with me," Elizabeth replied, turning her face up for his kiss. He bent to oblige.

"Sure?" he said against her mouth.

"Sure," she replied.

He took her at her word, easing her onto her back and kissing her deeply, pushing the bedclothes aside. Elizabeth wound her arms around his neck and pulled him to her, running her hands down his muscular back under his loosened shirt. She felt him, heavy and ready against her thighs, and the need to feel him inside her was overpowering.

Sean kept his flooding desire in check with an effort. He knew Elizabeth shouldn't be rushed, but he was used to more experienced women who urged him onward and were as eager as he was for completion. From boyhood he had been pursued, first by older women and then by village girls who took their pleasure as they found it. He had never in his life been with a virgin.

Elizabeth sighed as he moved his mouth to her neck, and she urged herself against him, tugging on his shirt. Sean lost control for a moment and pushed her down almost roughly, stripping his shirt off with his free hand and then letting her take his full weight for the first time. He kissed her body wildly, moving from her breasts to her stomach to her thighs, lifting her slightly to let his hand seek the damp warmth between her legs. Elizabeth shut her eyes and moaned deeply.

"Yes?" he muttered thickly.

"Yes," she gasped.

He bent and used his mouth to arouse sensations in Elizabeth that she had never imagined, much less experienced. She dug her fingers into his hair and bit her lower lip so hard it almost bled, crying out with disappointment when he released her.

"Sean?" she said wildly, her eyes flying open.

He stood, hastening to remove his pants, and Elizabeth felt cold from the loss of contact with him. When he rejoined her, she wound her arms and legs around him lightly, imprisoning him within her limbs. Shocked by the feel of Sean's naked body all along the length of hers, she was still too carried away by the intensity of her need for him to hold back.

"I want . . ." Sean said thickly. "Oh, Lizzie . . ."

"I know, darling," Elizabeth whispered, stroking his damp hair, suddenly feeling older and wiser than her far more experienced lover. The depth of his need stripped him bare, making him seem open and vulnerable, a different person from the firebrand labor organizer who had driven her father to distraction.

"I love you, Liz," Sean murmured.

"I'm not afraid anymore, Sean," Elizabeth whispered tenderly, and she wasn't.

When he entered her, she gasped and clutched his shoulders, slippery with perspiration. He stopped as he felt the sting of her nails and looked down at her anxiously.

"I'm all right," she said quickly.

"Am I hurting you?" he asked, his face flushed, his mouth swollen from her kisses.

"No, no, just be still for a second."

"You seem so slight beneath me, I feel like I'm crushing you," he said, drawing back from her.

"I'm not as fragile as all that, Sean," she said, holding him down with all her strength.

He drew her close again, and Elizabeth savored the feeling of union with him, running her fingers down his arms and up his back, from the patch of down at the base of his spine to the wealth of hair at the nape of his neck. She shifted her weight to accommodate him and he groaned brokenly, dropping his head to her shoulder.

"Love me, Sean," she said in his ear. "I want you to love me."

And so he did.

Elizabeth woke in the middle of the night to find herself alone. She was tucked in nicely, with a pillow under her head and the spread drawn up to her chin. A fresh log was blazing on the fire but Sean was gone.

She got up and felt around for her dressing gown, then slipped into it. She pushed the sleeves up on her arms and shook her hair back, gathering the loose folds of the gown in her hands as she walked barefoot into the parlor.

Sean was sitting on the sofa with one arm draped across its back, wearing only his trousers and staring into the fire. He looked up as Elizabeth entered and held out his free arm. She sat next to him and snuggled against his side as his arms closed around her.

"How do you feel?" he asked quietly.

"Wonderful."

"Bleeding?"

"Just a little."

He shook his head. "I feel like I . . . violated you."

Elizabeth giggled. "Sean, no one ever felt less violated than I do right now."

"You're not sorry?" he asked worriedly.

Elizabeth sat up and looked at him. "Of course not. Have you been sitting out here brooding and convincing yourself that I was going to regret this?"

His silence was her answer.

"Sean, what's wrong? Tell me."

"Lizzie, what's right? We're living in a dreamworld here. Once we get back to Langdon, we'll be plunged right into the middle of all that mess..." His voice trailed off miserably.

"You promised me that we weren't going to think about any of that tonight."

"I'm trying, but we took a big step in that bedroom. I want to love you and take care of you...."

"And you will."

"How? By continuing this charade? Aside from the fact that your da is my sworn enemy and we'll probably wind up at loggerheads before long, I'm just no good at playacting. How can I live in the same town and pretend I don't love you, pretend that I hardly even know you? Am I supposed to sit and twiddle my thumbs while you get engaged to Charles Brandon, or some fool like him?"

"Sean, I will not get engaged to Charles Brandon, or some fool like him."

"And how do you propose to avoid it? That's what your father has in mind. He wants to marry you off to somebody he considers 'suitable,' and unless I miss my guess, young Charles has been working away madly on the same idea."

"Sean, I have to humor Charles and accept his attentions to keep my father happy. But I'm of legal age and I assure you I can't be forced to do anything I don't want to do."

Sean sat forward with his elbows on his knees, staring at her morosely. "I'm afraid of what the future will bring, Lizzie. There's too many things to come between us, too many obstacles. I know if I lost you I'd go stark gibbering mad.''

Elizabeth moved to kneel in front of him and took both of his hands in hers.

''Then let's take a solemn vow, right now. We won't be separated, no matter what happens. Say it.''

''We won't be separated, no matter what happens,'' he repeated, his eyes on hers.

Elizabeth reached up to remove a tiny gold cross she wore on a thin chain around her neck.

''I want you to have this and wear it always. My Aunt Dorrie gave it to me when I was baptized and she stood as godmother. I've had to change the chain for a longer one a few times as I grew, and I think it may just fit you.'' Elizabeth slipped the chain over his head, where it fell short as it encircled his muscular neck, causing the cross to nestle snugly in the hollow of his throat.

''I'll wear it,'' he said flatly, ''but I'll have to hide it. We don't go in much for gold jewelry down in the mines. I wouldn't want such a bauble to be noticed, and I wouldn't want to get killed for it.''

''Everything is a problem, isn't it, Sean?'' Elizabeth said quietly.

''Seems that way.''

''We just have to be strong.''

''I'm trying.''

He leaned down to embrace her, and they tumbled to the rug, limbs in a tangle, kissing desperately.

"Make love to me again," Elizabeth said.

In the morning Elizabeth woke up back in bed with no memory of returning there. Sean was sleeping next to her, his arm thrown across her waist, the bedclothes bunched around his hips.

She touched his shoulder and he stirred.

"Good morning," she said.

He smiled and kissed her.

"How did I get back here?" she asked.

"I carried you in after you fell asleep on the floor last night," he answered.

"I don't remember."

"You were out like a snuffed candle."

Elizabeth hooked her arms around his neck and put her head on his shoulder.

"You exhausted me," she said happily.

"I'll say one thing. You're very cooperative when you're dead to the world."

"Thank you very much," she said, sitting up, insulted. "I suppose you have a great deal of experience carrying unconscious women around in the dark."

"You're the first," he replied, moving up to kiss her nose and then standing, assembling his clothes.

"I'm relieved to hear it." Elizabeth got up and rummaged in one of her bags for her long velvet robe—the fire had gone out and the room was chilly.

Sean strolled toward the hall, opened the door and then paused in the doorway, turning back to Elizabeth with a wide grin.

"What?" she said, looking at him.

He pointed into the parlor.

Elizabeth brushed past him and stopped when she saw Maureen on the sofa, fully dressed and frozen like a statue. Her skin was the color of parchment, and there were heavy blue shadows under her eyes. She was staring straight ahead, as if contemplating an unpleasant vision.

"Well, hello," Sean said, laughing.

Maura pressed her fingertips to her temples.

"Do you have to scream?" she said.

"Stop cackling, Sean. Can't you see that she's not feeling well?" Elizabeth said.

"She's feeling the effects of imbibing," Sean announced gleefully.

"Oh, be still. You've been in this condition once or twice yourself that I can recall," Maura snapped, then winced.

"I'm so sorry," Elizabeth said, sitting next to the other girl. "I should have told you that alcohol was in that punch."

"How much of that poison did I drink?" Maureen grumbled.

"Enough, apparently. But you'll feel better soon," Elizabeth said soothingly.

"If I live that long."

"I'm in mind to have a big breakfast," Sean said to them, rubbing his hands together. "Eggs and praties, a rasher of bacon, some of that French cheese..."

Maura groaned faintly, turning a delicate shade of green.

"Sean, stop teasing her," Elizabeth said sharply.

Sean subsided, still grinning.

"Should I ring for the maid?" Elizabeth asked Maura. "Maybe there's a house doctor, or maybe the concierge has some headache powder or a dose of laudanum."

"Laudanum will just put her to sleep," Sean advised. "Black coffee is the ticket."

Maura made a gagging sound and became even greener.

Elizabeth rang for the maid and motioned Sean into the bedroom. Maura inched forward on the seat and put her head in her hands, mewing softly.

"Maura," Elizabeth said gently, "one of us has to go to the fabric store this morning."

Maura said something unintelligible.

"What?" Elizabeth prodded.

"I said I'll go if this little man inside my head with the pickax gives up his job."

"We'll see what we can do about that," Elizabeth replied. When the maid came she gave the breakfast order and asked for a packet of analgesic powder. Sean emerged from the bedroom to find his sister stretched out on the sofa with her eyes closed and Elizabeth sneaking around like a nurse humoring an invalid.

"Is she going to be all right?" Elizabeth asked him, gesturing to the prone figure on the couch.

"Nobody ever died of a headache, Lizzie. If this carries her off, she'll make the history books."

"I heard that, Sean Jameson," Maura said from the sofa.

"You see?" Sean said. "She's perking up already. Her mouth is working fine."

When the maid brought their order, Maura swallowed the headache powder and two cups of coffee as Sean plowed through the food and Elizabeth nibbled a piece of toast. Maura's color gradually returned to normal, and she recovered enough to say acerbically to her brother, "Looks like you've been working up an appetite, Seaneen."

Sean stared at her for a long moment, then dropped his fork onto his plate and stood. "I think I'll have a wash," he announced, and headed for the bathroom.

"Touchy, isn't he?" Maura said. "I was just getting some of my own back. He was enjoying my . . . illness a bit too much."

Elizabeth waved her hand dismissively. "He's worried. He's picturing me married to Charles Brandon, at the very least."

"And why would he be picturing that?"

"He knows that's what my father wants, and he knows about the ball I'm going to at the Brandon house the day after Thanksgiving—the reason we're making the dress, remember?"

"I remember. It is a dangerous game you're playing with Charles, you know. Your father is imagining announcing the banns at this very minute, I'm thinking."

"There's nothing I can do about it, Maura. I don't flatter myself that Charles is in love with me. Once I'm out of the picture he'll move on to the next likely candidate. He just wants a wife to organize Christmas parties for his employees and produce sons to inherit his retail empire. He doesn't want *me.*"

"Not the way Sean does," Maura said softly.

"Not like that," Elizabeth agreed.

"Was it everything you hoped it would be?" Maura asked. "Last night, I mean?"

Elizabeth nodded, flushing slightly.

"It's glad I am to hear it," Maura said, rising, "for the chance all three of us took to get here." She retrieved her cloak from a chair and slipped into it, saying, "So where is this store I'm bound for?"

Elizabeth gave her directions and a stack of bank notes. "You have my measurements, right?"

"Right. But can you give me some idea of what style you want?" Maura asked.

"Mmm, let me see. A velvet bodice, maybe, with a sweeping skirt in a different material, and a full draped bustle. Oh, and a sheer shawl, the same material as the skirt?"

Maura stared at her. "You don't want much, do you?"

"That shouldn't be a difficult order to fill. The magazines—*Leslie's Weekly* or *Harper's*—are full of sketches like that. Find one in the lounge and show it to the clerk. She'll direct you to similar patterns and help you measure out how much material you'll need to cut each piece."

"Lounge?"

"You know, the waiting area where you sit until the clerk comes to serve you."

It was obvious that Maura didn't know, and for a few fleeting seconds Elizabeth considered going herself. Maura could read her expression and said briskly, "I'll work it out. You shouldn't miss this time with Sean. Who knows how long it will be before you can see him again?"

Elizabeth said nothing, aware that she was right.

"Lord, how did I get myself into this?" Maura muttered to herself, tucking a straggling wisp of hair behind her left ear. "Head pounding like a kettle-drum, can't even see straight and off to buy God knows what...."

Elizabeth watched her go, smiling, and then walked over to the balcony. She was looking out the window when she heard Sean behind her and turned to see him buttoning a clean shirt and tucking it neatly into his pants. His hair was damp and combed off his fore-head, and he was freshly shaved.

"Did Maura leave?" he asked.

Elizabeth nodded. "Sean, don't you think you were a little bit hard on her?"

He shrugged, unable to suppress another grin. "Ah, Maura's always putting the mickey on me for one thing and another. It's about time I could let her have it for a mistake she made.''

"She loves you and she's been a good friend to both of us. I think you should remember that.''

"I do,'' Sean replied, putting his arm around her. He smelled of Pears soap—supplied by the hotel—and the starch in his shirt. "Come and sit with me over here,'' he said.

They sat together on the sofa, Elizabeth waiting apprehensively for what he had to say. She knew she wouldn't like it.

"I have to go in a little while,'' he said.

She didn't like it.

"Why so soon?'' she protested.

"Because it's going to take me a lot longer to get home. I'm not traveling by coach. And I have to get off at Mauch Chunk and make my way back, or else Thurston at the train station will report to your father that I returned to Langdon the same day you did.''

Elizabeth couldn't argue with the logic of that, but she still wasn't happy.

"We'll have another time like this,'' he said gently.

"Will we?''

He pulled her close, and for several seconds they sat in silence, listening to the sound of each other's breathing and the steady beating of their hearts.

"I'll get word to you through Maura,'' Sean said.

Elizabeth nodded.

"I have to ask you something.''

"What is it?'' Elizabeth drew back to look at him.

"Elizabeth..."

Just his calling her by her full name alarmed her. "Sean, what? You're frightening me."

"If I could get a better job, out of the mines, I mean, and I could go someplace else and get some money together..."

"Yes?"

"Would you marry me?"

Elizabeth threw her arms around him. "Sean, what a question! Of course I'll marry you, under any circumstances."

"You shouldn't say that until you know what those circumstances might be," he replied soberly, his cheek against her hair.

"Nothing could change the way I feel."

"Lizzie, you're a hopeless romantic."

"I think you've pointed that out to me already."

He held her off and gazed into her eyes. "I won't let too much time pass before sending you a message."

"All right."

"I must go." He released her and stood up, looking around for his jacket. He put it on and draped his scarf around his neck, stuffing the ends of it inside his coat.

Elizabeth rose also and stood looking at him forlornly, her expression a mask of tragedy.

"Ah, cheer up now, Lizzie. Will you give me a face like that to remember all the way home?"

She looked at the floor, unwilling to let him see that her eyes were filling with tears.

"Don't cry," Sean said gently, not deceived, reaching out his hand to her.

"If you touch me that will only make it worse," Elizabeth said. "Just go."

He obeyed. She remained staring at the pattern in the rug, which blurred into a fog, until she heard the door open and close and realized that Sean was gone.

Then she sank into a chair and cried until Maura returned.

"Don't you think you'd better have a look at this lot?" Maura demanded, holding up the parcels she had brought. "I know you'd rather float away on a river of tears, but if you wind up a laughingstock at the Brandon ball, it will be no one's fault but your own."

Elizabeth sobbed.

"You were interested enough before I left."

"Sean's gone," Elizabeth wailed.

"He hasn't gone far. I believe his destination is the same as ours. Now pay attention." She collapsed into the chair across from Elizabeth and assembled her packages on the floor.

Elizabeth drew a handkerchief from the pocket of her robe, wiped her eyes and blew her nose.

"That's better. Now give my splitting head a moment's ease and see if you like this sketch," Maura said.

She handed Elizabeth a drawing of a Worth gown which had obviously been clipped from a magazine. It featured a fitted green velvet bodice with a scalloped neckline and a cream brocade skirt striped with pink sprays.

"Very nice," Elizabeth said, hardly glancing at it before handing it back.

"Oh, give me strength. I've spent the last two hours nattering with clerks and seamstresses and bought out half the store. You'd better go over all of it this minute, because if something is not right when we get back to Langdon, it will be too late."

"Let me see," Elizabeth said tonelessly.

Maura opened a parcel and handed her a length of forest-green cotton velvet, soft as eiderdown.

"It's lovely," Elizabeth said, impressed in spite of herself.

"And this is the brocade for the skirt, with the silk tulle overlay," Maura added, rummaging in the paper sacks and then holding up the sheer fabric for Elizabeth's examination. "I got enough of the tulle to make a shawl, and the bows for the flouncing are in that box."

"Did you get the right amount of everything?"

"I showed the clerk the numbers we figured, and she said they seemed right."

Elizabeth nodded. "You did a fine job. It's a beautiful dress. I just hope we can put it together."

"I can do it," Maura said confidently. "I was a little skittish at first because I never worked from a design before, but the pieces all fit the same way."

"Good."

"Elizabeth?"

"Yes?"

"Don't you think you'd better get dressed? We have to catch the train in a little while."

Elizabeth nodded and got to her feet, sniffling. "Would you clear up this mess and put the fabrics in my bag—the bigger one? I'll get myself together and we'll go."

"All right."

"And Maura, thanks for everything."

Maura watched Elizabeth go back into the bedroom, then bent to gather up the litter on the floor.

The return train trip to Langdon was quiet, with neither woman talking very much. The anticipation was gone, and all they had to look forward to were the difficulties they had left at home.

Elizabeth knew something was wrong when she smelled smoke as they pulled into the station.

"What is burning?" she said to Maura as they descended the steps from the train.

"I don't know. It smells like it's coming from outside." They left their bags on the platform and hurried into the open air, where Todd was waiting with the carriage.

A gray pall of soot hung over the valley, and the acrid tang of coal smoke was thick in the atmosphere. The two women exchanged anxious glances.

"Miss," Todd said, touching his cap.

"Todd, what happened?" Elizabeth said. "Is there a fire?"

"Fire in the mines—out of control underground. All the stored coal is burning," Todd replied shortly.

"How did it get started?"

"Mr. Langdon sent in replacement workers for the strikers, and there was a riot. The strikers set fire to everything. The CIPs couldn't control them. One of the new CIP patrolmen, Hastings, was killed."

Elizabeth looked at Maura, an icy finger tracing the back of her neck. All of Sean's work, gone for nothing. The moment he was not around the very thing he'd feared had happened.

Maura opened her mouth to speak, but Elizabeth shook her head slightly, warning Maura not to talk in front of Todd. They bit their tongues until he went to collect their bags, and then Elizabeth said in a rush, "This isn't a coincidence. My father waited until Sean wasn't around to send in those scabs."

"And Kelly went wild with Sean not there to control him," Maura replied knowingly.

"Oh, God, Maura, I feel like this is my fault," Elizabeth moaned. "All I could think about was myself and how much I wanted to be alone with Sean. I never dreamt it would lead to this."

"Sean doesn't know," Maura said. "I'm sure he isn't back yet. It will take him hours to walk home."

They became quiet as Todd returned, and the drive to the house was conducted in tense silence. Once in the front hall they saw that the doors to Arthur Langdon's study were closed, and they could hear the rumble of male voices inside.

"Please take my bags up to my room, Todd," Elizabeth said.

"Yes, miss." He went up the stairs.

Mrs. Tamm appeared to take Elizabeth's cloak. "Such doings since you left, Miss Elizabeth," the housekeeper said excitedly. "We were afraid for our lives in the house—"

"Mrs. Tamm, I'm very tired after my trip. I think I'd like a glass of hot milk, if you don't mind," Elizabeth said, cutting her off in midsentence. She wanted to be alone with Maura.

"Yes, miss," the housekeeper replied, looking hurt but obeying. Elizabeth felt a moment's regret at her curtness but then turned to Maura as the study doors slid apart and Tom Rees emerged from the room. He stopped short when he saw the two women and then hurried to Maura's side.

"Where is Sean?" he demanded in a whisper.

"On his way back to town," Maura replied.

Elizabeth glanced at her, puzzled.

"Do you know what happened?" Rees asked.

Maura nodded. "But not the details."

"There's a warrant issued for Sean's arrest. He's being charged with inciting a riot and involuntary manslaughter in the death of one of the CIP patrolmen, George Hastings."

Elizabeth sagged against the wall, the breath knocked from her body. "For Heaven's sake, he wasn't even here!" she exclaimed in protest.

"Do you think that matters?" Maura demanded bitterly. "He was behind the strike and everybody knows it. Your father will make it stick." She grabbed Rees's sleeve. "He can't come back here, Tom. You have to stop him. He's getting off the train at Mauch Chunk and walking back. You can intercept him on the way."

"Maura, what are you talking to him for?" Elizabeth demanded, aghast. "He's one of them. He'll turn Sean in."

"No, he won't," Maura said quietly, and Elizabeth saw the look that passed between them. She filed it away for future study, her concern for Sean obliterating other considerations.

"Will you help?" Elizabeth asked Rees.

He nodded.

"Can you take one of the CIP wagons and stop Sean before he gets here?" She fumbled in the reticule she still held and withdrew the rest of her money. "Give him this and tell him to go . . ."

"Where?" Maura asked in despair.

"Tell him to go back to Philadelphia—not by train, they'll check that," Elizabeth said rapidly, thinking as fast as she was talking. "Tell him to go to my Aunt Dorrie's house in Wynnewood. Dorothea Hunter, 32 Ambercrest Drive. Have you got that?"

"Thirty-two Ambercrest," Rees said, glancing nervously at the study, where the rest of the men were milling around, ready to spill into the hall.

"Tell him my aunt is not back yet from her trip, but the housekeeper, Bessie, is there. He's to show Bessie the cross I gave him and tell her that I sent him, and I want him to stay there. I'll write a letter as soon as I can," she concluded, pushing Rees toward the door as two of the company managers came out of the study.

"Go!" Maura whispered.

He slipped through the front door just as Arthur Langdon emerged from the room to greet his daughter.

"Elizabeth! So nice to see you back. Did you have a profitable trip?" Langdon said.

Maura turned her back and made her way to the kitchen, her spine ramrod straight.

"Yes, Father," Elizabeth replied, watching the door close behind Rees's tall form. "I'd like to tell you all about it."

Chapter Ten

Elizabeth wrote two letters the day she returned from Philadelphia and gave them to Maura to post: one to Bessie, confirming that Elizabeth wanted Sean to stay in her aunt's house, and one to Sean, telling him to remain there until she could arrange to help him. But she still had no idea if he had reached Dorothea's home in safety, since Rees had only been able to give Sean the message that he was wanted by the police and then turn him around for Philadelphia.

On the morning after the two women got back, Elizabeth waited nervously for Maura to arrive and begin working on her dress. When Maura finally appeared, lugging a tapestry bag full of fabric and fitting materials, Elizabeth hurried the other girl into her room and then locked the door behind them.

"Well?" she said anxiously.

"Tom mailed the letters in Ealing," Maura replied, setting her bag on the bed.

"And Sean?"

Maura shrugged. "I know no more than you. Tom told him what had happened, he took the money you sent him and turned back the way he'd come."

Elizabeth groaned. "I can't stand not knowing if he got to Wynnewood safely. I simply can't stand it."

"Well, you'll have to bear it since you can do no other. He can't write back to my house. The peelers will be watching the mail."

"Do you think he'll be safe there?"

"Your father has a few tricks up his sleeve, but even he won't suspect that Sean is holed up in his own sister-in-law's house." She glanced over her shoulder, as if a spy might be lurking in the corner. "Now stand up straight and let me get started with this. We have two weeks to produce a dress like that sketch, God help us all."

"What if Bessie wouldn't let him in the house?"

"She would let him in if he showed her the cross you gave him."

"What if she didn't recognize it? Worse yet, what if she thinks he stole it?" Elizabeth said.

"Sean has landed on his feet many times before you knew him, and he will yet again," Maura said tartly. "He has always known how to take care of himself. He'll get there, and if Bessie throws him out he'll find another place to hide."

Elizabeth stared at Maura as she stuck a row of pins in her mouth. "Are you angry with me?" she said quietly. "Are you blaming me for what happened to Sean?"

Maura sighed and shook her head. "No, it's Tom," she replied, speaking around the objects in her mouth. "He knows how worried I am about Sean, and he chooses this time to pressure me about..."

"About what?"

Maura was silent.

"What exactly is going on between you and Sergeant Rees?" Elizabeth asked.

Maura met her eyes. "Just what you think," she said.

"Maura," Elizabeth breathed. "And you never said a word!"

"If I remember, you and Sean were talking enough for an army," Maura said dryly.

"That's true," Elizabeth said, shamefaced, aware that her troubles had taken center stage for a while. "But what has Rees been pressuring you about?"

"He plans to go west, either to work on the railroad or get a parcel of land through the Homestead Act."

"And?"

"He wants me to go with him."

"Maura!"

"Hold still," Maura commanded, holding a length of green velvet up to Elizabeth's shoulder.

"Are you going to do it?"

"And what becomes of my mother and Matthew? And my brother Sean, who may wind up on the end of a hanging rope?"

"Oh, please don't say that," Elizabeth moaned, forgetting Maura's troubles in light of her own.

"It's true," Maura said grimly.

"I won't let it happen," Elizabeth said desperately, wincing as Maura stuck her with a pin.

"And how do you plan to prevent it?"

"I'll go to my father. I'll tell him everything."

"Which will only make him more eager to see Sean swinging, and well you know it."

"Maybe I could convince him to drop the charges," Elizabeth went on, not listening.

"The charge is capital now. The state takes over to prosecute. Your father couldn't stop it if he tried."

"How do you know that?"

"Tom told me."

"Then what's the answer?"

"Sean needs a good lawyer, someone who could challenge the system that allows your da to exploit the miners and then throw them in jail when they rebel. And the Jamesons can't afford that. We don't even know how to find such a person."

"My Aunt Dorothea would know what to do. She's not due back home for several weeks, but she knows everybody in Philadelphia. I'm sure she could help. She's very progressive and keeps up with all the causes. She knows lots of city lawyers."

"Is she likely to go against her brother-in-law?"

"To help me? It would be no contest. She's never been overly fond of my father, and she's devoted to me."

"Would she be devoted to Sean?"

"If he were my husband she'd have to be."

Maura stopped pinning and met Elizabeth's gaze. "What are you saying?"

"Sean asked me to marry him at the hotel. I'll accept him and we'll fight this together."

"Elizabeth, your father will move heaven and earth to take his revenge if you do that."

"I'm of age—he can't stop me."

"I'm not speaking of stopping you. He owns the newspapers and all the politicians—you said it yourself. Your da will line up everything against Sean when he comes to trial, especially if he blames him for taking you from him."

Elizabeth shoved Maura's hands away and threw the draped fabric onto the bed. "My father's going to do that, anyway, whether I marry Sean or not! Don't you see? He has too much to lose. His whole empire will collapse if the miners acquire any power. He'll make a test case of Sean and try to bury him, and that has nothing to do with me. At least if I get Dorothea on our side, we'll be able to fight back."

"That's a poor reason to get married."

Elizabeth looked at her. "Don't be silly. I'm going to marry Sean in any case. It was just a question of when."

"Does Sean have anything to say about that? If I know my brother, and I do, he'll not let you ally your life with his when he's in this kind of trouble."

"What am I supposed to do? Desert him just when he needs me the most?" Elizabeth demanded indignantly. "What would you think of me then?"

Maura just shook her head wearily, picking up the bodice she was fashioning and holding it against Elizabeth's torso.

"How can you concentrate on that when the whole world is crashing down about our ears?" Elizabeth asked irritably.

Maura threw up her hands and the fabric slid to the floor. "Fine. Forget it. It's no never mind to me."

Elizabeth caught the other girl's arm as she turned away. "Maura, I'm sorry. I guess you just have a little more experience at dealing with misfortune than I do."

"I'll not disagree with that," Maura said sarcastically.

Elizabeth bent to retrieve the material and straightened with it in her hands.

"Let's get on with it," she said, sighing. "By the time I get to the Brandon party, I'll be ready to strangle Charles with the shawl from this dress."

Maura laughed, the awkward moment passed, and they went back to work.

Langdon settled down into an uneasy peace during the days that followed. The strike ringleaders, Kelly among them, were rounded up and shipped off to jail, the scabs dismissed. The miners returned to work under a court order that threatened arrest if they didn't. The fires were eventually doused, but the pall of dissipating smoke drifted through the clearing air to remind everyone of what had happened.

And Sean remained at large.

Arthur Langdon was expansive in his triumph, presenting Elizabeth with an exquisite string of pearls to wear to the Langdon ball.

Two weeks went by, during which there was no word of Sean. Elizabeth and Maura worked feverishly on the gown and finished it on the morning of Thanksgiving Day. Maura then went home to her family, and Elizabeth endured a tense holiday meal with her father.

He was in fine spirits and discoursed on various subjects as Elizabeth pushed Mrs. Tamm's roast goose with chestnut stuffing around on her plate. Arthur Langdon preferred goose to turkey, and in his house his wish was obeyed, tradition be damned.

"Not hungry, darling?" her father asked, noticing her lack of interest in her food.

"Oh, uh, no. I think I ate too big a breakfast."

"That Jameson girl is not upsetting you, is she?" Langdon inquired, spearing a yam with his fork.

Elizabeth tensed but replied mildly, "Why would you say that?"

"I thought she might be harassing you about her brother."

"No."

"I'm not sure we should continue to have her working in the house, in view of what's happened, but Mrs. Tamm vouches for her and says that she'll cause no trouble."

"Oh, please don't send Maura away," Elizabeth said quickly, terrified that her avenue to Sean might be blocked. "She's been such a help lately, and I don't see how I could do without her."

"All right, my dear," Langdon said mildly. "But you let me know if there's any discussion of her brother, and I'll nip it in the bud. He has no one to blame but himself for his situation, and I won't have his relatives garnering sympathy for him in my own house."

Elizabeth squashed a cranberry with the flat of her fork and said nothing. Sometimes she felt a stab of guilt at the way she was misleading her father, but then she remembered his unfair treatment of his workers and strengthened her resolve to combat it. Her long years away from Langdon had distanced her from him emotionally and had given her an objectivity about his behavior that she might have lacked if she'd been raised by him. He was cruel and unfair, and that enabled her to continue the deception.

"What are you thinking, Elizabeth?" he asked abruptly, as if reading her mind.

"I was thinking about the Brandon party tomorrow night," she said, selecting a safe subject.

"Oh, yes? Are you looking forward to it?"

She nodded.

"May we expect an announcement soon?"

Elizabeth coughed and took a sip of claret from her glass. "An announcement?"

"Regarding Charles's intentions toward you."

"Father, I think that's premature."

"Why so? I'd wager that Charles has made up his mind."

"Maybe I haven't decided. I hardly know him, really. I've only seen him a few times."

"What do you need to know? How often do you have to see him?" Langdon asked in an even, reasonable tone. "He comes from a good family. He could provide for you most generously. You would never want for anything if you married him."

And that was the end of it as far as her father was concerned, Elizabeth knew. No mention of her feelings, mutual interests, love. A union of two prominent and prosperous county families was all that Langdon could see.

"I'm not going to live forever, Elizabeth. You should be thinking of your future," he added. "You will need someone to manage your fortune, a strong and capable man of the world to take good care of you. Charles fits the bill."

Oh, God, let me get through this with my sanity, Elizabeth prayed silently. Her father was dreaming of a wedding to Charles Brandon while her heart was longing for his worst enemy—who also happened to be a fugitive from justice. And Langdon wondered why she had so little appetite.

"I think I have some time, Father," she said in a conciliatory tone, smiling slightly.

"Don't take too long. Charles won't have to look far to see other young women eager for his hand."

"Is that what this party is going to be, Father?" she asked. "A parade of the hopefuls, with me leading the procession?"

Langdon put down his fork and eyed her balefully. Elizabeth realized that she'd gone too far and wished she had kept her mouth shut.

"You have no appreciation of your position, Elizabeth," her father said wearily. "I'm sure if your mother had lived, your upbringing would have been more suitable. I left you with Dorothea, and her influence has not always been good."

It was typical of her father to dump Elizabeth in Dorrie's lap for eighteen years and then complain about the job his sister-in-law had done. "Please don't start on Aunt Dorrie, Father. I won't hear anything against her. I would rather not ruin the holiday. Can't we please talk about something else?"

Langdon sighed, then nodded distantly, and Elizabeth knew he was thinking about what a disappointment she was. Well, that worked both ways.

Mrs. Tamm came in to clear the dishes and then served pie with a jug of clotted cream. Langdon dug in heartily while Elizabeth broke the piecrust into crumbs and desultorily pushed them around on her plate. Then she noticed her father watching her disapprovingly and so she took a huge bite. There was no point in annoying him any further.

When dinner was over she went up to her room and lay down on her bed, staring at the ceiling in despair and wondering if she would ever see Sean again.

* * *

Maura helped Elizabeth to dress for the Brandon ball the next evening. The finished gown fit as though it had been made by a Paris designer. Elizabeth draped her new pearls around her neck as Maura put the final pins in her hair. Elizabeth added earrings designed with a pearl on the lobe and a cascade of marcasites dangling from it and then stood, twirling as Maura inspected her.

"What do you think?" she asked.

"A vision. Charles will be overwhelmed."

"That isn't funny. What if he *does* propose to-night?"

"Maybe you should have worn a gunnysack."

Elizabeth slipped a silver ring with an enameled setting on her fourth finger. "This isn't helping me, Maureen. What am I supposed to do if he does ask me?"

Maura shrugged. "Keep him dangling. Tell him you need time to think it over. I hope you know you're asking the wrong person about dealing with marriage offers from rich young swells."

"I do need time. I have to keep my father placated until Dorrie gets home and I can enlist her to help Sean."

"What's 'placated'?"

"Happy, satisfied."

"Hasn't it come to you yet that your aunt may be no happier with Sean as your choice than your father would be?"

"She'll respect my wishes."

"She mustn't fit into your family too well."

"She's my mother's sister, not my father's. Remember that." Elizabeth placed a folded linen handkerchief in her reticule. "If Sean were to try to contact us, how do you think he would do it?"

"He wouldn't write to you or me, that's for sure," Maura answered. "There's nobody else he can trust."

"Considering that all of his friends are in jail," Elizabeth said bitterly.

"True enough."

Elizabeth donned her blue cloak and put her hands into the matching muff. "I wonder if my father's ready," she said.

"He was all dressed and pacing downstairs when I came in," Maura told her.

"Then I'd better hurry," Elizabeth said briskly. "He never likes to be kept waiting."

She went into the hall and Maura followed. Elizabeth turned and said to her in an undertone, "Let me know if you hear anything. I don't care when it is."

Maura nodded, and Elizabeth turned to sweep down the stairs and join her father.

"Elizabeth, you look lovely," he greeted her, taking her arm and steering her toward the door. He was wearing a black cloth redingote over his tailcoat and carrying his top hat in his hand. Mrs. Tamm beamed approvingly in the background as they went outside to the drive.

The night was cold, the last of the autumn leaves blowing underfoot. A frost lay on the grass, and a harvest moon shed its glow on the landscape, making the lawn leading down from the house and the patch below it almost as bright as day.

Todd opened the coach door for them, and Elizabeth's father handed her inside. As they drove away from the house, Langdon said, "I want you to ask Emily Brandon to visit us over Christmas, Elizabeth. You should encourage friendships with the right kind of young women at your age. You spend too much time with the servants." Elizabeth supposed that was a reference to Maura and let it pass.

"And be sure to thank Priscilla Brandon for her hospitality. An invitation to her home is prized throughout the whole county, I can assure you."

Elizabeth looked out the window of the coach.

Her father issued a few more directives about her behavior and then, seeing that she was not responding, fell into his own reverie. The rest of the ride was conducted in blessed silence.

The Brandon home streamed light onto the gravel drive, and a train of coaches pulled up to the front door one by one, disgorging passengers. As Elizabeth alighted from hers she could see Charles standing just inside the door next to his mother, greeting the arriving guests.

Charles was wearing a black double-breasted tailcoat with velvet lapels and a striped silk neck cloth. His boiled shirt was of a dazzling, polished whiteness, and his expertly fitted trousers made him seem taller and slimmer than he actually was. Elizabeth thought with a brief stab of regret how wonderful Sean would look in such beautiful clothes, and then she smiled as Charles spotted her coming up the steps and raised his hand in greeting.

His mother, Priscilla, drew the eye in a wine-red velvet ball gown trimmed with ivory lace around the deep square neckline and on the edges of the cap sleeves. Its apron front descended into a cascade of ruffles of the same lace at the hem, and the draped bustle fell in several tiers to a slight train on the floor. The dress was obviously designed to display jewelry, and exquisite diamonds blazed at her ears, around her bare throat and on both wrists.

Elizabeth went through the routine of greeting everyone and surrendering her wrap, then drifted through the crowd with Charles at her side. The house was banked with fragrant, out-of-season flowers, and all the rooms were open, allowing the guests to move through them freely. Chamber music drifted down the spiral staircase from the ballroom on the second floor.

"Would you like a glass of wine?" Charles asked as they approached the dining room, where a butler was handing around a silver tray of crystal flutes filled with claret and Madeira. Elizabeth shook her head, but Charles took one and then led her to a window seat in a small study off the main hall.

"This is my mother's sewing room," he said unnecessarily, as the consoles were stacked with embroidery hoops and an incomplete cross-stitch sampler was stretched on a stand in the corner. A Grover and Baker sewing machine stood nearby with a stack of varicolored fabrics piled next to it. "I wanted to get away from the crowd," Charles added. "I've been waiting for you to arrive."

Elizabeth watched as he took a sip of his wine.

"I've been thinking about you a great deal, Elizabeth," Charles continued.

Elizabeth sensed what was coming and realized that he wasn't planning to waste any time. In a panic, she stood abruptly and said, "You know, Charles, I'm really hungry. Would you mind getting me a plate from the buffet in the other room?"

Charles looked understandably startled, but ever the gentleman, he rose at once and said smoothly, "Of course. I should have thought of your comfort first. What would you like?"

"Anything you choose. I'll just wait here for you."

Elizabeth's mind raced as Charles left the room. He had acted as if she were expecting what he was about to say; his father and her father must have planned all this in advance. They had probably settled the dowry already, she thought gloomily. So that was the source of Arthur Langdon's little talks; no wonder he had been annoyed that she wasn't receptive. He must have decided to let Charles handle it.

Elizabeth began to feel like the pawn in a paternal chess game, and she didn't like it.

"What are you doing in here all by yourself?" said Emily Brandon from the doorway.

Elizabeth groaned inwardly but forced herself to smile. "I'm waiting for Charles. He went to the buffet to get something to eat."

Emily advanced into the room with little mincing steps, lifting the hem of her dress off the floor as if it could collect dust from the spotless oak. She would never be the beauty her mother was, but when dressed up she could look very attractive. She was wearing an elaborate dress of gold brocade with an amber velvet panel down the front, banded with the same velvet on the three-quarter sleeves, which ended in a triple cascade of gilt lace. Lace trimmed the rounded neckline and the hem of the full bustle, which fell to the floor in a sweep of draped flounces. The style was more elaborate than anything Elizabeth would choose, but she had to admit that it suited Emily's southern fragility. Even her jewelry was delicate: topaz and citrine stones set in a tracery of gold filigree. She looked like a belle transplanted from the plantation to the frozen north.

"How rude of him to leave you alone," Emily said.

"Oh, no. I sent him. I didn't feel like facing the crush in the dining room."

"I understand completely," Emily said, removing a silken handkerchief from her sleeve and fanning herself with it. "I always tell mother that she banks the fires too high on these occasions—the body heat of all these people just makes it too warm. But Mother's been cold since she left the South, and she thinks everyone finds the winters here just as frightful as she does.''

''I can imagine that it must be quite an adjustment,'' Elizabeth murmured, wishing for Charles to return and rescue her from this inane conversation.

''We really get snowed in here—I guess I don't have to tell you,'' Emily said, giving no sign that she was bored. ''Last Christmas it took the footmen two days to dig us out.''

Elizabeth nodded, feeling a stirring of sympathy for Charles's sister, who must be lonely. It had to be difficult living in this vast house with her self-absorbed mother and two men to whom business was an all-consuming passion.

''Speaking of Christmas, my father suggested that you might like to visit us over the holidays, Emily.''

Emily brightened visibly, and Elizabeth was glad she had mentioned it. She wasn't sure she would be able to entertain Charles's sister when the time came, but she would certainly do so if she could.

Charles returned to the room with a loaded porcelain plate and a folded napkin.

''Emily, have you been keeping Elizabeth company while I was gone?'' he said cheerfully.

''Yes, indeed, Charles, but I'll leave you to it. Mother must be missing me by now.''

Emily made a graceful exit as Charles sat next to Elizabeth and handed her the plate. Elizabeth pretended interest in the food and braced herself for the interchange she could no longer avoid.

* * *

When Maura returned home from the Langdon house that evening, Rees was waiting for her on the porch. She knew from his face that something had happened.

"What is it?" she said.

"Inside," he replied, nodding toward the CIP patrolman walking on the street in the distance.

They went through the door and discovered Matthew hard at work at the table. He was laboriously copying letters into a ruled book by the light of a coal lamp.

"Time for bed," Maura announced.

"You just got here!" Matt protested.

"That does not change what time it is," Maura replied. "Is Ma sleeping?"

The boy nodded, shuffling obediently to his feet.

"Got something for you," Maura said, removing her woolen shawl and tossing a wrapped package onto the table.

"What is it?"

"A present from Mrs. Tamm—leftover pie from yesterday."

The boy seized it eagerly and raced up the stairs.

"That's one way to get rid of him," Rees said dryly.

Maura turned to face him, folding her arms. "Well?" she said.

"I've heard from Sean."

"How?" she said excitedly, advancing on him. "Tommy, what did he say?"

"Take it easy. He sent me a letter."

"He sent *you* a letter?"

Rees nodded, chuckling at Sean's audacity. "I guess he thought no one would expect it. I certainly didn't."

Maureen grinned. Sean's courage, his sheer raw nerve, never ceased to amaze her.

"Where is it?"

Rees reached into his pocket and glanced at the stairwell. "Is it all right?"

Maura nodded eagerly.

Rees unfolded a piece of notepaper and read aloud. "'I am safe where I was meant to go. All is well, awaiting word. Torchlight.'"

"He must have made it safely to Elizabeth's aunt's house," Maura said delightedly.

"So it seems. Notice how carefully he worded it in case it was intercepted. And look at this—it was mailed from Reading. If anybody checked the postmark, he wanted them to think he had gone the opposite way!"

"I wonder how he managed to get it mailed from Reading," Maura marveled.

"With your brother, who knows?"

"I have to tell Elizabeth," Maura said, starting for the door. Then she stopped. "I forgot. She's at that Brandon party tonight."

"I'll tell her."

Maura looked at him.

"Langdon has me giving him reports at all hours on the conduct of the men since they've returned to work. He's expecting some repercussions, as well he might. He asked me to stop by at the beginning of the late shift. I'll find a way to see Elizabeth."

"Not at all shy about keeping you running in the middle of the night, is he?" Maura said nastily. "When are you ever going to quit that bleeding job?"

"When you say you'll come west with me," Rees rejoined smartly. "I'll resign the same day."

"I thought you were going with or without me."

"At the moment, I'm holding out for 'with.'"

Maura sighed and looked away from him. The temptation was great. "You know what my situation is here," she said. "How can I make a decision like that now?"

"And if Elizabeth's aunt can help Sean? What then?"

"Then we'll talk about it. I'll still have my mother and Matt to think of—that won't change."

"I've told you before, we'll take them with us," Rees said impatiently. "Could they be any worse off than they are right here?"

His unassailable logic always undid her; she found her eyes filling with tears.

Rees saw them and came to put his arm around her. "There now, Maura, don't cry. We'll be together some way, I promise."

She turned into his arms and took what comfort she could have for the moment in his embrace.

"So what did you think of the party?" Arthur Langdon said to his daughter as they rode home in their coach.

"Very nice."

"Didn't you think the house looked lovely?"

"Yes."

"And the food! Priscilla Brandon is an excellent hostess. Did you ask Emily to visit over the holidays?"

"Yes."

"And how did you get along with Charles?"

"He asked me to marry him, which I'm sure will come as no surprise to you."

"What do you mean?"

"Oh, please, Father, I'm not a child. Give me some credit," Elizabeth said disgustedly.

"Don't take that attitude with me, young lady," Langdon said sternly. "I always knew you were spoiled, but your behavior is a disgrace. Charles Brandon is the toast of the state. You should be filled with gratitude for a proposal from him."

Elizabeth jammed her hands inside her muff. She didn't reply.

"What did you say to him?" her father asked, curiosity overcoming his annoyance.

"I told him I would give him an answer by Christmas," Elizabeth said stonily.

"Was he agreeable to that?"

"Well, he obviously expected me to accept immediately." Elizabeth turned to face her father. "I can't imagine why."

"That's enough sarcasm from you. I don't know why you need a month to think over a proposal that would have any other young lady your age in a state of ecstasy, but so be it. Maybe it's a good thing. We can't have Charles thinking that you were too easily won, can we?"

Elizabeth gave a snort of derisive laughter, but when Langdon turned on her furiously, she looked away.

A confrontation with her father wasn't going to help.

When they got inside the house, Tom Rees was waiting in the front hall, cap in hand.

"Well, Tom, right on time," Langdon said. "Why don't you go on into the study, and I'll be with you in a minute."

Langdon turned away to put his hat on the tree in the hall. Rees mouthed over her father's shoulder to Elizabeth, "Wait for me." Then he walked ahead into the room.

Elizabeth stood rooted, her heart beginning to pound. It was news of Sean—it had to be.

"Are you all right, Elizabeth?" her father asked, noticing her expression.

"Yes, yes, I'm just tired. I think I'll go right up to bed."

"Very well. Good night."

"Good night, Father." Elizabeth walked slowly until she heard the study door close, then scampered up the rest of the stairs. Once in her room she stripped quickly and put on a dressing gown, then ran back down the stairs and into the kitchen. She got a glass of milk from the larder and stood with it just inside the kitchen door, waiting until she heard voices in the hall. Then she wandered out as if interrupted on a trip for a soporific.

"Elizabeth!" her father said. "I thought you went to bed."

"I did, but I couldn't sleep. I thought a glass of milk might settle me down, and I didn't want to disturb Mrs. Tamm—she's already retired for the night." She nodded at Rees, who looked uncomfortable.

"All right then, sleep well," Langdon said.

Elizabeth headed for the staircase and then bobbled the glass just as she was passing Rees. The milk shot out of the glass and onto the floor, splashing his boots.

"Oh, my goodness," Elizabeth said. "I'm so sorry. I can't imagine why I did that! I must be more tired than I thought."

"Elizabeth," her father said in exasperation.

Elizabeth and Rees both bent to swipe at his boots, and she whispered, "Come to the kitchen door when you leave."

"Go to bed, Elizabeth," her father said behind her, adding to Rees, "I'll get a towel."

Elizabeth left meekly, with profuse apologies, and then listened at her bedroom door for Rees's departure. She heard him go and then, a couple of minutes later, her father's heavy tread on the stairs. She waited for what seemed a safe interval, then crept back to the kitchen, unlocked the door and admitted a shivering Rees to the pantry.

"Cold out there," he said, rubbing his arms.

"Is it Sean?" she demanded.

He nodded. "He's all right. He's at your aunt's house."

Elizabeth clasped her hands at her breast and closed her eyes. "Thank God," she breathed. "How do you know?"

"He wrote to me. I guess he thought no one would expect that."

Elizabeth smiled. "Hide in plain sight," she murmured.

"What?"

"Nothing. Something Sean once said. Do you have the letter?"

Rees handed her the piece of paper, glancing around restlessly. "I have to make this short," he said. "This meeting would be a little difficult to explain to your father."

Elizabeth held the paper up to the window, trying to catch the moonlight, but all she could see was a bunch of squiggles on a white background.

"I can't make it out," she whispered, disappointed. "Was there anything else?"

"Keep it and read it later. Just make sure you destroy it afterward. The gist of it is that he's waiting for word from us."

They both looked up at a soft noise from the second floor. "I'd better go," Rees added.

Elizabeth threw her arms around his neck and kissed his cheek. "This means more to me than you know," she said. "Thank you."

Embarrassed, Rees disentangled himself. "You're welcome. Tell Maura I'll see her tomorrow night." He loped off into the darkness. Elizabeth pulled the door closed and clutched the paper to her breast.

Sean was safe. Now she had to work on setting him free.

Chapter Eleven

Waiting for Dorothea to return from her trip was an agony for Elizabeth, and as November faded into December, her anxiety about Sean increased to the point of torture. His letter reassured her for only a few days, and then she began to wonder how he was getting on in Dorrie's big, empty house, what he was thinking and whether Bessie would let slip something at the market that would bring the police to the door. From what Rees said and what she overheard in her father's study, she knew that the search for Sean continued unabated. He had caused a lot of trouble for Arthur Langdon, and Langdon was not about to forget it.

Elizabeth's unquiet mind was further disturbed when she missed a period at the end of the month. It was early December and she was two weeks overdue when she finally mustered the nerve to say to Maura, "Have you ever been late?"

"Late?" Maura said, folding a stack of underthings and dropping them into a drawer. "What do you mean?"

"Late for your monthly, you know."

Maura turned to look at her, eyes widening.

Elizabeth nodded, meeting her gaze.

"Are you usually regular?" Maura asked.

Elizabeth nodded again.

Maura sat down hard on the edge of the bed.

"I think I'm pregnant," Elizabeth said, unnecessarily.

"Trust Sean not to miss the opportunity," Maura observed dryly. She sighed and looked pensive.

"Well?" Elizabeth said.

"I don't know what to say."

"That's a first."

"Are you happy about it?"

Elizabeth smiled. "The thought of Sean's baby fills me with such joy, but..." She sighed, also. "You know what the situation is."

"It could hardly be worse."

"Not exactly." Elizabeth grinned.

Maura looked at her.

"He can't refuse to marry me now, no matter how much trouble he thinks he's in."

"I see. So that's the reason you're looking so smug." Maura stood and closed the drawer she had opened. "When is your aunt returning from her trip?"

"Five days."

"I wonder what she'll think of her houseguest."

"That reminds me." Elizabeth went to her armoire and retrieved a sealed envelope that had been buried under a pile of shirtwaists. "Can you give this to Tom to mail? I've written Dorrie a letter explaining everything, and I want it to be waiting for her when she gets home."

"That must be some letter."

"It's a long one."

"I hope that housekeeper doesn't get into trouble for letting Sean stay there."

"Bessie's like family. Dorrie won't blame her for doing what I asked. She had to make a decision in Dorrie's absence, and I think she made the right one."

"So you've said," Maura replied, unconvinced. In her experience servants never had much latitude with their employers.

"Oh, Maura, in less than a week I'll be with him," Elizabeth said, hugging the other girl.

"Are you going to see your aunt as soon as she returns?"

"The next day. I want to give her a chance to adjust to Sean being there before I descend on her, too."

"I'm sure that's wise." Maura stepped back and looked at the other girl levelly.

"What?"

"Elizabeth, are you positive there's no chance that your aunt will turn Sean in as soon as she realizes what's happened? I know that you love her and she's been good to you and all of that, but harboring a wanted man is not quite the same thing. We're staking Sean's freedom on the choice she makes."

Elizabeth didn't answer.

"Should we send word for Sean to get out before your aunt returns? He's had a chance to rest, and he could be far away before she gets back home."

"And then what does he do?" Elizabeth asked. "Run for the rest of his life? We have to face this and clear his name, Maura, and I need Dorrie's help to do that. It's not just Sean's fate at stake here, but that of all the miners. If no one challenges the hold my father and people like him have on the industry, this system will go on and on."

"But why does my brother have to be the test case?" Maura demanded heatedly. "I'd rather see him alive and on the run than lose this gamble you're taking and wind up in jail, or dead."

"It's not a gamble, Maura," Elizabeth said quietly. "Have a little faith, can't you?"

"I'm sorry. It's just hard for me to trust your family."

"I can understand that, considering the splendid example my father has been setting lately," Elizabeth said wearily.

They both fell silent as they heard Mrs. Tamm's voice in the hall, instructing one of the other maids.

"I'll be off before she comes looking for me," Maura said in an undertone.

Elizabeth nodded.

Maura grinned. "I'm going to be an aunt."

Elizabeth smiled as Maura slipped through the door.

* * *

"Aunt Dorothea!" Elizabeth said. "Welcome home."

The older woman embraced Elizabeth warmly. She was a tall, spare figure in her mid-fifties with graying dark hair and the snapping dark eyes of the Hunter family. She was dressed conservatively but expensively in a navy wool jersey dress with crisp white collar and cuffs and a modified bustle.

"Oh, and Bessie, hello," Elizabeth said, kissing the plump and bespectacled housekeeper. Bessie took Elizabeth's wrap as aunt and niece surveyed each other.

"Did you get my letter?" Elizabeth asked Dorothea.

"Oh, yes." Dorrie raised her brows sagely.

"How was your trip?"

"We'll discuss my trip and everything else later. Right now I'm sure you're much more interested in seeing my houseguest."

Elizabeth blushed and nodded.

"He's in the drawing room."

Bessie opened the paneled door off the front hall, and Elizabeth paused in the doorway, her aunt just behind her. Sean was standing on the Aubusson rug in front of the fireplace, and he turned at the sound of their steps.

Elizabeth and he gazed at each other for a few seconds, and then Elizabeth rushed into his arms. He caught her high and whirled her in a circle, his eyes closed, his cheek pressed against her hair.

Dorothea and Bessie looked on for a moment, then exchanged glances. Dorrie motioned with her hand and Bessie closed the door, leaving the young people alone.

"Lizzie, darlin'," Sean said brokenly. "I thought I might never see you again."

Elizabeth pulled back to examine him. "Ah, you look thin."

"Bessie's been working me terrible hard. Chopping wood, hauling coal, shifting paving stones in the courtyard. The woman is a slave driver, that she is."

Elizabeth laughed and hugged him again. "Oh, I missed the feel of you. Nobody in the world feels like you."

"And who else have you been hugging lately?"

"Maura."

"A poor substitute."

"I couldn't agree more."

Elizabeth took both of his hands and led him to the Queen Anne sofa by the fire. "Sean, we have to talk."

He nodded wearily. "Aye."

"What did Rees tell you when he sent you back here?"

"Everything. The riot in the mines, the warrant for my arrest, the whole bloody story. I didn't know what to think when I saw Rees coming after me, but I gather his interest in saving my neck has something to do with my sister."

"They're involved, Sean. I think he's asked her to marry him."

"You think."

"Well, she's pretty tight-lipped about it, but it's clear to me that he's crazy about her."

"Well enough, I suppose. He's a decent fellow, for a peeler."

Elizabeth studied his much missed face. "Sean, we must plan what we're going to do to get you out of this mess."

He released her hands and stood. "There'll be no 'we' about it. I appreciate what you've done for me so far, letting me stay here and all, but I'll not drag you through the muck with me. I'll be on my own from here out."

Elizabeth stared at him.

"I spent most of last night talking with your aunt," he continued, pacing up and down on the rug. "She knows a lawyer—John O'Brien. He's just one genera-tion out of the mines himself and likely to support my cause. Your aunt says he's as well connected as your father, and rich, too, from some land deals he made in the past. Your father would never expect me to turn up somebody like O'Brien to fight him. Dorothea con-tacted O'Brien and he's coming here to see me to-night. If he takes my case, you and your aunt have been a powerful help, and that's the last of it I'll take from you."

"I see," Elizabeth said quietly. "You've got it all planned, haven't you? And everything you said to me in the past, all that palaver about loving me and tak-ing care of me, that was just a bunch of blarney to get me into bed?"

Sean's face darkened furiously. "How can you even say such a thing?" he demanded, his eyes narrowing. Elizabeth knew that look; he was really angry.

"How can you kiss me off this way?" she countered.

"For the love of God, Lizzie, I'm not kissing you off. It would be my dearest wish to spend the rest of my life with you," he burst out in exasperation. "But can't you see that things have changed? I'm a wanted man now. Would you tie yourself to me when I might well wind up in prison?"

"Yes," she said simply.

"Well, I'll not let you do it."

Elizabeth, who was prepared to handle this argument, said flatly, "I'm pregnant."

He stared at her. "What?" he said feebly.

"You heard me. I'm pregnant."

Sean sank into a Chippendale chair and thrust his hands into his hair. "Lord, Lizzie, you do beat a man down," he finally murmured.

"Try and get rid of me now," she said with satisfaction.

"I was not trying to get rid of you—I was trying to spare you an uncertain future," he said.

"Save the nobility for your causes. You're stuck with me. I'll be part of any plans you make, so get used to the idea."

"All right, then. Will you marry me as soon as possible?"

"As soon as possible."

"Are you sure about...?" he asked quietly, his eyes traveling to her still flat abdomen.

She nodded, smiling slightly. "Pretty sure. I'm three weeks overdue and I was sick this morning. I plan to see a doctor while I'm here in town, but that's just for confirmation."

"Come here to me," he said, holding out his arms.

Elizabeth walked over to him. He put his arms around her waist and placed his cheek against her belly as she stood next to his chair.

"A baby," he whispered.

"Yes."

"Our baby."

"No one else's."

Elizabeth tangled her fingers in his hair, and he closed his eyes. They were frozen in this attitude when Dorothea tapped on the door, then opened it.

Sean raised his head and Elizabeth stepped away from him.

"Excuse me," Dorrie said.

"Not at all," Sean said, standing. He wiped his eyes quickly with his fingers and added, "I'll be off now to help Bessie with that laundry tub. I'm sure you two have some talking to do." He paused in the doorway and said over his shoulder to Elizabeth, "We'll be needing a parson as well as a lawyer, I'm thinking." He went into the hall, smiling at Dorrie as he passed her.

"Quite something, isn't he?" Dorrie said to Elizabeth when he was gone. She sat gracefully on the sofa and gestured for Elizabeth to sit next to her.

"I think so."

"I agree with you. It's the rare man who'll take on your father almost single-handedly. I had long conversations with Sean yesterday and last evening, and he certainly has the raw material to go a long way. He just needs a little polishing."

Elizabeth startled both of them by bursting into tears.

"I'm sorry," she sobbed. "I didn't realize how much I was counting on your approval until I arrived here today and was afraid I might not get it. I thought you might be angry about the way I sprung Sean on Bessie. She was technically breaking the law by taking him in...."

"Oh, Bessie has a mind of her own. You could hardly expect her to turn away that handsome devil when he showed up at the door half-frozen, clutching the cross I gave you like a talisman."

"You heard about that," Elizabeth said sheepishly, sniffling.

"Yes, indeed."

"I had to make a decision in a hurry. It was the only thing I could think of at the time."

"You did very well. And Bessie tells me he's been a big help. The coal bin is full and the woodshed is bursting at the seams."

"Sean's not one to sit around twiddling his thumbs," Elizabeth said, wiping her cheeks with her palms. "I could have predicted that he'd find something to do."

"Bessie's thrilled with him," Dorrie announced. She removed a handkerchief from her sleeve and handed it to Elizabeth. "After cooking for my birdlike appetite so long she finally has someone in residence who really appreciates her meals."

Elizabeth smiled and blew her nose, then looked away.

"All right," Dorothea said briskly. "I think you'd better tell me what's been going on and how this great romance came about."

Elizabeth recapped the events of the past couple of months for her aunt, who interrupted often with pertinent questions. Bessie came with a tea tray and then sat to listen, chuckling at the mention of several of Sean's escapades. She got up and left just as Elizabeth concluded her narrative.

"I could have told you it would end up this way," Dorrie finally said, setting her teacup into its saucer with finality. "That boy had no chance of overcoming the forces your father has at his beck and call."

"There would have been a chance if the miners had listened to Sean and avoided violence," Elizabeth responded vehemently. "But the riot erupted when he was away."

"I hate to say this, but it probably would have erupted anyway, eventually," Dorrie observed. "One man, a lone voice, wouldn't have much chance of outweighing the miners' long tradition of handling their problems with force. I'm not saying that Sean was wrong, just that it was impossible for him to stand by himself indefinitely against so many. It speaks well for him that he was able to forestall the mayhem as long as he did.''

Elizabeth sighed.

''Now what did he say about a parson?'' Dorrie asked.

''We want to get married.''

''While all this is up in the air?''

Elizabeth swallowed and licked her lips. ''Aunt Dorrie, I'm going to have a baby.''

Dorothea nodded slowly. ''I see.''

''Are you shocked?''

''Well, I'm not surprised. I witnessed your reunion earlier, and it was clear to me that you're deeply in love.''

''Yes, we are.''

''You do realize what your father's reaction will be when he finds out about the two of you. And he *will* find out once you're married. He'll be called as a witness in the state's case against your husband.''

''Will my father be able to do anything once we're married—to Sean, I mean?''

Dorothea pursed her lips. ''Well, that's a question more for Mr. O'Brien than for me. Did Sean tell you about Mr. O'Brien?''

''Yes.''

''But I don't think so,'' Dorrie continued. ''You're of age. You'll come into the small trust fund your mother left for you when you turn twenty-one in two months.''

"Can my father block me from getting that?"

"I'm the trustee," Dorrie reminded her.

"Yes, I know, but you're familiar with his tactics. Can he file papers or anything to prevent the money from being released?"

"He might try, but I'm in charge of it, and I'm sure O'Brien has as many tricks up his sleeve as your father does." Dorothea poured more tea from the silver pot on the table into her cup. "Speaking of money, you do know that your father will cut you off without a penny if you go through with this marriage."

"Yes, I know. My mother's trust fund is enough to live on until Sean is cleared."

"Does Sean know about it?" Dorrie asked.

"The trust fund?"

"Yes."

Elizabeth shook her head, avoiding Dorrie's eyes.

"I assumed not. Don't you think you'd better tell him?" Dorrie said gently. "I have a very strong feeling that he'll object to taking your money."

"Yes, I know. He expects me to be as penniless as he is once my father cuts me off."

"And?"

"And I want things to be settled between us, his defense all planned, before I tell him about the trust fund," Elizabeth said directly.

"Do you think it's right to deceive him until then?"

Elizabeth stood and threw up her hands. "Aunt Dorrie, Sean is a wonderful man and I love him to distraction, but his stubbornness borders on stupidity sometimes. It takes money to fight a court case. It takes money to *live*."

"I know that, but if you want my advice..."

"Yes?"

"Don't let it go too long. Trust is very important to that boy. Don't abuse his."

"I won't."

Dorrie rose also, setting her cup on the tea tray. "Now I'm going to call on Reverend Danielson and see if he can perform a wedding ceremony this evening. Mr. O'Brien can take care of the legalities. He's due here at eight."

Elizabeth kissed her aunt on the cheek and said, "I was sure you'd come through for me, Aunt Dorrie. I don't know what we would do without you."

"Oh, nonsense. If what you've told me about Sean is true, he's one of the most resourceful creatures who ever lived. He would have found a way through this maze."

"But you've made everything so much easier. Thank you."

"You're welcome. Now let me get on with my errand. I'll send your fiancé in to you."

Fiancé. She liked the sound of that. She liked the sound of husband even better. Elizabeth sat again and waited for Sean to return.

Elizabeth and Sean were married that evening at sunset in Dorothea Hunter's drawing room. Elizabeth carried a spray of gladiolas taken from one of her aunt's vases, and Sean wore a frock coat borrowed from a neighbor of Dorrie's. Afterward they had a celebration dinner and Dorrie toasted the couple with a vintage wine she had been saving in her cellar.

Then, at eight o'clock, Mr. John O'Brien arrived. He was a portly, florid man in his sixties, with a crest of creamy white hair.

"So this is our young firebrand," he said in a booming voice, extending his hand to Sean. "Been cutting a few capers challenging the law of the land, have you?"

"Uh, yes, sir," Sean replied uncertainly.

"And this, of course, is the blushing bride," he added, beaming at Elizabeth.

Elizabeth smiled back.

"So you two have landed in a peck of trouble from what Miss Dorothea tells me," he added cheerfully.

"Yes," Sean said, glancing at Elizabeth.

"Well, we'll see what we can do about that."

Dorrie showed them into the drawing room and then withdrew, leaving Sean and Elizabeth alone with the lawyer.

"First thing," O'Brien said as he sat in a chair across from the young couple, who were on the sofa, "is to put an end to this fugitive from justice thing."

"You mean turn myself in?" Sean said, aghast.

"Just that. Langdon will ask for an exorbitant bail—"

"And get it," Elizabeth interjected. "The judges are all his longtime pals."

O'Brien waved his hand dismissively. "I've a few friends myself—don't fret yourself about that. I'll claim prejudice and get a change of venue to Philadelphia County, where the bail will be reasonable and Sean, a first offender, will be out in hours."

"Can you do that?" Sean asked, impressed, glancing hopefully at Elizabeth.

"Why, son, of course. Why do you think I'm here?" O'Brien shuffled a stack of papers he'd brought with him and went on, "Now the charges are inciting a riot and involuntary manslaughter in the death of a CIP patrolman. He died in the Langdon riot?"

Sean nodded.

"But Dorothea told me you weren't even there."

"I wasn't, but I was well-known for organizing the miners in the work stoppage that led to the riot. The law says that's enough of a connection for me to be responsible."

"Right you are, and that's a law that wants changing," O'Brien said sternly.

Sean sighed deeply. "Mr. O'Brien, I wish that I'd met you a long time ago."

"Well, you've met me now, so let's get to work, shall we?" O'Brien replied.

For the first time since she'd heard of the warrant out on Sean, Elizabeth felt a fierce surge of hope.

"Do you think that old geezer really knows his business?" Sean said to Elizabeth when O'Brien had left. "He sounds just a mite too good to be true."

"Sean, this is what it's like to have some control, some power over your life. My father doesn't own the world. It only seemed that way when we were back in Langdon. O'Brien has just as much clout as Arthur Langdon, and it's on your side, for a change."

"He wants me to turn myself in tomorrow morning."

"He'll get you back out."

"I'm sure you know that my instinct is to turn tail and run as far away from here as I can get," Sean said flatly.

"I know. Resist the urge and do it the right way, the legal way. For me and the baby, Sean."

Sean pulled her into his arms and held her close. They were up in Elizabeth's old room on the second floor, where Sean had been sleeping during his stay.

"Your da won't half kill Dorothea when he finds out what a hand she had in this," he said.

"She's not afraid of him, and neither am I. Not anymore."

"Don't look for too much from O'Brien, Lizzie. He's not a miracle worker and it's a serious charge."

"Whatever happens, we'll be together, and that's the important thing," Elizabeth said.

"Did you hear what he said about exposing the plight of the miners during the trial?"

"Yes, as part of your defense. He wants to show the conditions that drove you to organizing for a strike."

"Do you think it will matter? I mean, will people listen? Does anybody outside the pits really care?"

"People would care if they knew, Sean. Your problem is isolation—everything is controlled by the mine interests, and my father is trying desperately to keep it that way. It's the only chance for survival of the system that made him rich."

Sean released her and sat on the edge of the bed, watching Elizabeth as she unbuttoned the bodice of her dress.

"I'm not frightened of jail, you understand," he said, his mind returning to his imminent incarceration. "I've been in the clink often enough that it holds no terrors for me. I just hate to leave you, especially now. Some honeymoon it is for you."

"I'm giving thought to our entire future, Sean, not just the next few days."

"Still no regrets about choosing me over Prince Charlie?" he asked, studying her expression.

"Oh, please, no more of that."

"It's a natural question from a man on his way to jail. Your life would be very different if you were with him."

"I want to be with *you* and I always will."

"So you say now. Wait until I'm shut up for months in a cell and you with a baby on the way."

Elizabeth dropped her shirtwaist on a chair and came to sit next to him. "Will you stop being so gloomy? O'Brien said there was an excellent chance you'd be out in a few days."

"Chances. I don't believe in chances."

"What do you believe in?"

"You," he said gently, touching her cheek.

"Then believe in my opinion. I know a little better than you how things work in the big world outside Langdon. O'Brien knows what he's doing."

Sean sighed and lay back on the bed. "Will poor old Charles throw himself into the Schuylkill River over his lost love, do you think?" he said dryly.

"He asked me to marry him."

"No surprises there," Sean said darkly.

"I told him I'd give him an answer by Christmas."

"And what will your answer be?" Sean asked, grinning.

"Is bigamy against the law in Pennsylvania?" Elizabeth asked teasingly.

"I'm not laughing. Don't you think you owe that poor sod an explanation?"

"Oh, now he's a 'poor sod.' A very short time ago you wanted to kill him."

"I'm the victor so I can be generous."

"I see. I do think he merits an explanation, and he'll get one. I'm going to visit the Brandons and have a talk with Charles and his sister. I invited her to come to the house for Christmas, and now it looks as though I won't be there."

"If it doesn't go well with me and I remain in jail, where will you stay?" he asked soberly.

"Here."

"And what will you do for money? Your father will disown you, I won't be working, and my defense will cost money, not yield it. You can't live off Dorothea forever.''

Elizabeth moved up on the bed until she was sitting right next to him. ''Didn't you hear O'Brien say he would be conducting your defense *pro bono?*''

''Whatever in blazes that means.''

''It means for free.''

Sean stared at her. ''Indeed?''

''Oh, yes. *Pro bono* is Latin, meaning 'for the good.' Sometimes a lawyer takes on a case without charging for it because the lawyer believes in the principles his client's case exemplifies.''

''That sounds like a direct quote from Dorothea,'' Sean said with a sly smile.

Elizabeth chuckled. ''It is. I asked her.''

Sean shrugged. ''That still doesn't tell me how we'll provide for the baby and you if I'm locked up.''

Elizabeth looked down at her hands. ''There's something else.''

Sean sat up, alerted by her manner. ''What?''

''It's true that my father will probably cut me off, but my mother left me some money, and I'll be getting it in two months, when I turn twenty-one,'' she said rapidly.

Sean's eyes narrowed. ''Have you known this all along?''

She nodded.

He sprang off the bed and turned his back on her. ''So that was your plan?''

''Plan?''

"To have me as a kept man?" She could hear the nascent fury in his tone.

"Oh, for heaven's sake, Sean, I knew you would react this way," Elizabeth said in disgust. "For anyone else but you this would be good news. Do you want your child and me to starve if anything goes wrong with your trial?"

"So you admit it could go wrong?"

"There's always that chance. We should be ready for it."

He nodded in grudging agreement, then said, "You still should have told me about the money."

"All right, I should have told you. But can you blame me for delaying this scene until after some of our other problems were solved?"

"Dorothea probably thinks I'm a fortune hunter," he said murderously.

Elizabeth fell onto the bed in a fit of giggles.

"Oh, go ahead, kill yourself laughing. It's a good joke on me," he tossed at her.

Elizabeth controlled herself with an effort and said, "Dorrie is aware that you didn't know about the money until now. And I'm sure she couldn't imagine anyone less like a fortune hunter than yourself."

"And why is that?" he said, whirling to face her.

Elizabeth got up and walked over to him, putting her arms around his waist and laying her head on his shoulder.

"Trust me," she said, amusement still in her voice.

His arms came around her reflexively.

"Do you forgive me for keeping it from you?" Elizabeth asked.

"Oh, aye," he said wearily.

"I had to get you to marry me first, you know," she said in a mischievous tone.

"Were you worried that I wouldn't?"

"I was pretty confident that after sampling my charms you'd have to come back for more."

He held her off to look at her.

"Cocky, aren't you?"

"Only where you're concerned."

He took her by the hand and led her to the bed.

"We have to get word to Maura about the wedding, my defense, everything that's happened," he said as he unbuttoned her skirt.

"She wants to go west with Rees, and I think she should," Elizabeth replied.

"And take my mother and Matt with them?"

"Yes."

"She won't go as long as I'm on trial."

"Then we have to get you off as quickly as possible so she'll be free to leave." Elizabeth's skirt fell to the floor.

"This may be our last night together for a while," he said softly, peeling her chemise off her shoulders.

"Then let's make it count."

Epilogue

Summer, 1875

Elizabeth Jameson struggled through the entrance to her husband's office, balancing her packages precariously and holding her four-year-old son by the hand.

"Come along, John," she said to the boy, who was lagging behind, staring up at the gold lettering on the glass door. Behind them the August bustle of the downtown Philadelphia thoroughfare continued unabated; the clop of horses' hooves, the whistles of cabbies, the shrill cries of the vendors combined to form a noisy backdrop.

"What is the man doing, Mommy?" the child asked, referring to the artisan who was stenciling a new name on the door.

"He's adding your father's name to the firm's list," Elizabeth explained, pausing a moment to admire it herself.

The workman touched his free hand to his cap, and Elizabeth smiled at him.

"Why?" the boy said.

"Well, since your daddy passed the bar examination, he doesn't have to work as a clerk anymore. He's a full-fledged lawyer with Mr. O'Brien's firm."

The child lost interest in the subject. He directed his attention to the secretary sitting behind the oak desk in the reception area as the outer door swung closed behind them.

"Hello, Marjorie," Elizabeth said to the woman.

"Hello, Mrs. Jameson." Marjorie grinned at John and reached into a drawer, putting her hand behind her back with a flourish.

"Got a treat for you," she said to John.

The boy looked at his mother.

"Oh, all right," Elizabeth said, sighing. The way everyone in the office spoiled the child, by the time he was ten he would be an insufferable brat—and weigh two hundred pounds.

Marjorie produced a licorice whip, which John seized and then jammed into his mouth.

"What do you say?" Elizabeth asked him.

"Thank you," he said, chewing.

Elizabeth looked at Marjorie. "Is Sean free?" she asked.

"Go on in," Marjorie said. "He's waiting for you."

Elizabeth walked down the hall and tapped lightly on a door that had once been marked Law Clerk. That lettering had been chiseled off and a new outline replaced it. Sean P. Jameson, Esquire.

The letters had yet to be filled in; that was obviously the painter's next job.

"Come," said Sean's voice from inside.

Elizabeth opened the door and John scampered ahead of her, running up to his father and clutching his legs. Sean, who was seated behind a cluttered desk piled with files, dropped the book he was holding and grabbed the child, hoisting him onto his lap. John squealed in mock protest and flailed his legs, laughing.

"Well, how's my boy?" Sean demanded. "What have you been doing with yourself?"

"Tormenting his mother," Elizabeth said dryly, setting her packages on the floor.

Sean stood, setting the boy down smartly and walking over to kiss Elizabeth.

"How so?" he asked her.

"He wants that carousel horse in Brandon's. Every time we walk past the display window, he screams and carries on like a banshee."

John wandered over to the desk and started playing with a glass paperweight.

"A banshee, is it?" Sean said, amused.

"Yes."

"Why don't you try staying out of the place yourself?" he asked teasingly, gesturing to the bags she'd brought.

"Well, we needed a few things."

Sean chuckled knowingly.

"Sean Jameson, you know about the dinner Dorrie is hosting Saturday night. You can't appear there without a decent set of clothes."

"You'll turn me into a gentleman yet," he said in an undertone.

"You were always a gentleman," she replied tenderly.

"Indeed?"

John punctuated the conversation by sending a stack of files flying onto the floor in a blizzard of papers. He looked up at his father, dismayed.

"It's all right, son," Sean said, bending to pick up the scattered material.

"What's all that?" Elizabeth asked.

"The latest *pro bono* case for the miners," Sean replied. "O'Brien just sent these depositions in to me. Some poor bugger got killed in an improperly hung cage over in Mauch Chunk, and his family is suing the company. It's the third compensation case this year."

"I guess getting you acquitted of your charges gave him a taste for bashing the mining companies," Elizabeth said.

"Well, he hasn't forgotten where he came from."

Elizabeth hugged him. "And neither have you. I know you're always at him to take these cases. You needn't make it look as if it were all his idea."

Sean grunted noncommittally, restoring the files to his desk. "So what time is Dorrie's dinner?"

"Eight o'clock."

Sean winced. "I hate those bloody things."

"I know you do, but for my sake you can make her happy and be civil to her friends."

"I am *always* being civil to her friends," he grumbled. "Sculptors, writers, crusaders, every artist with a new style or reformer with his hand out is lined up in your aunt's drawing room every time she gives a party."

"And you're one of them!" Elizabeth said, laughing. "How much money has she donated to your benevolent organizations for the miners? Not to mention her efforts to draft new members for them...."

"Leave off me, woman—O'Brien's just as bad as she is. This committee, that organization—it's a wonder we have time to practice law around here."

"And I would like to remind you that O'Brien saved you from jail, took you under his wing and let you work as a clerk when you knew nothing...."

"I learned fast," he protested.

"And so if he wants you to join a few committees, you should count yourself lucky to do so."

"All those politicians kissing each other's—" he glanced at his son "—hands," he concluded.

Elizabeth rolled her eyes at him.

"Still, I suppose we should indulge him. And Dorrie, too. She's your only family since your father's not speaking to us."

A shadow crossed Elizabeth's face. "He's never seen his grandchild," she said sadly, looking at John, who was now playing with the brass handle on a desk drawer.

Sean put his arm across her shoulders. "He'll come around," he said quietly.

Elizabeth shook her head. "I don't think so." She brightened. "Speaking of family, I got a letter from Maura today."

"Oh, what does she say?" Sean asked, gathering the files he needed to take home.

"Let's see," Elizabeth said, trying to remember. "The farm is doing well, the baby has a new tooth, your mother is working on a quilt. Oh, and Tom is teaching Matt to string a bow, which is something I would pay money to see."

Sean nodded, smiling.

"Do you think we'll ever get out to Oklahoma to visit them?" Elizabeth asked wistfully.

"Trains run all the time," Sean replied. "If I ever get caught up around here—"

"Fine chance of that."

He thrust a final file into his leather carryall and said, "I'm ready to leave."

"Let's go." Sean picked up Elizabeth's bags as they left his office. Their apartment was on the ground floor of a brownstone a few blocks away.

On their way out, Marjorie looked up and said, "Mr. O'Brien said to tell you that he'll be in court first thing in the morning, but he'll meet you for lunch at McGarrity's tomorrow at noon."

Sean nodded and handed Marjorie a letter to copy. "By Friday," he said to her.

"Where is the great man?" Elizabeth asked as they passed through the door to the street, John walking between his parents and holding on to Elizabeth's hand. The painter had finished, and Sean's name gleamed on the door alongside O'Brien's.

"He's in Scranton—he'll be back tomorrow." People swarmed around them, carrying bundles and hurrying past, as the trio made their way down the street toward their house.

"Sean?"

"Aye?"

"Do you ever look back on where we came from and then examine where we are now?"

He stopped walking and glanced at her. "I do."

"And what do you think?"

"I think I'm the luckiest cuss who ever got off the boat," he replied seriously.

Elizabeth smiled at him.

His expression changed. "John, did I ever tell you what your mother was wearing when I met her?" he said mischievously, looking back at Elizabeth.

"Sean Jameson, don't you dare!" Elizabeth said.

"What, Daddy?" the child asked, intrigued.

And Sean proceeded to tell his son about a mine fire, and a starry harvest sky, and a dark-eyed girl on a crisp October night.

* * * * *

**THIS JULY, HARLEQUIN OFFERS YOU
THE PERFECT SUMMER READ!**

Sunsational

EMMA DARCY
EMMA GOLDRICK
PENNY JORDAN
CAROLE MORTIMER

From top authors of Harlequin Presents comes
HARLEQUIN SUNSATIONAL, a four-stories-in-one
book with 768 pages of romantic reading.

Written by such prolific Harlequin authors as Emma Darcy,
Emma Goldrick, Penny Jordan and Carole Mortimer,
HARLEQUIN SUNSATIONAL is the perfect summer
companion to take along to the beach, cottage, on your
dream destination or just for reading at home in the warm
sunshine!

Don't miss this unique reading opportunity.

Available wherever Harlequin books are sold.

SUN

Harlequin Superromance®

This August, don't miss Superromance #462—STARLIT PROMISE

STARLIT PROMISE is a deeply moving story of a woman coming to terms with her grief and gradually opening her heart to life and love.

Author Petra Holland sets the scene beautifully, never allowing her heroine to become mired in self-pity. It is a story that will touch your heart and leave you celebrating the strength of the human spirit.

Available wherever Harlequin books are sold.

STARLIT